I Heard a Rumor

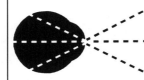

This Large Print Book carries the
Seal of Approval of N.A.V.H.

I Heard a Rumor

Cheris Hodges

THORNDIKE PRESS

A part of Gale, Cengage Learning

GALE
CENGAGE Learning®

Farmington Hills, Mich • San Francisco • New York • Waterville, Maine
Meriden, Conn • Mason, Ohio • Chicago

GALE
CENGAGE Learning®

ALL RIGHTS RESERVED
Thorndike Press® Large Print African-American.
The text of this Large Print edition is unabridged.
Other aspects of the book may vary from the original edition.
Set in 16 pt. Plantin.

LIBRARY OF CONGRESS CATALOGING-IN-PUBLICATION DATA

Names: Hodges, Cheris F.
Title: I heard a rumor / Cheris Hodges.
Description: Large print edition. | Waterville, Maine : Thorndike Press Large
   Print, 2016. | © 2015 | Series: Thorndike Press large print African-American
Identifiers: LCCN 2015041056| ISBN 9781410485779 (hardback) | ISBN
   1410485773 (hardcover)
Subjects: LCSH: African Americans—Fiction. | Large type books. | BISAC:
   FICTION / Romance / Contemporary.
Classification: LCC PS3608.O473 I15 2016 | DDC 813/.6—dc23
LC record available at http://lccn.loc.gov/2015041056

Published in 2016 by arrangement with Dafina Books, an imprint of
Kensington Publishing Corp.

Printed in Mexico
1 2 3 4 5 6 7 19 18 17 16

I Heard a Rumor

CHAPTER 1

Chante Britt filled her favorite pink and green mug with Ethiopian blend coffee, which had been a gift from her best friend and sorority sister, Liza Palmer-Franklin. *That girl knows coffee,* she thought as she inhaled the fragrant aroma. She almost didn't want to pour the creamer into the coffee. She took a sip and realized that it was perfect black. Reaching for the remote to the small TV set mounted over the stove, she sighed as she turned it on. This was her morning routine, and it was getting on her last damned nerve.

Chante was bored, mad, and tired of the purgatory her life had become since her suspension from the law firm she'd worked for, Myrick, Lawson and Walker.

She had been considered a distraction, according to managing partner Taiwon Myrick, because of her relationship with former senatorial candidate Robert Montgomery, who lost his bid for a senate seat after she and Liza exposed the fact that he was a liar and paid for sex with prostitutes. When Chante and Robert had been dating, she'd lobbied for her firm to support his candidacy, which they did. Taiwon liked Robert's pro-business stance on several issues and threw a lot of money his way, even after Chante had expressed her doubts. But as always, Taiwon chose not to listen to Chante. Over the last two years at Myrick, Lawson and Walker, Chante had been working herself ragged to become a partner. But she'd been constantly looked over — despite the fact that she'd delivered over a million dollars in billable hours, boasted a ninety percent winning ratio, and brought in more than a third of the firm's new clients.

Taiwon was from the old-school law community and just didn't believe a woman could be a partner with the firm his family had started. Though she couldn't point to any provable sexual discrimination, she knew it was her gender that had been holding her back at the firm.

So when Jackson Franklin won the senate seat after it was revealed that Robert had been involved with a hooker during the campaign, Taiwon had been happy to blame her for the firm being mixed up in the controversy.

Bastard, she thought as she lifted her head and saw Robert's image on the screen. Chante started to turn the set off. But curiosity got the best of her, so she unmuted the set to hear what he had to say.

"Wonder if he's still out there buying sex," she muttered, then took another sip of her coffee.

"I'm standing here today because of grace and forgiveness," Robert said into the camera. "I made mistakes in my quest to become senator, and I hurt a lot of people. But those people, including the love of my life, have forgiven me. And their forgiveness has given me the courage to throw my hat into the ring to be Charlotte's next mayor."

Chante spit her coffee across the kitchen. Was this man daft? Who was going to support him to be mayor, let alone the city's dogcatcher? And who was the love of his life? Poor woman. She didn't know what kind of mess she was going to be in as the pretend love of Robert Montgomery's life. The only person Robert loved was Robert.

She reached into her robe pocket and pulled out her smartphone to text Liza.

"Last night, as I talked to my future wife, Chante Britt . . ."

"What the . . . !" Chante exclaimed.

9

Forget texting Liza; she was going to have to call her friend and hope that she wasn't interrupting anything going on between the newlyweds.

"This is Liza," her friend said when she answered the phone.

"Robert has lost what's left of his blasted mind," Chante exclaimed. "This fool just . . ."

"Calm down," Liza said. "I'm sure no one is taking him seriously."

Chante's phone beeped. "Hold on, I have another call coming in," she said. Clicking the TALK button, she answered the unknown number.

"Chante Britt."

"Ms. Britt, this is Coleen Jackson. I'm a reporter with News Fourteen. I wanted to ask you a few questions about Robert Montgomery."

Click.

"People were paying attention, Liza," Chante said. "That was a reporter."

"Oh my goodness. While you had me on hold, they showed a clip of his announcement on the news here. He really called you the love of his life. Have you two been seeing each other?"

"Hell no! I haven't spoken to that man since two days after the election, and that was last year."

"I can't believe him. What does he think is going to come of this, and why would he think that you would agree to being . . . ?"

Chante's phone beeped again. She looked at the incoming caller's number and saw it was another unknown one. "I'm guessing that's another reporter," Chante said. "What am I going to do?"

"Issue a statement. I'll write one for you to e-mail to all the media outlets in Charlotte. This will blow over. Let's just take control of the narrative and wait for the next news cycle. Everyone will move on to the next thing and you can get on with your life."

"Thank you, Liza. I'm going to go for my run now."

"Has your suspension been lifted yet?"

"No. And I'm guessing this latest stunt from this asshole is going to give them another reason to keep the suspension going."

"I still think you should start your own firm," Liza said. "You don't need them."

Chante sighed. Part of her agreed with her friend, but there was something about the security of becoming a partner at an established law firm. Maybe she wanted that partnership so that she could prove her

11

mother wrong.

Allison Louise Cooper-Britt had grown up as the ultimate southern belle. She attended South Carolina State College for one reason — to obtain her MRS. That happened when she'd met and married Eli Britt. He'd been the crucial catch: wealthy family, right complexion, and a member of all the right organizations.

When Chante had graduated from college and decided that law school was more important than a husband and a family, her mother wished her failure. Thankfully, her smarts and a few of her father's connections had given her the blueprint for success.

She and her grandmother, Elsie Mae, had a much better relationship than she had with Allison. Probably because they were so much alike. Elsie Mae Cooper had carved out her niche in Charleston, South Carolina, by selling her handwoven baskets to tourists. In 1972, she began adding unique pieces of South Carolina culture to the baskets and opened a gift shop on Folly Beach. Elsie's Gifts and Goodies became one of the beach's most popular tourist attractions.

When Elsie Mae retired from running the shop, she sold it to a historical group while keeping a forty-nine percent stake in the company. The residual income allowed her to travel the world at will. Of course, Allison thought her widowed mother should spend her time in a rocking chair on the front porch. That was not Elsie Mae's style at all, and her world traveling and adventure seeking became a bone of contention between mother and daughter.

Chante wished she had her grandmother's fearless nature. She knew for a fact that Elsie Mae would've started her own firm without giving it a second thought. Her grandmother wouldn't have taken all the grief she'd subjected herself to for that partnership. Part of her knew she'd be fine if she struck out on her own. She had a huge client base, and she was a proven winner who'd made millions for her clients. But she was afraid. Afraid that if she failed, her mother would lord it over her, just as she'd always done with the fact that she isn't married.

As if that was the only thing she was supposed to do with her life. Rolling her eyes at the ringing phone, Chante hit the IGNORE button on another unknown call, then shut the phone off.

When she received Liza's e-mail with her statement and a list of contacts to send it to, Chante was ready to pound the pavement and Robert's face. Lacing up her sneakers and popping her ear buds in, she opened the front door and was blinded by flashbulbs.

"What the . . . ?"

"Ms. Britt, have you forgiven Robert?"

"When is the wedding?"

"Will Senator and Mrs. Franklin be there? Have all of you kissed and made up after such an ugly election cycle?"

"Get off my doorstep!" Chante exclaimed. When the members of the media took a step back, she thought they had heeded her demand. That was until she saw Robert walking her way. Narrowing her eyes at him, all she could think was that the media had just saved his life.

"Chante, darling, I didn't mean for this to happen," he said with a huge smile on his face. She watched in abject horror as he walked up the steps and stood in her face.

"You son of a . . ."

Robert wrapped his arms around her and attempted to kiss her. Chante kneed him in the family jewels before storming into her house and slamming the door. All she could hope was that the cameras had caught every minute of it. One thing was for certain: she wasn't going to stick around to be harassed by the media or Robert freaking Montgomery!

Zach Harrington downed a mojito as if it was a glass of water while he sat on the white shores of Folly Beach. It felt good to be an anonymous man in the crowd. In South Carolina, he was just a man on the beach. Back in New York, he was the ex-husband of the "Harlem Madame." Just thinking about the moniker the media had given his ex-wife made him cringe. And the circus! Cameras followed him around the city and camped out at his office building and his temporary home.

He couldn't even meet with the Crawfords about a tract of land they wanted to purchase in Manhattan for new office space. He was sure that Solomon and Richmond Crawford wouldn't want to be photographed outside his office after what their family had gone through in the media lately. Solomon and Richmond had discovered that their father, Elliot, had a son — Adrian Bryant — before his death. Adrian had taken the story to the media around the same time that Richmond had been arrested in Los Angeles for solicitation of sex.

Then there had been Richmond's messy divorce. The businessman in Zach knew that any partnership they'd enter into right now would be a disaster. And he hadn't told the Crawfords that he and Adrian had been friends long before the scandal broke.

Just thinking about the media circus and the money it was costing him made him crave something stronger than a sweet rum highball. When he'd filed for divorce from his wife, Natalie, he thought she'd been having an affair. He had no clue that she was running an escort service from their home on Long Island. It had taken three months for him to clear his name and prove to the district attorney that he didn't have anything to do with Natalie's illegal empire.

She'd been clearing about a million dollars a year. At least she was sleazy enough to hide the money in an account that had nothing to do with his business or their personal accounts. Shaking his head, Zach brought himself back to what was in front of him: a beautiful shoreline, women in barely there bikinis, and the blazing southern sun.

Digging his toes into the warm sand, Zach tugged at his Brooklyn Nets ball cap and grinned. For the next seven days or more, he was going to be anyone he wanted to be, without worrying about the glare of the New York media. Just as he was about to close his eyes, his cell phone vibrated in his pocket. Grabbing it, he smiled when he saw it was his assistant, Kia Clarke.

"What's up, Special K?"

"Your final divorce decree just arrived. You are officially unattached."

"Been unattached. I'm just glad the state has approved it," he said. "Have the reporters stopped calling yet?"

Kia sighed. "You haven't heard the latest?"

"I've been listening to ocean waves. Do I even want to know?"

"She claims there's a black book and you know where it is. We've had a few agents stop by the office, but I told them that without a warrant they couldn't come in. And three more clients have dropped us."

Zach muttered curses that caused a few people to give him the side eye. "Why does she keep tarnishing my name?"

"She doesn't want to let you go, and she isn't trying to go down without taking a lot of innocent people with her. I've never liked Ms. Shady Boots, and I told you that from the beginning."

"I wish I'd seen her true colors years ago," he said, then expelled a sigh.

"Tried to warn you, boss. But you were blinded by something else."

"Don't remind me. How's the baby?"

"Still baking. I'm two weeks overdue, and Dave is stressing me out. That's why I came into the office today."

"Please don't give birth in my office," he quipped. "I'm so happy for you and Dave. I wish I could be there to celebrate with you guys."

"Zach, I'm not mad at you for staying away and getting your head together. And why not have some fun while you're out there?"

"That's my plan. When I come back to New York, hopefully this news cycle will be over and I can get back to my business and spoiling my godson."

"Excuse you, I'm having a daughter. So, you better get some of the southern girly-girl stuff while you're in Charleston."

"I'm bringing football helmets and shoulder pads," he said with a laugh.

"Anyway. Unless anything major happens, the next time you hear from me, I'll be calling with the news of your goddaughter's entrance into the world," Kia said.

When they said good-bye, Zach turned his phone off, leaned back in his lounge chair, and closed his eyes. The warmth of the sun did little to ease the chill he felt creeping up his spine. Even though he'd divorced his criminal wife and had had nothing to do with her sex peddling, his boutique real estate firm was suffering. A couple of clients had taken their business elsewhere, costing him fifteen million dollars. The loss hurt, but his company was strong — for now. If he kept losing the big clients, then he would be hurting, as well as his employees.

Part of him wanted to push Natalie into the Hudson River with a hundred pounds of weights attached to her Louboutins. But he was nonviolent, and he just planned to let everything blow over. He was going to have to diversify, and maybe he would find a great investment down south that would make up for his losses. Down here, he wouldn't be cast as the husband of the "Harlem Madame." He could create a southern branch of his business, buy some cheap land, and turn it into gold. After all, he knew his Midas touch was still intact. At least, he hoped so.

Groaning, Zach decided it was time for another drink and some more girl watching.

CHAPTER 2

"Open the door, Chante," Robert said as he pounded on the front door.

Chante closed her eyes and counted to ten. "Get off my porch or I will call the police," she replied.

"Chante, come on. We need to talk about this."

"Talk about you being a delusional asshole? Nah, I'm good."

"This can work out for the both of us," he said. "Open the door. The cameras are gone. It's just going to be me and you talking, all right?"

Chante rolled her eyes. Jesus could've come and gone forty times and she was not going to open that door. "Robert, why don't you go see Dayshea and act out *Pretty Woman*? That will play better for the press. I've already released a statement letting everyone know that you're a liar and I want nothing to do with you."

"I made a mistake. Don't you think it's time for you to forgive me? I've forgiven you."

"Forgiven me? Are you insane? What am I talking about? Of course you are."

"Can we just talk?" Robert pleaded.

"Talk about what?" she shouted. Chante closed her eyes and counted to ten again. "Robert, you need to leave and retract your statement. We are done. Have been done for a long time."

"You don't think I deserve a second chance?" He banged on the door again. Chante looked around for something to hit him with. She ran into the kitchen and grabbed a broom. She'd tried reasoning with him. She'd tried yelling at him. This was coming to an end right now.

Opening the door, she blindly swung the broom at him. "Go home! Leave me alone!"

"Chante, stop acting foolish! Stop." He tried to block the blows from the broom, but Chante kept swinging. Robert tumbled off the porch and landed on top of Chante's prized rose bush.

"You son of a bitch! That was my favorite rose bush." She put the broom at her side and watched Robert struggle to his feet.

"This is a six-hundred-dollar suit you just ruined."

21

"You ruined my life, and that's priceless."

Robert brushed the dirt, leaves, and petals from his heather-gray suit and glared at Chante. "You and Liza owe me."

She started to hurl her broom at him like a long dart. "I owe you?"

"You bitches ruined my life. I was a shoo-in to win that senate seat, but . . ."

This time, Chante didn't stop herself from throwing her broom at him. "I don't owe you a damned thing. It's because of you that I'm suspended from my law firm. Now you've put me in the middle of your hare-brained idea that the people of Charlotte want your lying ass to be their mayor. Do you ever think before you start talking? How did you even make it through law school? You're a damned idiot!"

"All I need is for you to just show up at a few appearances. We can tell everyone, after I get elected, that things didn't work out. I can't get people on board if you won't forgive me. We don't have to get married. I'm fine with that."

Chante blinked and shook her head. "You have truly lost your damned mind. Why would I help you defraud people?"

Robert narrowed his eyes at her, and Chante struggled to keep her hands to herself. "I was supposed to be the first senator for District Forty-five. You were supposed to be my wife . . ."

"And you weren't supposed to pay for sex from a hooker! Had that not happened, maybe you would've won and maybe I would've been stupid enough to marry you. Then you would've gone to Raleigh and turned into the asshole that people already know you are. I can't believe I thought I loved you."

"Please," he said with a snort. "You're desperate. You may have your career, but you want and need a man in your bed. I was just as much of a means to an end for you as you were for me. So don't stand there and act as if you were in love with me. You loved the image. You wanted the power as much as I did. It kills you that Liza is the one who ended up with it, doesn't it? You can say she's your best friend, but you're jealous. She has the life everyone thought was yours for the taking."

"Get the hell off my property and don't come back."

"Hurts to see Liza living your life, doesn't it?" He sneered at her.

Chante slammed into her house, shivering with anger. She wasn't going to allow him to do this again. She wasn't going to let him interfere with her and Liza's friendship, like he did when they were engaged.

Liza deserved her happiness with Jackson. Besides, what kind of life would she and Robert have had? It was clear that their engagement had been nothing but a political tool. She would've found out too late that he was a no good piece of cow dung, and then where would she have been? Depressed and divorced?

I bet my mother would accept me as a divorcée more than she would like me being single for the rest of my life, she thought bitterly.

Chante made sure Robert was gone, and then she headed to the uptown YMCA to take her aggression out on a heavy bag.

When she arrived at the YMCA, Chante realized that hiding out from the media wasn't going to be easy. Two photographers appeared out of nowhere as she walked into the gym. Chante sidestepped them and hid out in the locker room, where she overheard two women talking about Robert's interview on the news.

"I can't believe how desperate some women are," one said as she stuffed her feet into her sneakers. "That man slept with a hooker and she took him back?"

"So you don't believe in forgiveness?" the other woman asked.

"Hell no. He might have some STD, and she's so desperate that she's going to stand by him. Bye, Felicia."

"I mean, I would think she would have more pride, but who knows? That man looks like he can put it down."

"She's dick-matized, then?"

When Chante heard the women laughing, she made her presence known. "First of all, you can't believe everything you see on TV," she said. "And from the looks of both of you, I'm sure you would take any man who smiled at you into your arms and forgive him for all of his shortcomings. Don't judge me because you have no standards!"

Chante strode out of the locker room, leaving the two women with their mouths hanging open. As she walked into the lobby, she saw a cluster of cameras and reporters standing out in front of the Y.

"There goes my peaceful workout," she muttered when she locked eyes with one of the reporters.

She wasn't going to live like this, running from the media and arguing with strangers because of Robert's lies. As much as she wanted to go home to Summerville and hang out with her father, Chante knew she'd have to explain too much to her mother, who would somehow make this all

25

her fault.

Charleston. That's where she could go and snuggle up with her grandmother until all of this blew over. If she were lucky, while she was gone some athlete or another politician would make the news for something even more ridiculous than Robert's stupid press conference. She dashed out the basement entrance and avoided the waiting reporters.

Heading home, Chante made up her mind to go to her grandmother's house in Charleston and relax in the South Carolina sun. When she arrived at her house, she wasn't surprised to see a TV truck parked on the street. Part of her wanted to flip the cameraman and the reporter off, but she just walked inside and started packing for her trip.

"I'm going to enjoy getting out of this city," she muttered as she stuffed her clothes into her suitcase.

Sunset in Charleston was a sight to behold, Zach thought. Either that or he was very drunk and everything just looked gorgeous. As he stood on the balcony of his hotel room, he watched the golden light of the sun bathe the city. Maybe Charleston was where he needed to start over. No one here knew who he was or, more importantly, who his ex-wife was. But Zach couldn't deny that he was a son of the city. He'd grown up in the Bronx, in Riverdale, where his father, Zachary Sr., made the family's fortune in real estate.

After his father's death, Zach took over the company, moving into all of the boroughs of New York. The company grew to rival Donald Trump's empire, without the bankruptcies. Maybe he could have that success down south. It was nice not to be known and to be able to move around without being linked to Natalie's crimes.

Natalie, he thought. *How did I miss what was really going on with us?* When Zach and Natalie met, he'd been in a Manhattan nightclub nursing an overpriced drink with his homeboy, Adrian Bryant. Adrian had been in New York quasi-stalking photographer Dana Singleton. The Los Angeles club owner had broken up with his ladylove after his mother's deathbed confession about who his real father was — hotel magnate Elliot Crawford. Dana had abandoned the Corvette he'd given her at LAX, and he just wanted to make sure she was all right. What he'd been doing for the last three hours had been ranting in Zach's ear about how much he wanted revenge on his family.

Zach had started to tune his friend out, and that had been when he caught her eye. A chocolate-brown beauty with shoulder-length auburn hair and a full bosom that made his mouth water. She'd lifted her glass to him, and Zach turned to Adrian, "Bruh," he'd said, "hold that thought." Zach had risen from his seat and walked over to the beauty on the other side of the bar.

"Hello, beautiful," he'd whispered in her ear.

"I was wondering if you'd noticed me."

"How could I not? You're a hard woman to miss."

"I'm Natalie Norman."

"I think Natalie Harrington sounds a lot better."

"Excuse me?"

"I'm Zachary Harrington, and you're going to be my wife," he'd said with a wink.

"What if I'm one of those women who don't believe in marriage?"

"Then it's up to me to change your mind. Do you know that you're the most beautiful woman in the room?"

She'd smiled, and he'd felt his groin jump with anticipation. "I've heard that line before. How are you going to prove you're different?"

"Why don't we get out of here and talk

about it?" Zach had waved for the bartender and paid Natalie's tab.

"Sounds good to me."

Glancing over at Adrian, who was on his cell phone, Zach had given him the peace sign with his two fingers and left with Natalie. That night, they had gone to a diner, drunk coffee, and laughed about life and the other diners who'd come in.

It had been about six a.m. when they'd left, hand in hand. Zach wanted to take her to his penthouse in Harlem, but he'd played it cool. But damn, he'd wanted her. She'd been funny, smart, and beautiful. Who wouldn't have wanted to spend the night with her? Now he wished he'd stayed in the club and listened to Adrian bitch and moan about Dana and his new family.

Sighing, Zach headed back into his room. He glanced at the television just in time to see Natalie's image on CNN. Rolling his eyes and hating himself for being curious about the latest in her melodrama, Zach turned up the volume.

"Alleged Harlem Madame Natalie Harrington was in court today looking for a deal in her money-laundering and tax-evasion case, which stems from her alleged call-girl ring. But superior court judge Logan Beck was led away in handcuffs after the FBI burst into the courtroom," the anchor said. "Sources close to the investigation said Harrington and Beck both had a connection with the prostitution ring."

Zach shut the television off. He needed one more drink. Instead of raiding the minibar, he decided to try to salvage the sunset and headed to the hotel's restaurant.

Chante pulled into her grandmother's driveway and immediately decided that God was playing a huge practical joke on her. She knew Elsie Mae was getting the house renovated, but did she really have to have it gutted? Chante knew there was going to be no way she could stay there when she saw the tub and the toilet on the front lawn. Staying in the cottage where she and her grandmother used to have tea and talk about the future might have been an option, but that hadn't been her plan, and the workers were loud. She had come to Charleston to relax, and she wasn't going to go to her parents' house. There would be no relaxation in Summerville.

Still, she hoped there would be a slight chance that she could at least give her grandmother a hug as she stepped out of her car.

"Hello," she said as she walked up to the

porch. A portly man in a pair of dusty overalls crowded the doorway.

"Can I hep' ya?" he asked, then spat on the ground.

"Who are you?" Chanted asked with her nose wrinkled.

"Norman Locklear, foreman on this here site. What can I do for ya?"

"I'm looking for the woman who owns this house." Chante folded her arms across her chest. "And just what in the hell are you all doing?"

"Who are you, lil' lady?"

"Attorney Chante Britt. Now answer my question!"

The man laughed. "Miss Elsie told me about you, and she left you something. Hold tight." He turned and headed back into the house. Chante felt as if she was going to scream. This was not the escape she'd planned. And where was her grandmother? She should've taken heed of the fact that she couldn't reach her on the phone. Elsie Mae always answered her phone calls.

"Here ya go," the man said when he handed her an envelope.

Chante offered him a faint smile and said thank you. She walked off the porch and headed to her car. She ripped the envelope open and read her grandmother's note.

Chante,

Darling, I got your message while I was out in international waters, and I couldn't call you back. If you've made it to Charleston, you see that my house isn't fit to live in. This project has turned into a full-out restoration. So I decided to let my contractors do their job. I'm so sorry about all the madness you're going through. You're a better woman than I am because I'd string that Robert Montgomery up by his nuts. (Sorry, baby, I just don't like men taking advantage of women for their own personal gain.)

My cruise is thirty days, and don't tell your mother, but I'm not alone. Remember Mr. Theo?

Chante stopped reading and smiled. Oh, she remembered Theodore Tanner, the former R&B singer who had been good friends with her grandmother for years. She always wondered if there was more between them. But she didn't want to think about her grandmother, at her age, doing that!

She continued reading.

Theo and I are together. And that man is singing like it's 1954. I love it, and I love him. When we get back, we're probably going to be married. Don't give me that look. LOL. It cost me a lot to FedEx this letter from the ocean. Right now, you might not be feeling the love, but, baby girl, when the right man comes along — no matter what age — you will know it and be happy. That's what I want for you. I'm not trying to be like my daughter, telling you that your life is nothing without a husband. You are smart, beautiful, and damned good at your job. What you need to do is quit that law firm and start your own. If you need help, you know I'm in your corner. I've always believed in you, and you need to believe in yourself. You don't need anyone's approval, you're an amazing woman. How can you not be? You're my granddaughter. And working for other people is overrated, especially when you know more than they do.

I've made a reservation for you at Sheldon Richardson's hotel on Folly Beach. You're going to be fine. Relax and have fun. And by fun, I mean a lot of drinks and maybe a flirtation with a stranger for a week or so. I know, that doesn't seem proper, but think of it this way — your mother would have a heart attack if she knew this was the advice I was sharing with you. I love you, Chante. And this too shall pass, my dear.

Chante couldn't help but smile as she read her grandmother's note. She always knew how to lift her spirits. She remembered coming to her grandmother's house when she and her mother had had one of their many disagreements, and Elsie Mae would smooth everything over with banana bread and cinnamon tea.

Chante started her car and headed for the hotel. She was glad she could hide out in Charleston because her phone had still been blowing up with calls from the Charlotte media before she turned it off.

Of course, she told Liza that she'd be out of pocket for a week or so and that if her friend needed to get in touch with her she should send her an e-mail. She was sure that Liza wouldn't need her; if anything, she'd need Liza to give her another statement or advice on handling the media. But she didn't want to bother her friend with her issues. This was the first year of Jackson's term, and he was busy. That meant Liza was busy as well.

The couple were splitting their time between Raleigh and Charlotte while the General Assembly was in session, and the last thing Chante wanted was to be a bother to her friend. Liza had weathered a storm of rumors and lies, thanks to Robert, and Chante wasn't going to drag her into it again.

Robert. Just the thought of that bastard made her want to commit a crime of passion. Well, not really passion in the traditional sense of the word, but more in the legal sense. He had turned her life upside-down again with another lie. She wouldn't support him running from a dog, so forget running for mayor. And take him back? Please. Even if it was just for show, there was no way in hell she'd go along with that. She wouldn't take him to a trash can. And for him to think she'd help him hoodwink the people of Charlotte again. He was a damned fool! That would be stupid. And Chante Britt was not stupid.

She arrived at the hotel and sighed. It hadn't been what she planned, but Sheldon Richardson's Charleston Harbor Bed and Breakfast would be a great place to rest and relax. Maybe she would take her grandmother's advice and have some fun, but she wasn't sure about that flirting with a stranger part. As soon as she pulled underneath the entrance canopy, a valet and a bellhop appeared.

"Greetings, ma'am," the valet said. "May I park your car?"

"Thank you," she said as she handed him the keys.

"Do you have bags?" the bellhop asked.

"Yes," she replied, "they're in the trunk." The valet popped the trunk, and the bellhop placed Chante's luggage on a rolling cart and waited for her to enter the lobby.

"Good evening, and welcome to the Charleston Harbor Bed and Breakfast," the front desk clerk said with a huge smile on her face. "Do you have a reservation?"

"Yes, it's under either Chante Britt or Elsie Mae Cooper."

The woman typed some information and then looked up at Chante. "Yes, Miss Britt, I have a suite for you." She handed Chante a key card with the number to her suite on the front of it. "If you would take the guest elevators behind you, your suite will be the second door on the right."

"Thank you," she said, then walked over to the elevator with the bellhop in tow. As the doors opened, a tall brown-skinned man nearly bowled them over as he stepped off.

"Jerk," Chante muttered as she and the bellhop stepped into the elevator car.

"Everybody is in a hurry," the bellhop said.

"Not me," Chante said. "I'm just going to relax and take it slow."

"Sounds like a good plan. So you're on vacation in the Palmetto City?"

Chante smiled and nodded. Damn, it felt good to be unnoticed and unknown. When she left Charlotte, a crew from a local news station had followed her until she crossed the state line at Rock Hill. She couldn't help but wonder if the media were still camped out at her house. She almost felt sorry for the reporters who had been assigned to wait her out and get a statement. Hopefully they were getting paid by the hour.

"Well, I hope you enjoy your stay," he said as they arrived at her suite, breaking into her thoughts of Charlotte. Chante opened the door, and the bellhop took her luggage in. While he set her bags in the walk-in closet, Chante took the time to look around the suite. It was beautiful. Lush beige carpets, and a tan and beige comforter spread across the queen-size bed. Had she been in the room alone, she might have jumped on the bed.

Crossing over to the glass doors, she pulled the curtains back and saw that her balcony looked out onto the beach. The sky was turning purple, and stars were starting to sparkle in the distance. Chante was glad she was high enough up to be able to keep her curtains open and watch the night sky.

"Miss Britt, have a good night," the bellhop said. She crossed over to him and handed him a tip.

"Thank you."

Nodding at her, he left the room, and Chante broke out into a happy dance. Then she fell back on the bed, sinking into the softness. And she would've been fine going to sleep, but a rumbling in her stomach reminded her that she hadn't had a bite to eat since she'd left Charlotte earlier that afternoon.

There was no way she was going to sleep hungry, not when Charleston had so much food to offer. And she knew that Sheldon Richardson had a five-star restaurant in each of his hotels and resorts. Her mouth watered as she thought about getting some legitimate shrimp and grits — fresh seafood from the Charleston bay and perfectly seasoned grits with the right amount of butter and salt.

Heading to the bathroom to freshen up, Chante changed out of her jeans and T-shirt and put on a strapless maxi dress and a pair of gladiator sandals. After dinner, maybe she'd take a quiet walk on the beach, then go to bed.

Smoothing some lip gloss on her lips and giving herself a quick once-over, Chante headed down to the hotel restaurant.

Chapter 3

Zach was happy to see sports on the television above the bar as he sipped his whiskey. He had to stop drinking because he was supposed to be relaxing. Still, the news report about his ex had gotten under his skin. Would someone who mattered in Charleston see the national reports and put two and two together when he started to do business?

Forget about it. You haven't even found an opportunity yet, he thought as he waved for the bartender.

"Yes, sir?" the perky blonde asked with a smile.

"I think I need some food to go along with this drink. What would a pretty lady like you suggest?" Zach smiled, and she leaned forward.

"You can never go wrong with shrimp and grits," she said with a smile.

"Then I'd like an order of shrimp and grits."

"All right, sugar, I'll put that in for you. Want another Apple Crown?"

He shook his head and handed her a twenty-dollar bill for a tip. "Thank you for your suggestion."

"My pleasure," she said as she slipped the money in her pocket.

Zach turned his back to the bar as she walked away and glanced at the door. When he saw her walk in, he had to check his mouth for drool. Maybe it was the way her long dress hugged her curves, or maybe it was her shoulders. She had the gait of a queen, and that was just as attractive as her curly honey brown hair. *Southern girl,* he thought as she headed toward the bar. The restaurant was packed, which made him hope she was going to sit at the bar. And she did. Only it wasn't as close to him as he'd wanted. But he was able to drink in the brown-skinned woman's beauty.

As he watched her lips while she talked to the bartender, Zach tried to remember the last time he'd made love to a woman. Looking at this woman made him want to change that right now.

Sex had been one of the reasons he'd slid a three-carat diamond ring on his ex's finger

41

and asked her to marry him. But even before he found out what she had been doing, their sex life had dwindled. That was why he'd believed she was having an affair.

In the beginning of their marriage, Natalie had acted as if she couldn't get enough of him. They'd made love every chance they had. Even as his business took off, he'd never left his wife unsatisfied. Then, about three years ago, she had been the one who had stopped wanting intimacy. Having no idea why, Zach had thrown himself into his work.

Then, following her arrest on tax evasion charges, he'd learned the truth about his wife's activities. A prostitution ring? Part of him had wished there had been another man. Didn't she realize she wasn't Heidi Fleiss?

The arrest hadn't been the worst; that came when he read the arrest warrant, which said his wife had been more than the "Harlem Madame." Natalie had been accused of selling herself as well as pimping other young women. And some of the women who'd worked for Natalie were eighteen, which made him feel really awful. It might not have been child trafficking, but it was close enough. His twin sister, Zoe, had wanted to strangle Natalie when Zach had told her about the arrest.

Sex hadn't been in the forefront of his mind; in fact, Zach had taken a vow of chastity — in New York. But this wasn't New York, and the game had changed.

She glanced his way and — did she just roll her eyes at him? *So much for southern hospitality,* he thought, never taking his eyes off her pretty toes. He was a man with a minor foot fetish, and she had the feet of a goddess. That pink polish on her toes reminded him of strawberries.

"Excuse me," she said, her voice sounding melodic. "Will you please find something else to focus on?"

"What?"

"You've been sitting here staring at me as if you've never seen a woman or you were just released from prison."

"I can't admire a beautiful woman?"

"I don't give a damn what you do, as long as you do it someplace else and out of my face."

"Whoa, little mama, you need to relax. Maybe I was building up my nerve to offer to buy you a drink."

She gave him a slow once-over as if she was mulling over his statement. "Whatever," she snapped.

"You need to loosen up and smile. I know

you have a beautiful one."

She rolled her eyes. Unfazed, Zach eased closer to her stool and extended his hand. "Zachary Harrington."

Did she really just ignore his hand? Where did they do that? Obviously right here.

"Do you want my hand to fall off?"

She tried not to smile, but Zach saw her lips twitch. "Go ahead and smile," he said. "It's not going to hurt anything."

"Whatever. Just look at something over there."

"Why would I do that when the view here is flawless?"

She rolled her eyes again and waved for the bartender. "Are there any tables open yet?" she asked.

The blonde shook her head. "But you can order dinner here at the bar if you don't want to wait."

She glanced down at Zach. Did she really just size him up?

"Fine," she said. "May I have a menu, please?"

She looks good, he thought as he turned away for a second. *But she is uptight as hell. Probably an ice queen in bed.* He stole another glance at her — and this time he caught her staring right back at him.

Zach smiled and lifted his drink to her.

She turned away, and he couldn't tell if she was embarrassed or annoyed.

Chante wanted to slap herself for getting caught looking at Zachary Harrington. She couldn't think of a word to describe this man's looks. He was like a chocolate-dipped Adonis. He had dimples, and she was such a sucker for dimples. And those sparking whiskey-brown eyes.

But if he wasn't one of the most arrogant men she'd met in a long time! *To hell with Zachary Harrington and his gift to women attitude! Who in the hell does he think he is?* But something about him stirred an itch between her thighs. Crossing and uncrossing her legs, she couldn't help but think how long it had been since she had been touched by a man's hand, held in arms as strong as Zachary's looked. There she was, staring again!

Stop looking at this man. Who vacations alone? His wife or girlfriend is probably upstairs, mad because of something he did, Chante thought as she turned her eyes to the menu. As much as she didn't want to, she glanced at him again.

"Okay, now you're looking at me," he said with a brilliant smile.

"And?"

"When the shoe was on the other foot, there was a problem," he said.

Chante started to say something smart, but she held her tongue. "Listen," she began, "I'm trying to relax. I thought I was going to be staying someplace else, and I ended up here. Maybe I was a little harsh, but being looked at as a piece of meat isn't appealing to anyone."

"My apologies," he replied and smiled. "If you felt like a piece of meat, that was not my intention."

Chante wished she had a drink to cool the heat building in her stomach. What was it about this man that had ignited her passion, which had been dormant? She crossed her legs again and thought about the last time she'd been touched. Robert had been passionless, even the first time they made love. She'd excused it, assuming he was nervous; everything had been so new between the two of them, and she just knew it would get better. It never did.

Her gaze fell on Zach's hands. Big hands. Long fingers. How good would his touches be? Would he make her scream and moan in pleasure?

Stop it.

"So do I just call you beautiful, or are you going to tell me your name?"

"Chante."

"Chante. Just one name, like Madonna?"

She folded her arms across her chest. "Are you always this corny?"

"What did he do?"

"Excuse me?"

Zach folded his arms and smiled. "Come on, a woman doesn't just come to a place like this alone because her man made her happy."

Chante rolled her eyes. She didn't want to talk about Robert and why she'd hightailed it to Charleston. "Who said it was a man? Maybe my girlfriend and I had a fight."

Zach's eyes widened, and Chante couldn't stop laughing. "I knew you had a beautiful smile," he said. "A girlfriend, huh?"

"I wish I could've taken a picture of your face," she said, still giggling.

"Either way, whoever let you travel to South Carolina alone because they pissed you off, I thank them."

"And I'm sure your wife or girlfriend wouldn't appreciate you flirting with me to make her jealous." Chante looked over her shoulder. "Where is she anyway?"

"I'm happily divorced." He pulled out his cell phone and showed Chante the screen saver of his final decree.

"Wow," she said, then shook her head.

"Were you ever happily married?"

Zach seemed to ponder her question. "It doesn't matter. Didn't last. Wish I had known sooner who I'd married. Could've saved more money than switching my insurance to Geico."

"That I will drink to, finding out those true colors."

"And what are we drinking?" he asked as he waved for the bartender.

Chante shrugged. "Apple Crown Royal on ice."

"My kind of woman," Zach said, then gave her a fist bump. As she looked over the menu, Zach took the seat right next to hers. "So I told you a bit of my story, are you going to give me a little insight into you?"

Chante smiled. "Nope."

Shaking his head, Zach ordered the drinks and gave her a slow once-over. "You really have a girlfriend?"

"No."

"Good."

"Why?"

"Because now I know that I have a chance." He winked at her as the bartender set the whiskey in front of them.

She rolled her eyes. "Trust me, you don't have a chance."

Zach raised his right eyebrow. "That's

what you think."

Chante rolled her eyes, then took a sip of her drink.

"Wait," he said. "We're supposed to toast. Remember? To learning those true colors." She lifted her glass to his, and Zach leaned in to her. In a swift motion, he brought his mouth down on top of hers. She froze for a second, and then her body seemed to respond to Zach's hot tongue. She pressed against him, and her body tingled at his touch. The kiss went deeper than she'd expected, and Chante liked it. Liked it a lot.

Too much.

Pulling back, she pushed against his chest and then tossed her drink in his face. "You jackass," she said, then rose to her feet. Chante tore out of the bar and decided that she needed to avoid Zachary Harrington for the rest of her trip. Then she could pretend that everything she felt had never happened.

Zach wiped his face with the towel the bartender handed him. That kiss was worth the drink in his face. Chante was a hell of a woman, with lips like sugar. But she was obviously one of those women who believed in denying herself pleasure. She responded to his kiss just as he knew she would — like she needed it as much as he did — and he wanted to see what else she was in need of.

"Damn it," he muttered. "This is probably the worst thing I'm going to do."

"Excuse me?" the bartender asked. "Do you need something else?"

"Actually, I do."

"Another towel?" She didn't hide her smile, and while there was nothing funny about what had happened, he could understand why women got a kick out of such dramatic outbursts.

Pulling his wallet from his pocket, Zach grabbed a hundred-dollar bill and slid it to the bartender. "I want to do something nice for Chante."

She looked at the money. "What does that have to do with me?"

"The lady never got a chance to eat, and I want to send her some room service."

She laughed. "That little bit of money is not worth my job."

He added another hundred. "I just want to feed her, tell her that I'm sorry, and enjoy the rest of my vacation with a clean conscience."

She shook her head. "Add another fifty and maybe I'll help."

He dropped another bill on top of the stack, and the bartender smiled. "Are you sending her shrimp and grits? On second thought, no grits. I don't want to be responsible for Al Green part two."

This time Zach laughed. "You have jokes, I see. How about a nice seafood quiche or something like that?"

"That's a good choice," she said as she pocketed the money. "And you plan to deliver the meal to her?"

Zach winked. "That's the plan."

The bartender typed the order into the computer, then handed Zach a slip of paper. He read it and smiled. *Chante Britt, suite 615.*

Why did he feel the need to chase this woman? Because her kiss had heated him up like the sun, and because she had no idea what kind of baggage he had with his ex-wife.

Part of him said just let it go and keep doing his thing. He'd come to Charleston to rest and relax. But the other part of him wanted to have her legs and arms wrapped around him while she screamed his name. Yes, he was going to deliver her dinner, and hopefully she would be a lot calmer when he knocked on her door.

Chante turned on her cell phone with the intention of calling Liza. She had to tell somebody about that kiss. But a flood of messages caused her phone to explode with dings, beeps, and vibrations. She tossed it on the bed and groaned. Falling back on the soft mattress, she closed her eyes and licked her lips.

Zachary Harrington flashed in her mind like an erotic memory. That tender yet hot kiss triggered a desire inside Chante that scared and excited her at the same time.

She closed her eyes and allowed her mind to take her into Zachary's arms. His lips pressed against hers as his hands stroked her in the most neglected spot between her thighs. When her fingers brushed across her wetness, Chante opened her eyes and bolted upright in the bed. "What in the hell am I doing?"

A knock at the door shook her. Had the media found her? She started to ignore it, but the knocking persisted. "Damn it," she muttered as she padded over to the door. "Who is it?"

"Room service," a male voice said.

"I didn't order room service."

"It's complementary, ma'am."

Chante sucked her teeth and opened the door. When she saw the man holding the dish from the hotel's restaurant, she wanted to slam the door. "How — how did you find me?"

"When I put my mind to something, I can do anything."

"This is very stalker-like," she said.

"Actually, this is my apology. I wanted to bring you dinner, since you didn't get to eat. Notice, I didn't bring you any grits — just in case you decided to throw that too."

Chante wanted to ignore the food, but the enticing aroma made her stomach rumble. Even if she wanted to deny she was hungry, her body had just given her up. "Thanks for dinner. But that still doesn't . . ."

"You must be a lawyer," he said. "You have an argument for everything. Damn, woman, can't a man be nice to a pretty lady?"

"Not when said man kissed that woman as if he had a right to," Chante snapped. "If you want to be nice, give me the food, leave, and move on."

He held the covered dish out to her. "Yep, probably a district attorney. Bet you've never lost a case."

"I'm a corporate lawyer, and I never lose."

Zachary smiled, and Chante's heart thumped so loudly she knew he'd heard it. That man was finer than frog's hair and he knew it. She wondered how many women he'd blinded with that smile and those dimples. Weak. She was weak and wanted nothing more than to kiss him again.

Be cool, just be cool, she thought as she stared into his eyes. When he leaned in to her, the cool went away. She expected another kiss, but he brought his lips to her ear. "Breakfast?"

Chante's knees knocked from the heat of his breath on her earlobe. She nearly dropped her dinner, but quickly regained her senses. "I don't think so."

"Come on, Miss Attorney, you're going to have to give me a better reason than that."

"Here's the reason: I don't want to. Good night, Zachary," Chante said and slammed the door in his face. Leaning against the door, she took a deep breath. Why hadn't she said yes? Clearly, because this man was a temptation she couldn't resist.

CHAPTER 4

Zach smiled even though if he had had his way, breakfast with Chante would've been in bed. Standing outside Chante's door, he thought about just cutting his losses and moving on. This was too much work for a vacation fling. But there was something about her, something intriguing. And it didn't hurt that she was stunning. Especially when those full lips trembled.

It had taken everything in him not to kiss her again. Knowing that she wanted it just as much as he did made him hold back. She gave him just what he needed when he saw her lip quiver. That was so sexy and made him harder than a year-old fruitcake.

Then she wanted to act like the air between them wasn't charged with sexual energy. Whatever. She was just as attracted to him as he was to her.

Her scent seeped inside him, and now he wouldn't stop without getting a taste of her.

Yeah, he wasn't going to give up on Chante Britt. As a matter of fact, she wasn't going to know what hit her. Zach headed for the elevator and hyped himself up for the seduction of Chante Britt.

She moaned as he sucked her throbbing bud. Her thighs clenched as she screamed, "Zachary!"

When Chante heard her own scream, she bolted straight up in the bed. She was sweaty, but alone. "What the hell?" she whispered as she climbed out of bed. Padding over to the refrigerator in the corner of her suite, Chante grabbed a bottle of water and drank it in two gulps. The coolness did little to quell the heat between her thighs. Zachary Harrington.

How had that man invaded her dreams? She didn't even like him. He was arrogant but sexy as hell. Her grandmother's words taunted her. *Flirt with a stranger.*

"This is insane," she whispered as she opened another bottle of water. This time she sipped it slowly. What did she really have to lose? She was only going to be in Charleston for a short time, and she wanted to see if he could back up that kiss.

Besides, it had been so long since she'd had an orgasm. Hell, she couldn't even

56

remember the last time she'd dreamed about having an orgasm. But one kiss from Zachary had changed all of that. That was scary and exciting.

"Why not have breakfast with him?" Chante took another sip of water. How was she going to find him? Crossing over to the phone, she dialed the front desk.

"Good evening. How may I help you?" the front desk clerk asked when she answered.

"Could you please ring Zachary Harrington's room?"

"Hold please."

Zachary's groggy voice rang in her ear. "Yeah?"

"I thought about your breakfast offer."

"Chante?"

"Just how many women in Charleston have you invited to breakfast?"

He chuckled, and she felt her insides throb. "And you decided this at two in the morning?"

"Are you complaining?" she quipped. "I could've just stuck with no."

"You're funny, Chante."

She wanted him to stop saying her name, because it did something to her — made her thighs vibrate. "Does eight work for you?"

"It would have, had you not walked out of my dreams and woken me up."

"See you at nine, then," she said, then hung up the phone. Chante was tempted, very tempted to ask him if he wanted breakfast in bed. She had no idea where this all came from. Everything about that call was so unlike her. But what had being herself gotten her these days? Nothing she wanted. She did what she was supposed to do at work and still ended up suspended. Her dreams of being a partner at Myrick, Lawson and Walker were basically a pile of ash.

Then there was Robert. That slimy bastard was still causing havoc in her life so that he could make his better. She deserved to have some fun, and that's what she was going to do with Zachary Harrington. Fun with no strings. She wasn't looking at him as a man she might marry. He was simply a man who she hoped would give her a good time and allow her to let go of a pent-up wall of sexual frustration.

Smiling, Zach flipped on his back and stared at the ceiling. *Well played, Chante,* he thought. The only thing better than the phone call would've been her showing up at his door dressed like she'd been in his

58

dream. Silk bathrobe with nothing underneath. Just thinking about it made his mouth water and his body tingle with anticipation.

Part of him wondered why Chante had had a sudden change of heart. She'd said no and slammed the door in his face. It didn't matter. She'd said yes — at two in the morning. That gave him six hours to get ready to see her again, and hopefully she wouldn't throw coffee.

Drifting off to sleep, Zach's dreams were about Chante in different states of undress. Maybe he was on his way to making his dream come true.

Sitting in the restaurant, Chante glanced at her watch. It was nine forty-five. "I don't believe this," she muttered as she rose from her seat. "I've been stood up." She looked at her watch again. Nine forty-six. She returned to her seat, feeling foolish. She'd had her fill of coffee and was tired of waiting. Obviously, Zachary wasn't coming. She looked down at her plate, half filled with grits and salmon, but her appetite was gone. Maybe this had been a reminder. She wasn't this girl, the one making late-night calls and demanding that he meet her. This was the wake-up call she'd needed. There was nothing wrong with the way she'd been living her life.

"Excuse me, beautiful, can a late man get some breakfast?"

She looked up and locked eyes with Zachary. Oh, he had as much nerve as he had sex appeal. Standing there with a smug — at least in her opinion — smile on his face showing off those dimples. Those dimples had been the only things that kept her from tossing her unfinished breakfast in his face.

Those damned dimples made her weak. He made her weak. "I've already had my breakfast. You can sit anywhere you please." And as much as she wanted to rise from her seat and stalk out of the restaurant, she stayed planted in place because she couldn't take her eyes off him. He was dressed in a pair of khaki shorts, a baby-blue tank top, and a pair of brown leather sandals. To the naked eye, he looked ready for a day on the beach.

The old Chante would've been out the door more than half an hour ago. But if she was honest with herself, she'd waited for him because she wanted to see him. Needed to see him. She wasn't disappointed at all, even if she had to pretend she wasn't impressed.

Zach sat across from her and stared into

her eyes — or was it her soul? He didn't make her uncomfortable as he drank her image in, but she wasn't going to let him know that. *Be cool,* she chanted silently.

"I'm sorry I kept you waiting. Of all the days to oversleep. And to think, I almost missed out on seeing your beautiful scowl."

Chante rolled her eyes. "Some apology."

He winked. "I was hoping I could steal a smile." Zach folded his arms across his chest and leaned back in the chair. "So what's good here?"

This time she did smile. "Why don't you look at the menu and ask a waiter?"

"I knew it was beautiful. A bit sassy, but beautiful," he said.

"What?"

"Your smile."

Chante didn't roll her eyes; she just continued smiling. Her tough girl act either wasn't working or Zach didn't care.

"All right, Miss Advocate," Zach said. "What's your story?"

She raised her right eyebrow as she felt a jolt of electricity shoot through her body. "My story?"

He reached across the table and took her hand in his. "Yes, what's going on behind those beautiful brown eyes?"

Glancing down at his hand, she had a flash

of that hand between her thighs, those fingers touching her most intimate spots. "I'm running from my real life," she blurted out.

"So he pissed you off really badly, huh?"

"You could say that. Got me suspended from work and almost ruined my relationship with my best friend. But I don't want to talk about that." She brought her coffee cup to her lips, then realized it was empty.

"Were you two married?"

She shook her head as she set her cup on the table. "Thankfully, that wedding never happened."

"Well, congratulations to you. I married the wrong person and spent a lot of time and money trying to get her to go away."

Chante wondered if he was going to say more about his ex. When he didn't, she asked, "So what did you do to her?"

Zach shook his head; his smile faded, and those dimples went away. "Why do women always assume . . . ?"

"I'm sorry," she said. "I'm not saying that I'm bitter, but my judgment has been clouded."

"My ex-wife was the cause of our divorce, and if I'd let her, she'd have destroyed everything that I've worked for."

"Sounds like we fell for the same person,

only in different forms."

"Maybe that's why we want each other, to see what it's like to be with the right one." He winked again, and Chante's heart pounded like a bass drum.

"Getting ahead of yourself, huh? We're just here for a short time."

"And we should have fun, not pay any more attention to the ones who tried to take us down."

She smiled again. "I can get behind that, Zachary."

"Please, call me Zach. All my friends do, and you're about to be my best friend."

"All right, best friend. Why don't you order your breakfast, and then I can show you one of my favorite places in Charleston."

"You know a lot about this city, huh?" he said as he picked up his menu.

Chante leaned back in her seat, realizing that Zach was still holding her hand, and nodded. Sliding her hand from underneath his, she still felt the heat from his touch. "I grew up here. And Charleston is a magical city."

"Really? Where's your geechie accent, then?"

Chante laughed, remembering how her mother had forced her to speak proper

English from the moment she'd started talking. There had been diction lessons and the whole nine.

"My mother frowned on that," Chante replied. "Even though my grandmother proudly has that accent. There are certain times when I will reveal it. Usually when I'm really pissed off about something and I'm trying not to curse."

"Let me guess: your mom is a true southern belle."

She rolled her eyes. "I thought we were going to have fun? Talking about my mother is not my idea of a good time."

"Ouch. Sorry."

"Don't be. Anyway, if I'm honest with myself, my mother's ways helped me in my career. Even if she thinks that my main goal should've been finding a husband while I was in college."

"Seriously?"

"Yes. And that's all I'm going to say about that," she said as a waitress approached the table.

"Good morning, again," she said as she glanced at Chante, then focused her attention on Zach. "Would you like to order, sir?"

"Yes. I'll have what the lady had. And coffee. Lots of coffee."

She nodded, then turned to Chante.

"Miss, would you like a refill on your coffee?"

"Please."

Once they were alone, Chante quietly studied Zach. Dark chocolate with a small hint of milk chocolate mixed in. And those eyes. They sparkled in the sunlight with flecks of gold dancing in them.

"You're staring," he said. "I got chewed out for doing that last night."

"Well, it's a new dawn, a new day . . ."

"And you're feeling good. Got to love a woman who can quote the goddess Nina."

"You're going to sit here and pretend you know more than one Nina Simone song?"

Zach put his hand to his chest as if he'd been shot. "Woman, you wound me. Music was a big part of growing up Harrington. Good music played in our house every day. Nina Simone was always on the play list."

"And what part of New York did you grow up in, because you have an accent."

"The Bronx."

"You still live there?"

He shook his head. "I live on the Upper East Side, at least that's where my mail goes. I had a great house on Long Island."

"Lost it in the divorce?"

"You could say that," he said. What Zach didn't say was the feds had taken his home because of his ex-wife's illegal activities.

"Well, that sucks," Chante said.

"I know, but this isn't fun," he said.

"True. I've always enjoyed visiting New York. I second-chaired a patent case there once."

"How many states are you licensed in?"

"Five and D.C. Why? Do you need a lawyer?"

Did he need a lawyer? No, he needed Chante Britt's lips against his. Leaning forward, he locked eyes with Chante. "You know what I need."

"What?" she breathed.

"This." He brought his mouth on top of hers and kissed her with a slow passion that made her shiver and tremble. Moaning as his tongue mated with hers, Chante wanted to strip out of her clothes and allow him to feast on her for breakfast, lunch, and dinner.

That tongue was magical, amazing, delicious, and becoming addictive. It wasn't until the waitress cleared her throat that they broke the kiss. "Honeymoon?" she asked as she set Zach's plate of salmon and grits in front of him.

Never taking his eyes off Chante, Zach said, "A new beginning."

"How sweet," she said as Chante smiled.

"How long have you been married?"

"Umm," Chante stammered. "We're not married."

The waitress's lips formed the shape of an O as she poured coffee in their empty mugs.

"Awkward," Chante said once the waitress was out of earshot. "She should've known we weren't married. We're happy and having a good time."

"You sure you haven't been married before?"

"My close encounter of the matrimony kind was more than enough to open my eyes to the trauma I avoided. But I have to say, I've seen a happy marriage. My best friend is married and having the time of her life."

"And you didn't get the itch like most women do?"

She rolled her eyes and poured a bit of cream in her coffee. "I'm not like most women."

"I see that. I like that."

She spooned sugar into her mug, then took a sip. "This is good."

"You like coffee a lot, huh?"

"It's something I picked up over the last year or so. My friend Liza is turning me into a real coffee snob. Ethiopian beans are the best."

"That's because you haven't had Kona

beans fresh from Hawaii. I have some property there, a little industrial tract of land. Whenever I visit, I have coffee with breakfast, lunch, and dinner. And the pineapples. You know what they say about pineapples, right?"

"No, I don't," she said with a raised eyebrow.

"They don't get any better than in Hawaii."

"I'm sure that's exactly what you meant," she quipped. Still smiling, Chante watched Zach devour his breakfast. As his lips closed around the fork, she couldn't help but relive both earth-shattering kisses he'd treated her to. *Those lips should come with a warning label,* she thought.

"Do I have something on my chin?" he asked as he reached for his coffee cup.

"No. I'm just wondering how you eat so fast without burning yourself."

"One thing you don't get in Manhattan is real grits. I think I've eaten more grits since I've been in Charleston than I have in twenty years."

Chante handed him a napkin. "There's more to Charleston than grits."

"Good. Sounds like you just volunteered to show me everything that Charleston has to offer," he said as he wiped his mouth.

"Not just your favorite place."

Chante's smile turned into a smirk. "And you're going to show me what pineapples can do?"

CHAPTER 5

Zach was happy he had swallowed his food, because Chante's last comment would've made him choke. "Oh, really?"

"Mangoes too," she said with a wicked gleam in her eyes.

"I see I had you pegged all wrong."

She sipped her coffee, and when she put her cup down and licked her bottom lip, he was hard. Chante knew what she was doing, and she was doing it well.

"And how had you pegged me?" she asked after another sip.

"Will anything I say be held against me?"

"I'm a lawyer, not a cop."

"Beautiful but uptight."

"And now?" she asked as she softly drummed her fingers against her mug.

Zach smiled and leaned forward. "I'm intrigued. You have layers, and I want to peel them back until I reach the core."

The look on her face sent a jolt to his

groin. Something about that mix of minx and innocence turned him on like a light switch. Who was Chante Britt, and why hadn't some southern gent snapped her up? That was layer one. He'd have to peel that back immediately. Glancing at her left ring finger, he noticed there wasn't the telltale tan line. That was a plus. But he didn't get the cheating vibe from her, no matter how mad her man may have made her.

"Well," she said after a beat, "are we ready to go?"

Zach nodded and waved for the blushing waitress to bring them their check. After paying the bill, he turned to Chante. "She probably thinks we're having an affair."

"I bet most of the people in here are." Chante shook her head. "I should really think about becoming a divorce lawyer. Half the work and more money."

"No, you shouldn't. By the time my divorce was final, I hated my lawyer as much as I hated hers."

"Hate is such a strong word."

Zach shrugged. "In this case it fits."

"But how could anyone hate anyone as lovable as me?" She winked as they rose from their seats. Zach crossed over to her and took her hand in his.

"You're something else, counselor."

"Wouldn't you like to find out."

Zach kissed her hand. "And a mind reader to boot. I like you. You can handle my next divorce."

"Wow, planning a divorce, and you haven't even met the next Mrs. Harrington."

He gave her a slow once-over. "Never say never. I could be holding her hand right now."

"Then you'd really hate your divorce lawyer." Chante's throaty laugh was like a sensual samba.

"What are you driving?" he asked when they entered the lobby.

"Huh?"

"What kind of car are you driving?"

"A Jaguar F-Type, why?"

Zach let out a low whistle. "Please tell me it's a convertible."

"Sorry to disappoint you."

"All right," he said as he pulled out the keys to his car, "we'll take mine. It is a convertible."

"What kind?"

"Nothing as fancy as yours. The seventeen-year-old in me rented a Mustang GT."

Chante grabbed the keys. "I love a Mustang, and since I know where we're going, I'm driving."

"Bossy is another layer, I see," he quipped.

They headed for the parking lot and got into the blue convertible GT. "This looks like a lot of fun," she said as she started the car.

"There's a lot of power under that hood. Can you handle it?"

She sucked her teeth. "I can handle anything." Starting the car, she tore out of the parking lot, making the tires squeal, and Zach wondered if he would be able to handle the ride with Chante.

They drove into Folly Beach and headed for the historic Folly Beach Pier. "This is beautiful," he said as they got out of the car.

"And strong," she said. "My grandmother and I used to come here and fish over there." She pointed to a corner of the 1,045-foot-long pier.

Zach gave her a curious glance. "You fished with your grandmother?"

"Yes. Much to my mother's chagrin. I'd come home covered in fish scales and dirt underneath my nails, and she'd nearly have a heart attack. I think Elsie Mae did it just to get a rise out of my mother." They walked among the tourists until they found a spot where they could look out on the ocean.

"Must have been nice growing up around

all this beauty."

She shrugged. "You take it for granted until you move away from it." Chante leaned against the wooden railing and inhaled the salty ocean air. Zach leaned against her, pressing his nose into her hair. Damn, she smelled good. Sweet like a Carolina rose. Instinctively, he wrapped his arms around her waist. He expected her to push him away, but she fell into his embrace. Silence enveloped them as they watched the ocean waves.

Chante's thoughts troubled her, made her think of past mistakes — namely Robert. But something about Zach's touch put her mind at ease while making her body tremble with anticipation. It occurred to her, as they stood in the sun, that in the time they'd spent talking over breakfast and the walk up the pier, he knew more about her than Robert ever did. Not once during their courtship had she thought about bringing him to Charleston or telling him about Elsie Mae. Maybe if she had introduced Robert to Elsie Mae, things wouldn't have gone straight to hell. Her grandmother probably would've sniffed out that self-serving son of a bitch the moment she laid eyes on him.

Chante turned around and lost herself in Zach's brown eyes. What would her grandmother make of him?

"What?" he asked.

"I want to show you something special," she said.

"I'm already looking at it," he replied with a smile.

Chante rolled her eyes. "Are you always like this? I mean, if I didn't want to drive your car, I'd push you over the edge for being so damned corny."

"You sure know how to hurt a brother," he said, then feigned a pout. "This is your show; whatever you want me to see, I'm down for it."

"Good," she said, still basking in his touch. Zach felt his erection grow as she licked her lips. He wanted this woman more than he should have since he'd told himself he was taking a break from the opposite sex. But her lips drew him in like a magnet to metal. Kissing her softly, he slipped his tongue between her pillow-soft lips and reveled in the sweetness of her mouth. Chante moaned as his hands traveled down her back, resting right above her ample behind. She broke the kiss and looked up at him.

"We've got to stop doing this," she said.

"Why do you like to deny yourself pleasure?"

"Let's go."

"Answer the question."

"Ever think that people get into bad situations because they move too fast?"

"Maybe people miss out on a good thing because they don't live in the moment. We have a moment, Chante. Right here and right now. We don't have to look five or six years down the road. You want me and I want you."

She shivered, unable to come up with a rebuttal to him. Did she want him? Yes. Could she live in the moment? She didn't know. It wasn't her style. She was a planner; she did weigh her options and look toward the future.

And what has planning gotten you so far? You planned to be a partner at the firm by now. You're not. You planned to be married by now. You're not.

"Chante?" Zach asked, breaking into her thoughts. "Can we have this moment, no matter how long it's going to last?"

"Yes," she breathed. "Yes. We can."

He cupped her face in his hands and kissed her again. Slow. Deep. Passionate. She pressed her soft body against his hard one, losing herself in his kiss. Giving in to the pleasure of his tongue and his touch.

This man was kissing her senseless, and Chante liked it. Needed it. Wanted it. Breaking the kiss, his lips curved into a seductive smile. "So what's this special thing that you wanted to show me?" he asked.

"Umm," Chante began as clouds of desire cleared her brain. "My grandmother's legacy. She has a shop on Folly Beach that is a must-see tourist spot."

"Sounds like you're pretty well connected in this city. Why did you ever leave?"

Shrugging as they started walking down the pier, she replied, "Wanted to blaze my own path, and I couldn't do it in the shadow of my family's history."

What she didn't say was she wanted to be far away from her mother's judgment. Chante was sure that had she come up with a cure for cancer without being married, Allison would've found fault with it.

"Interesting. I knew that I wanted to follow in my father's footsteps. And leaving New York wasn't an option for me in my younger days. I wanted to be bigger than Trump. Then I realized I had the best role model ever because Trump is an idiot."

Chante laughed. "That is the truth. My mother and grandmother have different views on legacies. Figured it was best to make my own."

"Miss Independent. Bet you started walking when you were six months old," he said as they reached the car.

"Funny. I was about eight months old, thank you very much."

Giving her a slow once-over, he was thankful she had those hips and that round booty. He was thankful for those lips and the skillful way she used them.

"Let's go," he said, feeling the burgeoning of his growing erection against his zipper.

Chante locked eyes with him, seeing something that made her thighs quiver.

"Okay," she said, then did her imitation of Bo Duke and hopped in the car without opening the door. Zach's knees nearly buckled as he laughed.

"Did you just . . . ?"

"There is a seventeen-year-old in me who's having so much fun right now. Get in the car so we can go!"

Opening the door, he got into the car and buckled up. "Giddy up!" Chante took off like a bolt of lightning. Zach gripped the side of the door.

"Your seventeen-year-old is a little out of control," he quipped.

Chante eased off the gas. "Yeah, it is tourist season, and the last thing I need is a speeding ticket. My mother would call me a criminal."

"I get the feeling that you two aren't that

close," he said. "I thought that was a south-ern thing."

"You haven't mentioned your mother," she said, not wanting to get into her rela-tionship with her mother.

Zach nodded. "My mother passed away when my sister and I were young. I think the reason Dad and I were so close is because we felt we had to team up and protect Zoe."

"And how did she feel about that?"

Zach laughed. "My sister is a rebel, so she was none too pleased. I think that's why she became a private investigator — so she can take all the risks we tried to protect her from."

"She's older or younger?"

"Younger by about five minutes. Zoe's my twin."

"Wow," she said. "I wish I had a sibling, but to have a twin, that must be exciting."

"Eh, when she's not in one of her moods. But I love my sister, and I'm so proud of her. She's saved my ass more than once or twice. I still worry about her, though."

"Because she's a woman? I don't know why men think women aren't capable of handling ourselves. And if your sister is a PI, she's probably kick-ass and . . ."

"Whoa, whoa. I don't know where that

came from, but I don't doubt that a woman can do anything. At the end of the day, that's my sister."

"Sorry, it's just a bit of the feminist in me."

"There's a lot of things inside you," he said, while thinking, *I want to be inside of you myself.*

"Here it is," she said as she pulled up in front of Elsie's Gifts and Goodies.

"Wow. This was actually one of the places the concierge recommended I visit," he said as Chante put the car in PARK.

"See what I mean about shadows," Chante said when they exited the car, looking up at the white wooden storefront and the black script across the top of the fascia.

"Will your grandmother be here?" he asked as they walked up to the door and he opened it for her.

"No, she's on a cruise around the world and . . ."

"Chante Elaine?"

"Mother," Chante said, "what are you doing — hi."

Allison Britt offered her daughter a plastic smile as she crossed over to her as if she were the queen of Charleston. She gave her daughter a slow once-over, then smiled. "So you breeze into town and can't even say hello to your own mother? Is that how they treat their mothers in North Carolina?"

Chante blinked and swallowed the urge to ask her mother when was the last time she'd spoken to her own mom. "I was going to call you and Dad after I got settled in. But when I arrived and saw the state of Grammy's . . ."

"Your grandmother is trying to wipe out all traces of my father's history. She thinks this shop allows her to . . ." Allison glanced at Zach. "Oh, Chante, how rude of you. Who is your companion?"

Zach could feel the tension in the air like humidity. He could see why Chante and her mother weren't close. How were they even related?

"Zach Harrington," he said, extending his hand to Allison.

She smiled and gave him a limp hand-shake. "So how are you and my daughter acquainted?"

"Mother," Chante said.

"Are you dating, or is it time to finally start planning a wedding?"

Chante slammed her hand against her forehead. "We actually just met, and according to you, there's a certain time for a court-ship, right?"

"Your sarcasm is not welcome," Allison

said in clipped tone. "At your age, we'll just have to take what we can get."

Zach inhaled sharply and waited to see what Chante's response would be. When she didn't say a word, he was shocked. Then again, this was her mother, and he couldn't expect a verbal dressing down.

"Anyway," Allison continued, "Mr. Harrington, where did you and my daughter meet? Are you also a lawyer? I'd love to have you two over for dinner. Though it's short notice, I'm sure I could pull something together for this evening."

"Well, Mrs. Britt," Zach began, "Chante and I have plans tonight, and I wouldn't want to put you under that kind of pressure."

"Where are you from?" Allison asked, and Chante groaned.

"New York."

Allison looked at Chante and shook her head. "Ah, a Yankee."

"Mother, the war is over," Chante said, then rolled her eyes.

"Well," Allison said as she toyed with the pearl choker around her neck. "Please call me and your father once you've settled in. And how long are you going to be here, Chante?"

"I haven't decided yet."

Allison nodded. "Mr. Harrington, it was a pleasure. Chante, will you walk me to my car?"

"Sure thing, Mom," Chante said with forced gaiety in her voice. Once they were outside, Allison shook her head at her daughter.

"That's the best you can do?"

"Mom, we're not even dating. We're just spending some time together and having fun."

"Having fun? Don't you think you're a little too old to just be having fun? When are you going to have a family?"

Chante shook her head. "This is why I needed to get myself together before I called you. I'm . . ."

"Chante Elaine," Allison said touching her daughter's arm, "if you're going to get married, please don't let it be to a damned Yankee."

"I thought I didn't have many choices left," Chante said sarcastically.

"If you put a little more effort into looking like a lady, then men wouldn't just want to have fun with you. I mean, Liza Palmer married a senator. Yet you're still single."

"Tell Dad I'll give him a call." Chante turned back to the shop and counted to ten before walking inside. Zach was about to smile at her when he saw the look on her face.

"Everything all right?"

She waved her hand and forced a smile. "That's my mama," Chante said.

"You two seem like night and day."

Chante thought oil and water was a better description, but she didn't want to get into a discussion about her mother. She hadn't even wanted her mom to see her with Zach or any other man because she knew where the conversation would lead.

Changing the subject, she pointed toward a wall of handwoven baskets. "My grammy used to make these herself. She tried to teach me, but my fingers were too small." Chante held up her hand, and Zach took it in his bigger one. Soft, slender fingers linked with his, and he didn't fight the urge to spin her around as if they were on a ballroom dance floor.

"What are you doing?" she asked with a laugh.

"Trying to restart the fun. Your mama was pretty intense."

Chante wrapped her arms around his neck. "Let's not talk about my mama, and let's get a basket with chocolate in it."

All Zach wanted to do was hold her and kiss her until the sunset, but knowing the shop was her grandmother's place made him feel a little awkward about that. Still, it didn't stop him from copping a feel of her round bottom.

"Chocolate, huh?"

"Yep. Chocolate and biscuits. Best thing in the world."

"I think you're wrong on that one."

Chante raised her right eyebrow. "How can you say that when you've never had it?"

Zach pulled her against his chest. "I haven't had you either, but I know you're going to be better than chocolate and biscuits." Then he flicked his tongue across her ear lobe. Chante took a deep breath, then placed her hand on his chest.

"You know what," she began. "I think you're trying to seduce me."

"Yes. I am," he whispered. "I'd kiss you right now, but I feel like your grandmother is watching."

Chante brought her mouth level with his. "And if you kissed me right now, she'd give you a high five."

"In that case," he said as he brought his mouth down on top of hers. Chante welcomed his tongue, reveled in the sweet and spicy taste of his mouth. And those hands roaming her back, cupping her bottom and pulling her against him, should be outlawed.

"Really?" Allison exclaimed, causing Zach and Chante to break their kiss. "Is this a lawyer thing? I didn't raise my daughter to act this way."

"Mom," Chante said, "I thought you were gone."

Allison closed her eyes and counted to ten, causing Zach to laugh inwardly. Was she serious? She acted as if she'd just walked in on two sixteen-year-olds having sex in her bedroom.

"Mrs. Britt, I take the blame for what you just walked in on. I asked Chante a question, and she said yes."

Suddenly, Allison didn't seem so traumatized. Chante shook her head as she saw the sparkle in her mother's eyes. "Well, let me see the ring," Allison excitedly said.

"Mom, you . . ."

"I haven't had a chance to pick out the perfect ring for this woman, but that is next on the agenda. We really didn't want to say anything yet because it's just been such a whirlwind romance."

"What are you doing?" Chante asked through clenched teeth. Zach smiled at Chante.

"Were you trying to keep this a secret?" Allison asked. "I should've known that you weren't just . . ."

"Mom, Zach, can we talk about all of this later? In private? Without an audience?" Chante nodded to a few customers who were staring at them.

Allison nodded. "That would be proper. Let me call your father." She reached into her purse and pulled out her cell phone. Chante punched Zach on the shoulder.

"Do you know what you've done?" she asked in a tense whisper.

"Yes. I've gotten your mother off your back for a little while." Zach winked at her. "She thinks you're going to marry a damned Yankee."

Chante laughed quietly and shook her head. "How in the hell am I going to live this down?"

"Easy, when you go home, you will realize the error of your ways and move on to a more suitable mate or decide that marriage isn't your thing." Zach kissed Chante's hand. "When you get back to Charlotte, you tell your mother what an asshole this Yankee is, and you're golden."

She sucked her teeth. "You don't know my mother."

"I have an idea."

Chante pinched his arm again. "She's putting together a dinner party right now. This isn't going to work."

"I got this, dear."

Chante slapped her hand on her hip. "Don't call me dear; it's very condescending." Zach kissed her on the forehead.

"Darling or sweetheart? I mean, I have to call my fiancée something."

"How about Chante?" she quipped with a wink.

"All right, darling, I will see you later," Allison said as she walked over to Chante and Zach. Pointing her finger at her daughter, she smiled. "Your father said you've been holding out on him. So we're having a low-country boil tonight, and you two are expected to be there."

"What if we have plans of our own?" Chante asked.

"Then change them. You're going to have the rest of your lives to be together and do whatever it is that you have planned."

"You're absolutely right, Mrs. Britt," Zach said, and Chante wanted to strangle him.

"Please, call me Allie."

Chante could've been pushed over with a feather. *Allie? When in the world did she start going by a nickname?*

"Well, Miss Allie, I will make sure Chante and I arrive for the boil on time, especially since this will be my first one."

Chante rolled her eyes at the big Kool-

Aid grin on her mother's face. This time, making sure her mother was gone, she turned to Zach and shook her head.

"Have you lost your ever-loving mind? You know when we get to that house tonight it's going to be filled with her closest friends, asking about wedding dates, rings, and . . ."

"So?" He smiled. "Your mother looked so happy when she thought you were getting married."

"Did you just say *so*?"

"Yes. We're supposed to be having fun, remember? Your mother and her demands for you to get married put a damper on our tour. I'm all about giving women what they want."

Oh, I can tell you what I want, and it has nothing to do with a low-country boil, she thought as she looked at his lips.

"What?" he asked as their eyes locked.

"This is a bad idea."

"It's one night. You get your mom off your back, and you can spend the rest of your vacation with me without interruption."

"And what makes you think I want to spend the rest of my time in Charleston attached to you at the hip?" she asked as she picked a basket filled with chocolate and Firefly Sweet Tea. Zach looked at the goodies in the basket.

"What is Firefly Sweet Tea?"

"Oh, you're going to find out, my dear Yankee."

Zach was about to respond when his cell phone went off. Retrieving the phone from his pocket, he saw it was Kia calling him. "I have to take this," he said as he took a few steps away from her. "Hello?"

"Zach, the feds are here," she said frantically.

"What the hell do they want, and do they have warrants?"

"Yes. They're looking into her ties with that judge."

Zach groaned and muttered, "What the fuck does that have to do with me?"

"I asked, but not in those words. Everybody in New York is looking for you."

"Make sure they don't find me."

"Ooh," she moaned.

"What's wrong?" Zach asked, his voice laden with concern.

"Your goddaughter feels the same way about these feds as I do. They want to question you."

"Give them my attorney's phone number, and tell them to kiss my ass."

"Now, Mr. Harrington, is that anyway to speak of the United States government?" a male voice asked.

"Who is this?"

"Special Agent Carver Banks."

"Call my lawyer."

"Listen, Mr. Harrington, I understand that you and Natalie are divorced. I believe you're a victim, but I'm only doing my job. However, we need to find out how many people are involved in her operation, and if you're innocent, then you have nothing to worry about."

"I'm on vacation, and I've already told you people I have nothing to do with her criminal enterprise. The only thing I have to worry about is that you're in my office for no reason."

"True. But this is another crime, and having a judge in your pocket would make your business a lot easier."

"Go to hell and call my attorney." Zach hit the END button on his phone. When he slammed the phone into his pocket, he noticed that Chante was giving him the side eye.

"What was that all about?"

"Nothing for you to worry about."

She shook her head, thinking about the hushed conversations she'd ignored when she and Robert were together. Wait, why was she acting as if this was the same thing? She and Zach weren't a couple. He was right. Whatever drama he had going on was none of her concern.

"You really need this tea now," she said, keeping her voice light.

Zach offered her a weak smile. "Listen, that call was . . ."

"Nothing for me to worry about," she parroted.

"My ex-wife is in some more trouble, and it's come to my front door."

Chante shook her head, remembering the reporters at her front door and the reason for her trip to Charleston. "And you didn't ask for that. I just don't understand why people try to make the sins of others your problem."

Zach knew right then that Chante Britt was the phenomenal woman Maya Angelou wrote about in her poem. "You know what, you're amazing."

"Yes, and I've been on the other side of that. So before we go and pretend we're madly in love and going to break up after this vacation is over, let's get drunk."

"Sounds like a great idea. But know this: after this low-boil thing, I want to strip you bare."

His words sent a tingle though her body, but a warning voice in her head told her to chill. "You sure you haven't been drinking already?"

"No, but I've been wanting to see you out of these clothes for a long time." He brought his lips to her ear. "And I'm not talking about getting you into bed. I want you on the sand."

"Huh?"

"I want to see you in a sexy two piece on the beach, while we drink."

Smiling, she said, "Just so you know, indecent exposure in South Carolina can put you in prison for up to three years."

"All right, good to know. I'll make sure I'm really discreet when I untie your top," he said with a wink.

CHAPTER 6

Meanwhile, in Charlotte, Robert and his campaign staff huddled around a television watching an Erica Bryant report on the race for Charlotte's next mayor. Dominic Hall paced back and forth as the face of former Mecklenburg County Commissioner David Clemmons filled the screen.

"That lame duck. He was voted off the board of county commissioners. Why does he think people want him to be mayor?" he muttered.

"Calm down, Nic," Robert said, trying to hear what Clemmons had to say. Clemmons had lost his seat on the board of county commissioners after his affair with the former head of the Department of Social Services became public. But for as many people who wanted his head, there were just as many who cheered his comeback.

Robert knew he didn't have the long history that Clemmons did in Charlotte politics, but surely he still had supporters. And being that Charlotte claimed to be a family-oriented city, if he could get Chante on board, then he'd be able to mend those fences that Liza had brought down. *That bitch,* he thought. *All she had to do was mind her business. That senate seat was mine. Now I have to work my way up from the bottom as though I haven't been preparing to lead for my whole life.*

"You're up," Gabrielle Tanks, a young staffer on Robert's campaign said as she grabbed the remote and turned the volume up.

"Robert Montgomery seems like an unlikely candidate for mayor," Erica Bryant began as she walked in front of a picture of Robert on a big screen. "In the race for the North Carolina senate seat for District Forty-five, Montgomery was humiliated when it was revealed he'd had a relationship with a woman whom he paid to have sex with him. At the time, he was engaged to Charlotte attorney Chante Britt."

A picture of the smiling couple flashed on the screen. Robert had hoped to talk Chante into making amends for her role in sabotaging his senate bid. She owed him a chance to restart his political career. Had she not participated in Liza's smear campaign, then he might have been in Raleigh as the first senator from District Forty-five — not that blunt instrument Jackson Franklin.

"But," Erica Bryant said, "it was his former fiancée's forgiveness that inspired Montgomery to return to the public eye."

The camera cut to a pre-recorded interview of Robert and Erica.

"Robert, after what you went through last year, most people would think your political career would be over," Erica said. "What made you decide to run for mayor?"

"Charlotte needs a new voice. One that isn't afraid to stand up to policies in Raleigh that hurt our city. And Charlotte is a city that looks past rumors and lies, as did the love of my life."

"So there is no truth to you and Dayshea Brown having a sexual relationship that you paid for?"

"None at all. I was the victim of a smear campaign. Chante didn't believe it, and the people of Charlotte should follow her lead."

Robert smiled as he watched the interview replay, then saw Dayshea appear on the screen. He and Nic expelled more curse words than an Eddie Murphy stand-up routine.

"We didn't agree to this!" Robert exclaimed.

Dayshea had lost the glamor she'd had the last time she'd been on the news. She looked like a plain around-the-way girl.

"I only met Robert once, then his fiancée and her friend came to me. I told them when I was about that life that I had one rule: I didn't sleep with married men or men who had someone at home. I was a different person back then. But I've changed, and maybe Robert has too."

"Turn it off," Nic bellowed. "Just what we need, an endorsement from a hooker."

"What about all the people who were standing by me last year?" Robert asked, now on his feet and pacing back and forth.

"I've made calls," Nic said.

"Do more!"

The staff members in the room headed for the door. Robert turned to Gabrielle. "Wait," he said. "You're the head of my social media campaign. How many likes do we have on our Facebook page?"

She looked down at her iPad Mini. "One hundred and three."

"That isn't enough," Robert exclaimed.

Nic tented his hands underneath his chin. "Maybe this Chante angle isn't working, No one has seen you two together, and she's suspended from her law firm."

"But," Robert interjected, "if she doesn't

forgive me, how can I expect voters to do so?"

"Then we have to find her and get you two on camera."

"I need to talk to Gabby, alone," Robert said, basically dismissing Nic.

When he was alone with the young woman, he pulled her into his arms. "You are so sexy," he breathed against her ear.

"What about Chante?"

Robert slipped his hands between Gabby's thighs and stroked her womanly core. "Chante who?"

Gabby moaned, and Robert believed that free sex was the best sex ever.

Back in Charleston, Chante looked at herself in the mirror. She hadn't worn a bikini since she and Liza went to Cancun on spring break. Looking at her image in the mirror, she smiled. All the running and working out she'd done since her suspension had done her body good. She was impressed with the reflection she saw in the mirror and knew Zach would be as well.

"What am I doing?" she mused aloud. Chante knew her grandmother would get a kick out of this ruse. But Chante wasn't so sure that going to her parents' house with Zach on her arm, acting as if they were getting married, was a good idea. Lying to her overbearing mother was one thing, but her Dad didn't deserve this. Then again, he'd probably laugh too. *Don't overthink it. You're here to have a good time, and Zach is just a distraction.* Satisfied with her reflection, Chante tied a yellow sarong around her waist and headed for the lobby to meet Zach.

Zach was glancing at a brochure about Folly Beach as he heard the ding of the elevator. When he saw those legs, those thighs, and those pretty toes, he wanted to take Chante back upstairs and suck the polish off her toenails. If Zach had any weaknesses, Chante highlighted each and every one of them in that yellow bikini. "Well, I think I've found the highlight of my trip. Wow," he said, then took off his Brooklyn Nets hat and bowed.

Chante smacked him on his shoulder. "You're too much," she said.

"You look too damned good," he said as he gave her a slow once-over. "Let's get out of here before I change my mind."

"Change your mind?"

He nodded. "Change my mind and take you into the Jacuzzi, then put up an out-of-order sign."

Shaking her head, she headed for the door with Zach in tow. "Slow down," he said as he tugged at her sarong. When Chante took a step forward, the sarong came off in Zach's hand. Taking a look at her barely covered behind, he knew that God was a mighty, mighty good God.

"Zach!" Chante called out as she placed her hands behind her back. "I can't . . ."

"I was trying to slow you down," he replied as he twirled her sarong. "Ended up slowing myself down."

She walked up to him and reached for her sarong. Zach held it above his head. "No, ma'am," he quipped.

"Stop playing," she said as she reached for it again. But she was no match for Zach's height. As she reached up, he couldn't help but smile at how her assets bounced.

"All right," he said, handing her the sarong when he saw a man staring at Chante's luscious curves. "I guess we're putting on too much of a show for people."

"You think?" she snapped as she tied her sarong around her waist. "You're a bit of a jackass, huh?"

"That hurts," he said.

Chante rolled her eyes. "The truth usually does."

"Is this our first argument?" he asked with a smile.

"Oh, please," she quipped. "You don't want to argue with me. That's what I do for a living, and I'm good at what I do."

"All right, I will take note of that." Zach took her hand in his and gave it a gentle kiss. "I don't like to fight anyway. I do like the making up, though."

Chante laughed, and it felt good. But she had to remember, what she and Zach had was a farce. Getting this comfortable with him would most likely be a mistake. When she went back to Charlotte and he returned to New York, this thing would be over. Sighing, she leaned against his arm. He had great arms. Strong, hard. She closed her eyes for a second as the image of those arms holding her while they made love flashed in her mind.

"What's wrong?" he asked when she moaned slightly.

"Nothing. Just letting my mind wander."

Zach stopped walking and faced Chante. Cupping her face, he brushed his lips across hers. "Let me guess. You were thinking about you and me ditching the little bit of clothes we have on and having some real sex on the beach."

"You are so nasty," she said, though he

wasn't far off from what she was thinking.

"And you have the most irresistible lips I've ever seen." Zach covered her mouth with his. His kiss was slow and succulent. Chante pressed her body against his and felt every muscle harden. Why did she want this man so much when he was practically a stranger? How was it that he knew how to kiss her and where all of her hot spots were?

When his hand slipped between her thighs, Chante knew she was done for. She wanted him, and he was giving her all the reasons to believe this would be a magical moment. Her love-starved body purred as he stroked her womanly core through her bikini bottoms. Pulling back from her lips, he continued stroking her as if he wanted to bring her to climax right there in the parking lot.

And when he did, Chante thought she was going to pass out. She muted her scream as she fell against his chest. "How-how . . . wow."

"I can tell someone has been neglected for too long," he whispered against her ear. "We're going to have to change that."

Chante wanted to tell him to change it now, but she took a deep breath instead and waited for her body to stop twitching. "Let's get to the beach before . . ."

Zach scooped her up into his arms. "Before I decide to take you upstairs and make you come again?" He smiled, and she melted like ice on the sidewalk.

"You're too much."

"You might find out that I'm just enough." Winking, he took off with her in his arms toward the shore.

If Zach thought Chante was going to be one of those women who didn't want to get her hair and body wet in the ocean, he was wrong. When they made it to the water, Chante headed in and let wave after wave hit her. She reminded him of a mythological sea nymph as her hair curled up and her suit clung to her body. If he were a sailor, he'd be in trouble because he would've followed her to the edges of the Earth.

"What are you waiting for?" she called out. "This water feels so good!"

"The view is quite stunning," he said as he walked toward her. Chante kicked water his way when she noticed that he still had his shoes on.

"Come on, Yankee. You don't know good fun until you dance with a wave barefoot."

Zach splashed water on her. "Is that so?" Chante dashed away from him, and Zach easily caught up to her, wrapping his arms around her waist.

"You look good in the water," he said as he kissed her neck.

"Umm," she moaned. "This has always been my favorite place. Granny and I used to come out here and toss all the negativity away."

"You and your grandmother had a lot of good times," he said, slipping his hands from her waist and palming her ample behind. Chante moaned as his fingers drummed against her cheeks.

"Your hands should come with a warning label," she said.

"I'll keep that in mind. But your body is giving my hands all kinds of life."

She playfully slapped him on the shoulder. "Whatever. You know, I'm glad we're doing this," she said. "Maybe my dad won't see that we're a fraud."

"So you and your dad have a different relationship than you and your mother?"

Stepping back from him, she nodded. "He always encouraged me to follow my dreams — husband or not."

"We don't have to do this," he said. "I know that the relationship between a father and daughter is important."

"You're a lot sweeter than I thought you were. My dad will probably understand after I tell him the full story. Sometimes I wonder how my mother hooked him when they were college. She had to have dazzled him with her brilliance, because I don't even want to think about it happening any other way. I don't know why my mother decided that Margaret Mitchell's southern ideals were the way women were supposed to live."

"Seems like she picked the wrong author to follow," he said, pulling Chante closer to his chest.

"Anyway," she said, shaking her head, "my grandmother is much more inspiring than any woman ever written about in southern fiction. She did something that most women back in the day didn't do."

"Which was?" he asked.

"She left my grandfather and made her own way. When she found out that he had another family in Summerville, she wasn't going to stand for that. It's a part of the family history that my mother likes to gloss over. She pretends that Granddad passed away and my grandmother is trying to erase his memory."

Zach furrowed his brows. "So your grandfather is still alive?"

She shook her head. "No, he died in a train accident when I was five. That was when my mother started to rewrite her family history. My grammy wasn't going for it, and she wasn't going to play the role of the eternal widow."

"So how did your mom end up as a Scarlett O'Hara wannabe when your grandmother seems like such a force of nature?"

Chante shrugged. It was the same question she'd asked herself for years. "Did you ever meet your grandfather's other family?" Zach asked.

"Not officially," she said. "My mother likes to pretend they don't exist, but Grammy introduced me to a couple of the young men who were close to my age so we'd never end up dating."

Zach burst out laughing, and Chante kicked water at him. "What's so funny?" she snapped.

"Your grandmother seems really gangster. And she knew that you were an irresistible woman, so she did the right thing."

Chante rolled her eyes. "She wanted me to be rooted in reality. And there is nothing wrong with that. I'm blessed to have her in my life."

"I'd like to meet her."

"Now you're confusing a farce with reality," she said, wiggling out of his embrace.

Zach shook his head. "No, I'm not. Although meeting you has been one of the perks of my trip to Charleston, I'm also here for business."

Chante raised her right eyebrow. "What kind of business?"

"I'm looking for some property to develop."

"Oh," she said with a smile, "so this little farce idea is a way for you to get your foot in the door with old Charleston, huh?"

"When you say it like that, it sounds so dirty and deceitful."

"Listen," she said, "I'm glad we're both getting something out of this."

"A fair exchange is no robbery." He kissed her on the forehead. "What time are we supposed to head to your mom's?"

She shrugged. "Not until you take those shoes off and get those feet wet, son!" Chante splashed him with water, and Zach bent over to take his shoes off. He crossed over to her and scooped her into his arms as a wave crashed against them.

"The water does feel good," he said. "But holding you feels even better."

Chante smiled and kissed his lips. "I think I like you holding me."

CHAPTER 7

Nic walked into Robert's office and shook his head when he saw the young girl getting up off her knees.

"You still haven't learned a damned thing," Nic railed. "Miss, get out of here."

The woman adjusted her skirt and then walked out of the office. "What's your problem?" Robert asked.

"Your wayward penis is the problem. Do you want to be the mayor and use this position as a stepping-stone to something bigger?"

"What's the point of all of this?" Robert zipped his pants. "That interview with Channel Nine didn't help, I can't find Chante, and none of the support I had when I was running for state senate is there."

"One thing about Charlotte is this city will forgive mostly anything. But you have to show them you've changed. Getting your dick sucked in your office after the last scandal isn't going to do that. We have to find Chante and get her onboard with this. She owes you."

Robert nodded. "I tried to tell her that."

"Is she still suspended from the law firm?"

Robert shrugged. "After they pulled their funding, I stopped caring about those bastards."

Nic drummed his fingers against his chin. "Maybe I need to call Taiwon Myrick. He has a few skeletons I can put my hands on, and he might be able to help with the Chante issue. You need to become the dutiful fiancé again, and that means no more sex with campaign workers or random women! And for God's sake, no more hookers."

Robert rolled his eyes and pulled out his cell phone to call Chante. *Voice mail. Damn it! Bitch, you owe me this!* he thought as he slammed his phone onto the desk.

Chante and Zach walked into the lobby of the Charleston Harbor Bed and Breakfast feeling refreshed, having cleaned up after an afternoon of frolicking in the ocean. And though she was wearing a strapless maxi dress, Zach thought Chante looked even sexier than she had in her barely there bikini.

They walked out to the Mustang, and if Chante had plans to drive, Zach squashed them when he led her over to the passenger-side door.

"Ugh, this feels like prom," she said as he opened the door for her. "And why don't I get to drive? It's not as if you know where you're going."

"I know enough about the South to realize that there is no way a man pulls up to a father's house with his daughter driving," he said as he eased behind the wheel.

Chante laughed, thinking that her father would indeed give Zach a hell of a side eye if she rolled up to the Britt home driving while he sat on the passenger seat. "I guess you're not completely Yankee after all."

Zach laughed as he started the car. While they drove, Chante directed him to her childhood home. It wasn't lost on her that she hadn't taken Robert to her parents' house. She hadn't even told them about the engagement, but her mother found out about the breakup.

That was one of the main reasons Chante had planned to avoid coming to her childhood home while she was in Charleston. But as the old saying goes, God laughs when we plan.

Chante directed Zach toward Chateau Britt, a sprawling plantation house on the edge of Summerville, South Carolina. When he drove up the winding driveway, Zach was impressed. The wide porch was filled with people, and Chante groaned.

"I should've known."

"What?" Zach asked.

Chante pointed to the people milling about. "That the whole damned county would be here. I don't think this is a good idea, Zach."

When he saw her mother wave at them and then motion for the duo to get out of the car, he shrugged. "Too late now. We've been spotted."

"This is a hot mess," she said as she opened the door.

"Think about it this way, now you know what to expect when you bring your real man here to meet your family."

"Yeah, I know to skip this part," she said. Zach got out of the car and linked arms with her.

"Chante, smile. They just want to inspect the Yankee."

She laughed. "You are right about that." Chante leaned her head on his shoulder, and it felt so comfortable, almost like he was her fiancé. She blinked and dropped her hand from his.

"There you two are," Allison said with a wide smile. "I'm not even going to ask what delayed you."

"We were playing in the ocean," Zach said. "Chante is quite the water lily."

Allison shook her head. "I thought you would've outgrown that by now."

Chante rolled her eyes and held her tongue.

"Baby girl," a voice boomed as they approached the porch. Zach looked up and saw a tall caramel-skinned man with a bald head holding a glass and walking their way. When Chante smiled and rushed into his arms, he figured this was her father. Looking at him and Chante embrace, he saw more of a resemblance between the two of them than he did between her and Allison.

"Daddy," she said, "you look great. I see you've lost some weight."

"I love lawyers: y'all make lies sound so good," he said, draping his arm around her shoulders. Then he turned to face Zach. "All right, young man, how did you stop this speed demon from driving that Mustang up here?"

Zach laughed, realizing that this man would be a great father-in-law, unlike the one he'd had during his marriage to She-Who-Would-Not-Be-Named.

"It was hard, sir," Zach replied, then winked at Chante.

"Please, I'm Eli, and you are?"

"Zach."

"One name, like Prince, huh?" Eli said, then broke out into laughter. "Not your fault, son." He looked at Chante. "I should've met you a long time ago."

"Daddy," Chante said, "this is Zach Harrington. Zach, this is my Daddy, Eli Britt. And it's not as if we've been together that long."

"I see," Eli said as he took a sip of his drink. "Nothing either of you need to whisper about to me and Allison?"

"Eli, please," Allison said, "you're drunk, and that is not funny."

"We're waiting until our wedding night, sir," Zach said.

Eli laughed, and Allison looked as she wanted the ground to open up and swallow her. "You must be a lawyer too," Eli quipped.

"No, sir. I'm in real estate."

"Come on, let's get some of this low boil. Now I can tell you're not from around here. New York? You got that accent."

"Yes, sir," Zach said. "Born and raised in

the Bronx. But I came south to expand my empire and lost my heart." He looked at Chante, and she thought that Zach belonged on Broadway. Smiling at her "fiancé," Chante kept quiet. She hated weaving this yarn of a love story, but for the moment, it did feel better to introduce her family to a fake fiancé than to the one who'd cheated on her with a hooker.

"Let's get some food," Chante said. "I'm starving." She headed up the steps and spoke to a number of her parents' old friends.

"Congratulations, Chante," Anita Moore said as she stopped her. "Though I've always held out hope that you and my Marvin would end up together."

Chante simply smiled and quietly wished Anita would accept the fact that her son was gay. "How is Marvin?" she asked. "Is he still loving life in San Francisco?"

Anita took a huge gulp of her wine. "I guess. He, like most of you children, doesn't come back to visit."

Anita, if you're still trotting out random women for him to date when he comes home, I wouldn't come back either, she thought while smiling at her mother's closest friend. "The next time you talk to him, tell him I said hello," Chante said before walking away.

Allison and two of her sorority sisters had cornered Zach, and he stood there while they peppered him with questions.

"So," Deloris DeWitt, one of Allison's oldest friends, began, "how did you and Chante meet? Are you also a lawyer? She's the only attorney worth knowing, you know."

Zach smiled. "I've come to learn that."

"And what part of New York are you from?" Hannah Morgan asked. "I love to visit that city but living there, I'd just die."

"New York isn't as bad as you may think, ma'am," he said.

"You never answered the question," Deloris said.

"Yes," Allison said, "how did you and my daughter meet?"

"At a bar," he said. It wasn't a lie. They met at the hotel bar last night.

Allison shook her head. "I hope not at some tawdry speed-dating mess."

"No," Zach said as he looked across the room and saw Chante standing with her father. "I was having a late dinner, and this goddess walked into the bar. Bronzed skin and bright eyes. She seemed to look right through me. I was intrigued, because — not to brag — women don't usually ignore me."

Chante locked eyes with him and smiled. Deloris caught the look between the two of them and clutched her pearl necklace.

"Aww, look at that," she said as she glanced from Chante to Zach.

He winked at Chante, who held her glass up to him.

"And then what happened?" Hannah asked.

"She threw a drink in my face."

The women gasped and Zach laughed. "I was totally intrigued. And then I took her a quiche and everything seemed to work out just fine."

"You cooked?" Allison asked.

Zach shook his head and placed his hand on Allison's elbow. "No, ma'am. I wanted to impress your daughter, not run her away or to the hospital."

The group laughed, and Chante crossed over to them. "Sounds like someone is having fun over here," she said as she stood on the other side of Zach.

"Just having a great conversation with these lovely ladies," he said, then kissed Chante on the cheek. "I told them you threw a drink in my face when we met."

Chante's mouth dropped for a second; then she shook her head. "I hope you explained how you were being a super jerk when I did that." Her voice dripped sarcasm like honey. Zach could feel his dick thump. He wanted this woman more than he wanted to breathe. Her smile when she slipped her hand in his back pocket and squeezed his ass almost pushed him to full mast.

"Eh, I was getting to that," he said as he wrapped his arm around Chante's waist. Did he just feel her tremble? Glancing at her, there was an unmistakable look of desire in her eyes. Yep. He was officially harder than Chinese math.

"I'm going to get a drink," Zach said. "Will you show me to the bar?"

"With pleasure," Chante said. Zach walked behind her, keeping his hand around her waist.

"You are so sexy," he whispered. "I don't know if I'm going to be able to contain myself."

"You better try," she replied. "Thanks to your charming conversation, all eyes are on us right now."

When they approached the bar, she turned to him and asked, "What did you tell them?"

"A version of the truth. Like how you threw a drink in my face and that I took you a quiche, then won your heart."

Chante rolled her eyes and waved for the

bartender. She couldn't help but wonder if this party had been planned long before her mother saw her and Zach at the gift shop.

"What can I get y'all?" the older man asked.

"Two double bourbons," Chante said.

"Okay."

"You like your drinks strong, huh?" Zach asked.

"I'm going to need it. You were talking to the coven."

"That's mean."

Chante giggled as the bartender returned with their drinks. "Blame my grammy. She came up with that nickname. Those three went to college together with the same mission: find husbands."

"And how did it work out for the other two?" Zach took a sip of his drink while Chante took a huge gulp.

"Miss Deloris has three ex-husbands, each one richer than the other. She gets enough alimony that she doesn't have to work anymore. I bet her divorce lawyers are hoping that she gets married again."

Zach snickered and wiped his mouth. "You're a trip," he said.

"Then there's Miss Hannah. She wants to be married so badly that she ignores the fact that her husband has another family in

North Charleston."

This time, Zach nearly choked on his drink. "Seriously."

Chante took a sip of her bourbon. "Southern women are notorious for keeping secrets about their marriages, but small-town gossips find out the truth every time. We're lucky we don't live here." Chante stroked his cheek. Before Zach could respond, Eli and another man walked over to them.

"Zach," Eli said, "I wanted to introduce you to Mayor Jenkins."

The taller, caramel-skinned man extended his hand to Zach. "Mr. Harrington, I heard that you were in town on business. I had no idea you were here with one of my favorite lawyers. Hello, Taye," he said to Chante as he shook hands with Zach.

"Uncle Mike," she said with a smile.

He looked at Chante's hand. "Now, where is the ring?"

"We're waiting for the right one," Zach said. "A woman this special needs a wonderfully beautiful ring."

"That's true," Mike said as he gave Chante a hug. "So, my dear, how's the legal community in Charlotte?"

She sighed and thought about telling the truth. She had no idea. But she simply smiled. "Lots of lawsuits and contract negotiations."

"Guess that's why my baby girl doesn't come home enough," Eli said. "You don't know how proud of you I am."

Tears sprang into her eyes. He was proud of a lie, and she was telling him another one as she pretended to be Zach's fiancée. "Daddy," she whispered.

"Listen, if you ever decide that you want to work for the family company, I'd love to have you heading up the legal department at Britt Industries," Eli said. "And your mother would love to have you closer."

"Charlotte isn't that far away."

"She hates traffic, darling. Will you and Zach be making Charlotte home?"

Zach stroked Chante's shoulder. "We haven't decided yet."

"Have you taken the New York State Bar Exam?" Mike asked Chante. She looked down into her half-empty glass.

"Yes, and I passed it. But the thought of opening a firm there is a little scary," she replied. "There is a lot of competition."

"That's nothing for you, darling," Zach said. "You'd take New York by storm."

Eli and Mike nodded in agreement. "And if you moved to New York, it would give your mother and her friends a reason to go shopping more often."

Chante grinned and took a sip of her drink. "Then it's settled," she said after swallowing. "Zach, we're making Charlotte home."

The group laughed, and Allison headed in their direction. "Everyone seems to be having a good time," she said as she approached the group. She shot Mike an icy glance, and Chante shook her head.

It wasn't a secret that Allison and Mike didn't get along. Eli and Mike were fraternity brothers, and he was one of Deloris's ex-husbands. If it had been up to Allison, Eli would've turned his back on his friend after the divorce, but Eli had told his wife to stay out of grown people's business and remained friends with Mike.

"Yes, we are, darling," Eli said, then planted a kiss on Allison's cheek.

"Eli," she admonished, "we're in public."

"We're in our home," he said, then shook his head. Allison rolled her eyes.

"Allison, I see you're still pretending that the North lost the war," Mike said with a smirk.

She rolled her eyes, then turned to Zach. "I hope you're not fooled by this guy's so-called charm. He's a snake with a government job."

Mike clutched his chest. "Ouch, Allie.

You'd think I'd divorced you."

"Eli, it's almost time to eat. Do you think I can borrow our daughter for a moment?"

Chante groaned inwardly. "Mom, I wanted to show Zach your art collection. Can it wait?"

"It will only take a second, dear," Allison said, then gripped her daughter's elbow. Chante unwillingly followed her mother into the kitchen. As suspected, the kitchen was filled with caterers preparing the low-country boil.

"May we have the room?" Allison said to the kitchen staff.

The workers headed outside to prepare the tables, leaving Chante and her mother alone. "What's going on, Mom?"

Allison drew in a deep breath. "I don't want to alarm you, but how much do you know about Zach."

"Enough," Chante replied.

Allison pulled her smartphone from her pocket. "Did you know he was divorced?" She showed Chante a Google search that had pulled up Zach's Wikipedia listing.

"Yes, I knew this." She shook her head. "You do realize that most people my age are divorced or have children."

"And that's why you should've gotten married earlier. Like, right after college. I swear, I don't understand . . ."

"Mother. I just want to eat and enjoy the day. I don't need you and your friends judging my choices."

Allison folded her arms. "You haven't been making the best choices. Robert Montgomery, for example?" She held her phone up and showed Chante a headline about Robert's quest for mayor. "Were you going to tell me about this?"

Chante folded her arms across her chest. This was an argument she'd been hoping to avoid. Old ladies and smartphones were a dangerous combination.

"I'm going to walk away, Mom," Chante said.

"No, you need to explain this to me. He asked you to marry him and cheated on you with a hooker? Why couldn't you keep this man happy at home?"

Chante's right eyebrow shot up. "Are you serious? It's my fault that he didn't keep his dick in his pants."

"Language!"

"You know what, why don't you look at what I've done with my career. Show that to your friends who have daughters who are living off the taxpayers' dime and three baby daddies. I'm not doing this with you, and if I wasn't looking forward to having dinner with my father, I'd leave right now." Chante stormed out of the kitchen and rejoined Zach, her father, and Mike. Just like Allison, she put on a fake smile and pretended that she wasn't mad as hell.

CHAPTER 8

Taiwon glared at Nic. "How dare you come into my office with this bullshit?"

Nic smiled and smoothed his hand down his pant leg. "Listen, Mr. Myrick. You were one of our biggest supporters in the senate race."

"Until your candidate was exposed as sleeping with a hooker. How does a law firm look supporting a criminal?"

"As opposed to having one as a partner?" Nic smiled and leaned back in the leather chair. "Your juvenile record may have been expunged, but you were charged with armed robbery."

"And they had the wrong person. It's clearly written in the judge's dismissal of the case. What do you want from me?"

"Chante Britt."

"What in the hell does she have to . . . ?"

"I need her in Charlotte. I know her suspension hasn't been lifted. Maybe if . . ."

"She is the reason our firm was associated with your client, a man who solicited sex while running for office, as if no one would find out. Do you know how much money we tied up in that loser? Chante is lucky she still has a job." Taiwon snorted. "And she's dumb and desperate enough to stay with him? I told them she wouldn't be good candidate for partner."

"Obviously, they aren't together; otherwise I wouldn't be here. You'd better do all you can to get her back in Charlotte and working here."

"Why would I do that?" Taiwon asked as he leaned back in his chair. "She put us in the middle of Montgomery's scandal. We lost several conservative clients because of our endorsement of that louse."

"And how many more clients do you want to lose? Make no mistake, I will destroy you if you don't work with me in making sure Robert wins this mayoral race."

Taiwon shook his head. "And you think the people of this city will forgive him for sleeping with a hooker? Look at the last mayor. The voters want someone they can trust, and I don't think Montgomery fits that role."

"And how do you think your partners will feel about a lying lawyer who wormed his

126

way into the corner office? As a member of the bar, you were supposed to disclose your youthful transgressions. I know you didn't."

"Blackmail is how you want to handle this?"

"I haven't blackmailed you. All I've done is make promises. Trust me, Mr. Myrick, you want me as an ally. Lift Chante's suspension, and she'll come back to Charlotte."

"I don't take well to threats. Get the hell out of my office."

Nic rose to his feet and shot Taiwon an icy glare. "You don't want me as your enemy. If you want to think about this for the next twenty-four hours, I'll give you that. But you need to do everything in your power to get Chante Britt reinstated at this law firm." Nic walked out, feeling comfortable that Taiwon would do everything he ordered.

Once Chante and Robert were seen together, the voters would think she had forgiven him and would do the same. Nic wanted to show Teresa Flores, Jackson Franklin's campaign manager and political advisor, that he was still a player, and getting Robert elected mayor would do just that. If he had to use every dirty trick he'd invented, he would.

■ ■ ■ ■

Chante yawned as she listened to Zach tell stories about some of the deals he'd closed in New York. It wasn't that she was bored; just like all the other guests at the table, that man enthralled her.

She, however, was tired and a little drunk. Chante wasn't a big drinker, but after her conversation with her mother she'd downed two more glasses of bourbon. Of course, Allison blamed her for Robert's bad choice. She toyed with her fork as conversations went on around her.

"Are you all right?" Zach asked when he noticed she'd gone silent.

"Yeah, yeah, I'm fine."

"No, you're not," he said leaning closer to her. "What happened with you and your mother? Since your tête-à-tête with her, you've been quiet, and you seem kind of tipsy."

"I'm ready to go," she blurted out. "I'm tired of pretending I'm getting married and acting as if that's going to make my mother acknowledge that I've made something of my life."

A few heads turned in Chante and Zach's direction, and she didn't give a damn what they heard. When she saw her mother coming her way, she rose to her feet — in very wobbly fashion. Zach stood and held her steady.

"What's going on down here? A lover's quarrel?" Allison asked.

"No," Chante said, "Zach and I have decided we're going . . ."

"To head back to the hotel," he chimed in. "My fiancée had a little too much to drink and isn't feeling well."

Allison shook her head. "You are so much like your father," she said.

"Well, thank God for small miracles."

"Chante, why do you have to . . . ?"

"Ladies," Zach said, "let's table this for later. I need to get my baby into bed."

Chante and her mother looked at Zach with their mouths in the shapes of *O*s. Allison may have been scandalized by his announcement, but Chante was intrigued. In bed? Did he know that after this dinner party, that was a strong possibility? Did he know that she'd wanted to hop into bed with him right after they'd finished playing in the ocean?

Knowing him, though, he probably meant he was going to take her up to her suite and make sure she got into bed and slept off her bourbon-induced insanity. Still, Chante brought her mouth to his and kissed him with an unbridled passion that made her mother gasp and some of the dinner guests clap.

"It's so good to see young people in love," said one of the women sitting next to where Chante and Zach stood. Breaking the kiss, she looked up at him and smiled.

"Let's go."

"I can't believe you," Allison cried out, then dropped her head in her hands and started to sob.

Chante was sure her mother was faking it and didn't give her a second glance as Zach walked her to the front lawn.

"Chante, what was that back there?" he asked as he unlocked the Mustang.

"A lot of history and anger. Thanks to Jack Daniels, I just felt like telling her how I feel."

Zach helped Chante into the car. "You and your mother have some deep-rooted issues."

"And I've had too much to drink." Chante blinked. "I think I'm going to be sick."

Before Zach could move out of the way, Chante barfed all over his leather shoes.

When Chante woke up, she was sure that the last few hours had been a dream. She was wrapped in a blanket in her bed at the

Charleston Harbor Bed and Breakfast. She stretched her arms above her head and turned toward the double doors leading out onto the balcony. She saw how dark it was and realized she'd been dreaming about having an argument with her mother at the low-country boil. And there was no way that Allison knew about Robert, nor did she . . .

"Hello, Sleeping Beauty. You owe me a new pair of loafers."

"Oh my God," she groaned. "It wasn't a dream."

"It was quite real," Zach said with a chuckle. "I think the best part was when your mother started crying and you walked off like you were so unbothered."

Chante sat up and the room started to spin. "Oh no, I think I'm going to be sick."

Zach rushed to her side with a glass of water. "Drink this slowly," he ordered.

She took a quick sip of the cool water and then a slower one. The bile she felt rushing forward dissipated. "So," Zach continued, "what is Taiwan?"

"Why?" she asked.

"If you have connections to that Asian country, you pretty much ruined them. That phone call was brutal. Remind me to never wake you up."

The cup of water fell from Chante's hand.

"I have pretty much ruined my life. Taiwon is one of the partners at my law firm."

Zach released a low whistle. "I think you're going to be looking for a new job after the conversation you had with him. You made me blush, and I'm a New Yorker."

Chante groaned and shook her head. "This is just getting worse."

"Do you want to talk about what's going on?"

She swung her legs over the side of the bed. "Let's see, I pretty much ruined my life. Not much else to talk about."

"There has to be a reason behind it. You seem way too level-headed to spaz out the way you did."

I used to be. I used to have everything in control until I allowed the wrong man to ruin everything that was important to me, she thought as she turned away from Zach's glare.

"I have a headache, and I'm hungry."

"Good side step. But avoiding the question won't make me stop asking."

Chante rolled her eyes as she rose from the bed. "Zach, why are you here?"

"Making sure you didn't have alcohol poisoning. Bourbon is not water."

"You can see that I'm fine," she said, even though the room seemed to be spinning as she tried to cross to the bathroom. Zach's strong arms kept her from falling to the floor.

"Slow down. You need more water."

Looking into his eyes, Chante knew she needed his lips on top of hers. She knew she needed his arms around her until the sun came up. Sighing, she also knew that she and Zach didn't have to pretend they were getting married anymore.

"I'm fine. I have to go to the bathroom." She wiggled out of his embrace, though staying in his arms would've made her forget all the drunken bad decisions she'd made tonight.

"All right," he said as he watched her walk into the restroom. "But just so you know, I'm not leaving until we eat."

"Who said I wanted you to leave?" she called from behind the closed door.

Zach crossed the room, ordered an assortment of appetizers from room service, and opened the doors to the balcony to allow the salty warm air to blow into the room. Looking out over the ocean, he couldn't help but smile. Someone had a situation that was even more messed up than his, even if he didn't know the details yet. But from the short time he'd known Chante, he felt as if her actions were showing that she had something deep going on and was lashing out at everyone.

You're here to have fun. It isn't your job to figure out what's going on with a woman you barely know, he thought as he took a deep breath. Then he heard the shower start inside the bathroom. Part of him wanted to run in there with Chante and join her underneath the water and kiss her until whatever her issues were turned into afterthoughts. Just thinking about her wet and naked made him hard.

He couldn't remember the last time he'd wanted a woman this way. Over the last few months, Natalie had turned him against sex, which had become linked to her crimes. He had been ready to take a vow of celibacy, and he'd hoped to start it while he was in South Carolina. But Chante had to walk into his view. Those hips, lips, and dangerous thighs made him want her with a powerful longing.

The water stopped, and he walked back into the room. When the bathroom door opened, he expected a naked Chante to saunter out. He was disappointed when she walked out covered by a white terry-cloth robe.

"Where's the food?" she asked as she

caught his glance. "And I hope you . . ."

Zach crossed over to her and wrapped his arms around her waist. "You hope that I untie this sash," he said as he did just that, "then lay you on this bed and feast on you?"

He lifted her in his arms and walked backward to the bed. Gently dropping her on the bed, he knelt, pulled her thighs apart, and dove into her wetness. His tongue darted in and out the wet folds of flesh, greedily seeking her throbbing bud of womanhood. When he found it, he sucked it until she gripped his neck and cried out his name.

"Ooh," Chante moaned, "Zachary! Zachary!"

He replaced his tongue with his finger and looked into her eyes as he brought her to the edge of an orgasm. "Do you want me to stop?" he asked.

"Don't. Stop," she said as she writhed underneath his touch. Zach kissed the sensitive spot between her thighs. Her legs trembled as she thrust her hips forward.

Zach deepened his kiss, probed her deeper with his tongue as she moaned in pleasure.

"Come for me, baby," he groaned, then returned his mouth to her womanly core. With a few more licks and nibbles, Chante exploded. Her sweetness covered his face, and he licked his lips, savoring her taste.

"Whoa," she moaned, her body shivering from the aftershocks of her intense orgasm. "That was . . ."

"Delicious," he replied with a smile. "Feel better?"

Chante smiled, but before she could answer, there was a knock at the door. "I guess you better get that," she said.

"Room service," he said with a wink as he headed for the door. Chante tried to catch her breath as Zach signed for the food. Her body felt relaxed, and she'd almost forgotten about the earlier incidents. Was it wrong that she wanted more? After all, if she was making bad decisions today, she might as well go all the way. Besides, she was an adult, and she needed to feel him deep inside her. At least for tonight. In the morning, she'd try to fix the mess she'd made earlier.

Zach walked over to the bed with the tray of food. "Let's eat," he said. Chante stood up and took the food from his hands.

"Why don't we save this for later," she said as she set the tray on the nightstand beside the bed. "I have a taste for something else."

"And just what would that be?" he asked with a smile on his lips. Chante reached for his fly, and Zach was surprised by her boldness.

"You started this," she said as she unbuttoned and unzipped his slacks.

"And? I love the way you taste." He pulled her closer as his pants dropped to his ankles. Chante brushed her lips against his. And that was all the encouragement he needed to kiss her long, hard, and deep. Her soft moan made him harder than a concrete wall. Then he felt her soft touch on his penis. She had an expert stroke — her fingers gliding up and down the length of him like an expert musician playing a sax.

"Oh baby," he moaned as they broke the kiss and he stepped out of his pants.

"Need you. Inside," she moaned.

Zach nodded, unable to speak as she continued stroking him. Speechless and filled with desire, Zach felt as if he was about to explode with her touch. If she kept this up, he wasn't sure if he'd be able to hold back his climax.

"You're making me weak, babe," he whispered as they backed toward the bed. "You got the touch."

"Mmm," she said. "That's just a little payback for what you did with those lips and tongue."

"You're a saucy little minx. I like that."

137

Falling backward on the bed, Zach slipped his hands between Chante's thighs. She was so wet. And she was so beautiful. His eyes roamed her body, ripe breasts with chocolate-brown nipples. Her flat stomach lead down to those thighs; he'd already decided he liked her thighs a lot. His fingers danced in her womanly valley. Chante arched her back and cried out his name as his finger found her throbbing bud. With his free hand, he pushed the robe away, giving him an unfettered view of her naked body. That caramel skin made his mouth water, and he leaned in to get a taste of a diamond-hard nipple. Then she screamed as his tongue flicked across her sensitive nub.

"Zach!"

He responded with another lick and pressed his finger deeper inside her. Chante closed her eyes as she felt an orgasm tease her senses. If this man was about to make her come with his finger, she was going to have his tongue and hands bronzed so that she could remember this moment.

And there it was. A slow rumbling, then a huge explosion. "Zach, Zach!" she cried as she came.

"Was that good?" he whispered.

Nodding, Chante couldn't speak at all.

She hadn't even noticed that Zach had sheathed himself with a condom. "I want you to ride me, Chante," he said.

She smiled and almost told him she wanted to ride him all night. He eased up toward the head of the bed, and Chante placed her hands on his strong thighs. He clutched her hips and positioned her on top of his erection. She ground against him, and it felt so good. Zach sucked her nipples, alternating between the left and right as she tightened her thighs around him.

"Yes, yes!" Chante called out as he thrust his hips forward. She wound her hips as if she heard a steel drum band playing in her head. Zach fell in rhythm with her, and moments later they were collapsing against each other as they came in unison.

She expelled a satisfied sigh as Zach kissed her on the forehead. "You're amazing, woman," he whispered as he stroked her back.

"I had an equally amazing partner," she replied. "Wow."

He drummed his fingertips against her spine. Her skin was softer than silk. And when Chante wiggled her booty, he was hard again. "Umm," she said, "looks like someone caught a second wind."

"You're irresistible. You think I can hold

all of this and not want some more?" He squeezed her bottom, and then she shifted against his throbbing erection. "This time," he said, "let's take it a little slower. I want to savor every minute I'm inside you."

And with a slower tempo and Zach on top of Chante this time, they made love until the sun started to rise over the horizon. When the couple finally drifted off to sleep, sated and happy, Chante had totally put the night before out of her mind.

CHAPTER 9

When the ringing of her cell phone woke her up, Chante was pleased and a tad bit surprised to find herself still wrapped in Zach's arms. Such strong arms. He felt amazing, and that phone call was just going to wait.

She inhaled his masculine scent and started to run her tongue up and down his neck. She snaked her hands around his waist, gently stroking his hips. Her intention had been to reach down and stroke his morning erection, but the phone rang again.

"You'd better get that," Zach said, his voice thick with sleep. "I can't keep pretending to be sleeping while your phone is ringing."

"I don't want to."

"Obviously, someone wants to talk to you pretty badly."

Chante reluctantly climbed out of the bed and grabbed the ringing phone. She chided herself for turning the phone on again. When she saw the number on her touch screen, she groaned. It was the law firm. Maybe today was the day she'd be fired. Especially if she had talked to Taiwon the way Zach said she had.

"This is Chante," she said when she pressed the talk button.

"Chante, I hope you're in a better mood today," Taiwon said.

Clearing her throat, she said, "I want to apologize for anything I said last time we spoke. I hadn't been expecting your call and I guess I said some things that I shouldn't have."

"Setting your profane rant aside, I can understand why you're upset. This suspension has been just as hard on the firm as it has been on you. Many of your clients are asking about you and when you're coming back. You also have a few cases that are on the docket."

"So what are you saying?"

She heard Taiwon clear his throat. "The partners and I want to lift your suspension."

"I've been thinking about everything while I've had this time away from the firm, and maybe I don't want to come back."

"What do you mean? Have you taken another job?"

"What if I have? Obviously, you didn't think I was good enough to be partner, despite the millions of dollars I made for Myrick, Lawson and Walker. I could open my own practice or walk in the front door of any law firm in the city and start as a partner."

"You have a contract with us and if you . . ."

"My contract expired during this suspension," Chante shot back. "And I figured that's why it was taking so long for you to lift it. Then you could fire the distraction and not have to worry about being in breach of contract. So, no, Taiwon, I'm not coming back unless you and the other partners give me what I deserve."

"And you think you deserve to be partner after all of the undue scrutiny you brought to the firm with your relationship?"

"When I found out . . . You should've listened to me, but like always, all you could hear was your own voice." She glanced over her shoulder and saw that Zach was sitting up in the bed watching her. "I'm not doing this right now. I'm on vacation." She shut the phone off and tossed it in the top drawer of the dresser.

"That didn't sound much better than your other conversation," he said as he rose from the bed and crossed over to her. "And you look great in your birthday suit, all angry and indignant."

Chante shook her head and laughed. "I see we're wearing matching outfits."

He stroked her cheek. "That we are. Chante, is everything all right?"

"You want to talk while we're standing here naked?"

He winked at her. "I see what you're doing, distracting me with that body. I'm all over that." Scooping her up in his arms, he carried her over to the bed and laid her on the crumpled sheets. Chante wrapped her legs around his hips as he kissed her slowly and deeply. Feeling his erection growing against her thighs made her wet as a river.

"Umm," she moaned as his finger slipped between her folds. Chante needed him inside her. She wanted to feel good underneath his touch. "Protection," she said.

Though he wanted to dive into her wetness raw, he knew better. Unwrapping her legs from his waist, he reached for his discarded slacks and cursed when he came up empty.

"What?" she asked.

"No protection. Do you have any?"

Chante shook her head. Disappointment clouded her face. Zach crossed over to her.

"I have an idea." He parted her thighs then dove between her legs. Burying his face in her wetness, he lapped her sweetness, making her scream his name out over and over. After her third orgasm, she lost count. And Zach didn't stop. It was if he was addicted to her taste. Looking into her eyes as he licked the last of her desire away, Zach felt almost as satisfied as Chante looked.

"That was a hell of a breakfast," he said, then winked at her.

"So what are we going to do for lunch?" she asked once she caught her breath.

Taiwon stalked back and forth in his office. He couldn't believe Chante hadn't jumped at the chance to come back to the firm. Even without Nic breathing down his neck, the other partners wanted her back. They were losing money, and now he had to tell them she was going to quit.

And then there was Nic. If he leaked Taiwon's criminal record, he'd be ruined. "I guess I'm going to have to make that bitch a partner," he muttered as he dialed her number again. The call went directly to voice mail. Hanging up and tossing his phone across the office, Taiwon knew he had to fight fire with fire. Maybe he could get Nic and Robert before they got him.

Those fools picked a fight with the wrong person, he thought as he crossed over to his computer.

Meanwhile, across town, Robert woke up to another positive news story about his mayoral rival and his wife. Pushing Gabby's head away from his semi-erect penis, he grabbed the remote and turned the television up.

"Mayoral candidate David Clemmons and his wife, Courtney, have teamed up with A Child's Place to provide an ice cream social for the foster children who have made the honor roll at several Charlotte-Mecklenburg schools," the anchor said before the camera cut to the smiling couple scooping ice cream for kids in school uniforms.

"Son of a bitch!" Robert muttered as he pounded the mattress. "That should be me!"

Gabby jumped in with her opinion. "Why couldn't we do something like that together?"

Robert glared at her. "Because what we already do together is enough. I need to project an image like that. I need class and elegance. People need to look at me and my wife the way they look at Michelle and Barack!"

Gabby frowned. "So what are you trying

to say about me?"

Robert patted her head dismissively, treating her like a playful puppy that had peed on his suede boots. "Gabby. You're not the kind of girl a man takes home to his mother or to a political event."

She pulled away from him and hopped out of the bed. "You know what, you're a fucking fraud! That's why no one wants to support you. Everyone knows this act of yours is just that — an act. You want power, a title. I've heard your little power meetings with Nic. I hope Chante is smart enough to stay away from you."

Lunging over to her, Robert grabbed Gabby by the throat. "I'll be damned if I let another bitch ruin me. Nobody forced you to be here, and you knew from the start that all I needed you for was to get my rocks off." He let her go, and she fell to the floor. "Why don't you get dressed and get out of here. By the back door."

Gabby rubbed her throat and glared at him. "Who do you think you are?"

"I'm the last man you want to mess with. If you try to stand in the way of me and the mayor's office, I'll make you suffer like I should've done to Liza. So get out, and don't show your face here or at the campaign office."

She dressed quickly, actually feeling a bit of fear because of the way Robert glared at her. He didn't have to worry about seeing her ever again.

Alone in his house, Robert sat in the corner by the bay window in the living room. Had he been honest with himself, he would give up politics. But his loss of the senate seat had been so public and so embarrassing, like having a mother who'd left him at a fire station because her next high had been more important than taking care of her son.

He judged all women by the sins of his mother. When he'd been eight, he'd learned of his adoption. And since it was an open adoption, his parents — Selah and Patrick Montgomery — knew who his mother was.

Two years later, he'd seen the woman who'd given birth to him. She'd been in an alley with her head buried between some man's legs as he called her all kinds of dirty names and slapped her. When the man had had his release, he pulled his penis from her mouth and spilled his seed on her face. Robert had been so disgusted and embarrassed that he rode off on his bike and tried to forget about her and what he'd seen.

Three years later, his mother had cleaned herself up and tried to have a relationship with him. But all Robert ever saw her as was the whore in the alley. He hated thinking about her, hated being reminded that he was a crackhead's son. Maybe that's why he'd taken the loss to Jackson Franklin so hard. Here was a golden boy winning again, and he was on the outside looking in. Pounding his fist against his thigh, he thought about how Chante owed him, and he was going to make sure she paid him back for helping Liza humiliate him.

When the phone rang, he immediately knew who was on the other end.

"Yes, Nic," he said when he answered.

"We have to get some kind of press," Nic said, forgoing a hello. "Clemmons has the press sniffing his ass. Feeding kids ice cream — so damned clichéd. We need to do something that matters."

"Like what?"

Nic sighed. "I'm working on Myrick to get Chante back here so that you can counteract Clemmons and that wench of his. Last year, they were on the verge of divorce; now they want to be Charlotte's Michelle and Barack."

"Well, it's working," Robert growled.

"You need to get your head together. We're going to win this race. At least we don't have to worry about Liza Palmer inserting herself in this situation."

A light bulb when off in his head. Liza knew where Chante was. "Nic," Robert said, "I'm going to have to call you back."

Chante and Zach laughed as they sat on the balcony eating the cold leftovers from the night before as their breakfast. "We're worse than teenagers," she said.

"I didn't expect to meet a sultry sexpot while I was in Charleston."

"So why did you have one condom?"

He shrugged as he bit into a cold wing. "I believe in being prepared, and I was just setting up for a one-night stand."

Chante wiped the edges of her mouth. "And what's changed? I want you to know that last night and this morning didn't put you under any obligation to spend the rest of your time in Charleston with me."

"Whoa. That's not your decision to make, counselor. Then again, I could be stopping you from hooking up with your geechie boy toy."

Chante laughed. "That's funny. I came home, and you came to a place where people don't know your name. For all I know, I could be the fifth girl this week."

Zach leaned over the edge of his seat and reached for Chante's chin. Forcing her to look into his eyes, he said, "Trust and believe me. You're the only woman I've wanted to be with in a long time. And when we make love again, I'm going to be prepared."

"And you're just assuming you're going to get a second chance." She winked at him.

" 'Cause you like screaming my name. And I damned sure like screaming yours." Zach stroked her cheek. "Besides, we have a charade to continue, my betrothed."

"Ugh, how about we just avoid my mother for the rest of the time we're here?"

"And how much longer do you plan to stay here? Seems as if they want you back in Charlotte."

"You're pretty nosy, huh?"

"You weren't very quiet. What's going on? Because you sound like someone who's either throwing her career away or having an epiphany."

Chante leaned back in her chair and looked out over the ocean. "I guess I'm finally taking my life back. I let a man use me as a tool, and even though I was the one who got played, I'm the one who's suffering. You know what he's doing? Running for mayor and spreading the rumor that I've forgiven him and we're a couple."

"Damn. That's cold."

"No, that's insane. He had the unmitigated gall to show up at my house with the press."

"Wow, and I thought Natalie was the ex from hell. Your guy might have her beat."

Chante rolled her eyes. "I'm not trying to compare the two. I just want my damned life back, you know?"

"Weren't you offered your life back with that phone call this morning?"

She shook her head. "If I'm honest with myself, my life hasn't belonged to me in a long time. It's time for me to take it back. The problem is, I don't know how."

Zach studied her for a moment. He would never believe that about her for a minute. Chante Britt wasn't the type of woman who allowed people to tell her how she was supposed to live.

"I'd say you've gotten off on the right foot with that. You've come to Charleston, relaxed a little. Dare I even say you're having fun?"

"Some people would call this running away."

Zach shrugged, knowing that he had run away himself. The feds were still trying to connect him to Natalie's bullshit. Then there was the money he was losing while trying to establish himself in the South, where no one knew of his connection to Natalie's crimes. But in the age of Google Alerts, how long would it be before everyone in Charleston knew of his ties to the New York sex scandal?

"I guess we needed this distraction."

"You could call it that, but I prefer a sweeter term," she said with a smile.

"Which is?"

"Haven't thought of one yet. I know one thing, though. The water looks great. We should get in it."

"Good idea. I'm going to go to my room and get my trunks," he said as he rose to his feet. Chante stood and wrapped her arms around his waist and hugged him.

"Thank you for listening to me."

"You trusted me, and I get the feeling that isn't something you do easily."

She kissed his chin and let him go. "You're right. I've learned my lesson about trusting the wrong people."

As she looked into his eyes with a melancholy expression, Zach wondered if she'd forgive him for not being totally honest about his real reason for being in Charleston.

"See you in a little bit," he said, then headed inside.

CHAPTER 10

Liza Palmer-Franklin yawned as she read her Twitter timeline. It was good that she was bored with what she saw. That meant all of her clients had been behaving themselves on social media.

She actually felt as if she could unplug for a few hours and be ready to have dinner with her husband when the day's session of the General Assembly ended. It was still hard to wrap her mind around the fact that she was a state senator's wife. Smiling, she thought about how he woke her up to an exciting quickie because he knew he'd been neglecting her while fighting for the state Veteran's Employment Act. This was the first bill that Jackson had authored, and as a freshman senator, a lot was riding on this for him. Liza understood all of that, and as hard as it was, she didn't try to get involved. She simply did everything her husband asked her to do. Stay out of it and don't call

Teresa, their biggest political ally.

It had taken every ounce of self-control she had not to make that call to Charlotte. But she didn't.

Just as Liza was about to log off her computer, her business cell phone rang. She had never changed the number, even though she had a personal number that had the Raleigh area code. Only her inner circle had that number. So getting a call from an unknown number on her business cell wasn't a shock.

"Liza Palmer."

"I thought it was Franklin now?"

Her jaw tightened at the sound of the voice on the other end. "What in the hell do you want, Robert?"

"Aww, is that any way to talk to a friend? Remember, I've always been your best friend, right?"

"I'm hanging up my phone, you asshole."

"Wait, have you heard the news?"

Liza chided herself for not following through on her threat to hang up the phone. "Are you talking about your campaign to be mayor of Charlotte? That's not news, Bob, that's a joke."

"Until I win. And then I hope you and soldier boy will be able to let bygones be bygones so that we can work together to build a better Queen City."

"The people of Charlotte aren't stupid. And it would take five villages of fools for you to win anything."

"That's where you're wrong, Liza. I have a commanding lead in the polls as it is."

Even though she knew it was a lie, Liza did a quick Google search, and her suspicions were confirmed. But instead of rubbing the truth in Robert's face, she let him continue weaving his lies.

"So," she said, "did you call me to gloat, or are you trying to hire me to run your social-media campaign? Just so you know, you can't afford me."

"I've seen what your help can do. I'll pass. But I hope you realize that I don't have any ill will toward you and Chante. I think we should meet and clear up this ugliness between us."

"There is nothing to clear up, Robert. Don't ever call me again, you assclown."

"Such language. I figured you'd be a little more refined by now. Then again, you've always been a trashy bitch."

"You bastard. Let me do us a favor and end this conversation before I go get Chante and we give you the ass whooping that she should've given you when you admitted to paying for sex."

"So, Chante is in Raleigh with you?"

Liza hung up the phone. He was looking for Chante, huh? She wasn't going to tip him off as to where her friend was. But she was going to call Teresa now, because this was a favor that didn't have anything to do with her husband.

Chante and Zach lay side by side on the sand, enjoying the heat of the sun and some frosty iced tea. Zach glanced at her hips as Chante flipped over onto her stomach and took an ice cube out of her cup and popped it into her mouth. Those lips closing around that ice cube gave him an erection that he couldn't hide. Reaching into his cup, Zach grabbed an ice cube and ran it down Chante's back, stopping right above her behind.

"Oh, that felt so good," she cooed. "It's hot out here."

"Not half as hot as you look. But you already knew that. I'm glad you ditched the sarong today."

Chante giggled as he ran another ice cube down her back. "All right, too much of a good thing." Zach leaned over and untied the back of her bikini top.

"Don't move," he said, then slipped his hands underneath the loosened top. Chante moaned as he kneaded her breasts.

"You are so bad," she intoned.

"And you love it." His fingers played with her nipples, and she arched her back, slamming her booty into his erection.

"You keep this up and we're going to get arrested," she said as she pressed her body against his.

"Doing that is not helping the cause," he groaned. "You know I went to the store and I got a big box of . . ." This time it was Zach's cell phone interrupting their interlude. "Shit." He rolled over and glanced at his phone. It was Kia. "What's up, Special K?"

"Zach, it's me."

Launching to his feet at the sound of his ex-wife's voice, Zach was filled with anger and disgust. "What in the hell are you doing in my office?"

"Zach, why are you being so hostile?" Natalie asked. "I need your help, or I swear to God I will tell the feds that you were involved."

"Natalie, you can take the highway to hell. I'm not helping you do a damned thing, and I'm sure I will get to the FBI before you do, since they have my office under surveillance. Here's hoping they bust in there right now and haul you off to prison."

"Why do you hate me so much? I just wanted something of my own. I was tired of living in your shadow, being that perfect little housewife you wanted. Zachary, you neglected me. So, yes, you were a part of this because you didn't give me a choice."

"Have you lost your mind, and did it ever occur to you that we should've talked about this when we were still married?"

"Bastard!"

"Get out of my office." Zach ended the call, then dialed the building's main number. When the head of security answered the phone, Zach lit into him with a litany of curse words that would put to shame a native New Yorker stuck in a traffic jam at rush hour.

"If you allow that woman into the building or even on the sidewalk in front of my building again, I'm getting a new security company."

"But, sir . . ."

Zach hung up the phone, not wanting to hear any excuses for their incompetence. Natalie's clearance had been revoked from his office the day that she said she needed space. Sighing, he pulled up Kia's cell phone number.

"Zach," Dave said when he answered his wife's phone, "I'm glad you called. Kia just gave birth to a beautiful little girl and a handsome little boy."

Despite his anger, Zach smiled. "Twins, huh?"

"Yep. I'm so proud. We were going to call you when the hubbub died down around here. We have so many people in and out of this place right now. So what's going on? I know you have to be calling for a reason."

"Umm, nah, nothing, other than to see if Kia had given birth, and it looks like I called at the right time. I'll see you four soon."

Zach hung up and felt like a jerk because he was actually calling to chew out a pregnant woman. He should've known that Kia had gone to the hospital if Natalie had gotten up the stairs and into his office. But what in the hell had she gone there for?

The sound of Chante clearing her throat broke into his thoughts. Facing her, he could tell she'd heard a lot of his conversations.

"And I thought I'd cornered the market on cursing people out. I was drunk. What's your excuse?" she asked with her right eyebrow arched.

Zach smiled. "I really don't want to talk about it when we're having such an amazing time."

Chante tilted her head to the side. "My,

how the tables have turned. I think we had this conversation in reverse last night."

"You were drunk."

"And you're angry. I'd like to know why."

Zach sighed. How much longer could he avoid telling her everything? "Why don't we get dressed and have a few adult beverages? I'll tell you everything," he said.

Chante blinked, then nodded. "Wait," she said, "we're supposed to be having fun, and I've already let my issues intrude on that. So I say let's get dressed and take a ride in the Mustang."

Zach smiled. "I'm guessing you're going to be doing the driving?"

"Wouldn't be fun if I didn't," she quipped. He took her hand in his and brought it to his lips. He was thankful for the brief reprieve, but he knew it wouldn't last long.

Teresa Flores tried to hold back her response as she listened to Liza rail on about Robert Montgomery. "Liza," she said, then broke into laughter, "everyone in Charlotte thinks he's a joke. Why did you let him get to you?"

Sighing, Liza gritted her teeth. "He was so damned smug, and I'm just hoping that he isn't up to something that's going to hurt Chante again."

"She hasn't been around since the media descended on her after that fool went on TV and announced they were back together."

"She called me about that, and I sent a release for her. I thought that had done the trick," Liza said. "Chante isn't the one who should be running away. Maybe I should . . ."

"Stay out of the fray, Liza. If I need to get down in the dirt with Nic and Robert, then I will. But you and Jackson have bigger fish to fry in Raleigh."

"I know, but . . ."

"Friends and politics make strange bedfellows. But you and I know that anything that would distract from Jackson's bill would play into the hands of those who are against him. Remember all the rumors swirling around you during the election? Want all that stuff to be brought up again?"

"No."

"Then let me handle Charlotte. When I get some things going in the news, I'll send you links to tweet. I know you have an anonymous account somewhere."

Liza chuckled. "Can't keep anything from you, huh?"

"Nope, and that's why you and Jackson have me in your corner."

"Thanks, Teresa."

After Teresa hung up with Liza, she made a call of her own. She was going to beat Dominic Hall again, and Clemmons was going to accept her help, whether he wanted to or not.

Chante fluffed her hair after her shower and dressed in a white tank top and denim shorts. "What am I doing?" she thought aloud. "Obviously, Zach and I have issues that we're hiding from, and they're going to explode in our faces."

Smoothing gloss on her lips, she told herself this wasn't anything serious; she didn't need to worry herself silly about his issues. Grabbing her phone and heading for the door, she was ready to have a good time and drive really fast.

Riding down to the lobby, she groaned when her cell phone rang. And when she saw it was her mother calling, she didn't answer. The last thing she wanted was an argument.

She was about to turn her phone off when she got another call, this one from Liza.

"What's up, Mrs. Franklin?" she asked as the doors to the elevator opened.

"Why do you have your phone on when you're supposed to be chilling with your grandmother?"

"Grammy is on a cruise with her boo," Chante said. "So she got me a suite at the Charleston Harbor Bed and Breakfast."

"Well, I'm glad you're still out of Robert's reach. He had the nerve to call me."

"I'm surprised you don't have his number blocked."

"Creep boy has a new number. Anyway, he's looking for you, and he tried to pick a fight with me so that I would let your whereabouts slip."

"I guess he hasn't figured out that everyone around him has changed and he's the one who's still the same."

"Anyway, how is Charleston? I'm thinking after this session is over, Jackson and I have earned a relaxing getaway. He's been working so hard to keep up with his campaign promises and not get caught up in the BS that goes on up here. I wish some of these politicians were my clients. I could probably retire."

"And never get a moment's rest," Chante said. "Politicians are worse than athletes."

"I know, and that means I'll be able to have something to do while my husband is saving the state."

"So you're not in the honeymoon stage anymore?"

Chante heard a happy moan in her friend's voice. "I wouldn't say that. It's just that since he won the election, the work has gotten harder. And because my man doesn't play the game, he has a lot of people who are looking to bring him down."

"I know Senator Franklin can handle it. He's a man of conviction, and you have his back."

"He's lucky, isn't he?" Liza broke out into laughter. "I'm the lucky one. That man has actually shown me that slowing down is not always a bad thing."

"Elizabeth Palmer-Franklin, I can't believe you! You're actually happy and talking about slowing down. Marriage is really good for you."

"And I hate to sound clichéd, but I hope this situation with Robert hasn't turned you off to . . ."

"Don't go there. But I do have a confession: I met someone."

"All right, now! Is it . . . ?"

"A vacation fling. I'm not looking for that Claire Huxtable life anymore, even if I told my mother that Zach is my fiancé."

"Wait? What?"

Chante was about to tell her about her ruse with Zach, but as she walked off the elevator, she saw Zach standing in the lobby with a long-stemmed red rose in his hand.

"Liza, I have to go."

"Oh, you better call me back!"

Chante ended the call, then shut her phone off as she drank in the image of Zach in his white linen slacks and white tank top. He held out a long-stemmed red rose to her. "You look amazing," Zach said.

Smiling, Chante took the rose from his outstretched hand. "Thank you." She brought the rose to her nose. "I love roses."

"Haven't met a beautiful woman who doesn't."

She raised her right eyebrow. "Is that so?"

"Think about it, a rose is the symbol for beauty, love, and war."

"War? And why do you know this?"

"Got to know these things. You never know when you will be able to impress Chante Britt with it."

"Anyway."

"Okay, the florist told me when I bought the rose."

Chante broke out laughing. "I was about to be impressed."

"Ah, random facts impress the lady. Let me take note of that."

She playfully pushed him in the chest. "Taking notes, really?"

"Yes, I have to know how I can keep that

smile on your face." He stroked her cheek. "Where are you driving me to?"

"Jestine's Kitchen."

"Where?"

"You will see when we get there. Come on," she said.

Zach handed her the keys to the Mustang.

"I'd tell you to drive slow, but I know that would be a waste of breath," he said as they walked out of the hotel. They passed a film crew and a few photographers. Neither of them gave it a second thought as they climbed into the Mustang.

One of the production assistants for the film crew, which was recording a documentary about African American landmarks in Charleston, nudged the director.

"What?" the burly man barked.

"I think I just saw Zachary Harrington."

The director almost dropped his camera. He was a native New Yorker who'd been following the case of the "Harlem Madame." No one in the city had been able to find Zachary and discover what his involvement had been with the alleged sex ring. But if he could locate Harrington, get some footage of him, and maybe even ask him a few questions, CNN would pay him a lot for it.

"Hey, guys! Let's come back at sunset," he said. "It will be a better shot."

The crew groaned, since they had been up since six a.m. "Wrap it up!" the director yelled, then turned to the eagle-eyed production assistant. "What were they driving, and which way did they go?"

Smiling, the production assistant handed the director a slip of paper with the license-plate number written on it. "All right," the director said, "let's find him."

Meeting Street was packed, as Chante expected. But she found a parking spot about a block and a half from Jestine's Kitchen.

"What's so special about this place?" Zach asked as they got out of the car and walked toward the restaurant. A line of people stretched along the sidewalk.

"Well," Chante began, "it's named after Jestine Matthews, a woman who lived until she was one hundred and twelve years old. The family she worked for in the late 1920s opened this restaurant to keep Jestine's legacy of good food alive."

"You know your history of this city," he said with a smile.

"Charleston is filled with a lot of history. A lot like New Orleans."

Zach nodded. He'd considered going to the Big Easy before settling on Charleston for his great escape. Holding Chante's hand, he knew he'd made the right decision.

As they waited in the line, he couldn't help but wonder if things would change between them when she learned of the drama he was embroiled in back in New York. Glancing at Chante, he wondered if she would be forgiving, or would she take exception to the fact that he didn't tell her everything?

"What's with that look?" she asked.

"Huh?"

"You were staring again," she quipped.

"Have you seen yourself? I'm not the only one staring. But at least I know what's underneath the wrapping."

She pinched his arm. "Keep it up and you will never see underneath this wrapping again."

Zach snickered. "You and I both know that's a lie." Bringing his lips to her ear, he said, "You'd let me take those sexy shorts off your exquisite body right now and eat you for lunch."

The heat of his words and his breath made her tingle with excitement. She couldn't even jokingly deny what he said. "I don't know what I'm going to do with you."

"After we eat, I have quite a few ideas." His smile made her throb between her thighs.

"Takeout?" she asked.

CHAPTER 11

Though the sexual tension between Zach and Chante was hotter than the oil used to fry Jestine's famous chicken, the cozy atmosphere of the restaurant drew them in. And a coveted empty table made them stay. "I see this is a popular place," he said as they took a seat.

"Very. There's no telling whom you might run into here," she said as she placed her napkin in her lap. "And the cucumbers are to die for."

Moments later, a waiter set a bowl of pickled cucumbers on the table. "Welcome to Jestine's Kitchen. I'm Peter, and I'll be taking care of you today. Would you like to try Miss Jestine's table wine?"

"It's a little early for . . ."

"It's iced tea," Chante said with a smile as she interrupted Zach's question. "And yes, we'll have a pitcher."

Peter nodded and headed to the kitchen.

Chante was about to lean in and whisper something wicked to him when she heard someone call her name. Looking in the direction the voice came from, she groaned when she saw her high school nemesis, Rochelle Moore.

"Hi," Chante said as Rochelle and a heavyset man made their way toward her.

"Wow," Rochelle said when she reached the table. "You look amazing. I guess law school and all that stuff paid off."

Chante narrowed her eyes at the former cheerleader who looked as if she'd eaten her younger self. "Rochelle, I'm surprised to see you in Charleston. How did that modeling career work out for you?"

Rochelle laughed uncomfortably. "Well, you know that was a childish dream. I'm actually a principal at Hanhan High School."

"Nice. Good for you. I remember my childhood dreams of becoming a lawyer. I did that," Chante said smugly.

"Is this the fiancé who cheated on you with a hooker?"

Zach's eyes stretched to the size of quarters.

Chante's smile dropped, and she narrowed her eyes at Rochelle. "Still following my every move?"

"You want people to think you're perfect, and you're far from it. You've always been that way."

"And you believed it," Chante said. "Otherwise you wouldn't be standing here trying to make yourself feel good because I had a setback. Glad to see nothing — much — has changed about you."

"At least I can keep my man satisfied," Rochelle said, then stalked off. Chante wanted to toss the bowl of cucumbers at the back of her head. Why did she fall into that high school trap of childishness?

"You two have never been friends, huh?" Zach asked as he watched her eye the bowl of cucumbers.

"Not at all. I should've known the true story of my relationship with Robert wouldn't stay in Charlotte."

"So that jab was true?" Zach asked.

She rolled her eyes and sighed. "Yes."

"Then this Robert person is a fool. I don't understand how anyone could . . ."

"You know what," she said, cutting him off. "I don't even want to talk about it. I'm surprised she didn't seek me out on social media to let me know she knew about Robert's scandal."

Zach fell silent, wondering how his scandal would play out with her. She'd already dealt with her own sex scandal, and his drama in New York would only add insult to injury.

"I tell you what: we don't have to stay here."

"I'm not running from that . . . We're here and we are not leaving." Chante glanced in Rochelle's direction and wasn't surprised to see the smug heffa looking back at her.

"What's the deal with you and her?" Zach asked as he nodded toward Rochelle.

"The difference between being number one and number two. When we were in high school, she and I were always either number one or number two. Mostly, I was number one, and she tried to steal my boyfriend, and it didn't work out for her. She's been holding it against me ever since."

"Tom Petty and the heartbroken." Zach reached over and placed his hand on top of hers. "You're still winning."

Chante leaned over and kissed him on the tip of his nose. "You're sweet."

"Not as sweet as you are," he whispered, then winked at her. "But you already know that."

Part of her wished that she and Zach had something real. Something that would develop into the relationship they were pretending to have. It felt good and it felt real.

I have to stop this. I'm kidding myself if I think this is going to be anything more than a charade, she thought as she stared into his eyes. Before she could say a word, the waiter returned with their drinks and took their food orders. Chante wished that she'd actually ordered some wine instead of iced tea.

"Zach, when you got that call earlier from your ex . . ."

"Yeah. I thought we agreed we weren't going to talk about that?"

She held up her hand, "Let me finish. You were pretty upset with her, and I need to know if you're going to take that passion and turn it around and try to get revenge, or are you going to give her a second chance?"

"Neither of those is going to happen. I want her to be a distant memory in my life. Why do you ask?"

Chante shrugged. "I'm just being ridiculous. I know that what we have here ends when we leave Charleston, so whatever you do or don't do with your ex isn't my issue."

"Where did that come from?"

She took a sip of her tea. "Just overthinking things," Chante said. "You and I aren't real, so it doesn't even matter what you do when you leave."

Zach nodded and took his own sip of tea.

He started to ask her what she meant by not being real. Did she think last night wasn't real? Didn't she know that she had awakened something deep inside of him that he thought his ex-wife had murdered?

How could she question that? Maybe it was because she didn't plan to keep things going with him and found herself getting closer to him, or was the charade of their relationship getting to her?

"Do you think we should tell your mother that we're over?" he asked.

"What?" Chante pushed her glass away.

"Did she rattle you that much?"

She furrowed her eyebrows. "Are you serious?"

"You're the one who just made everything serious." Zach reached out and held her hand. "Why?"

"I need to go to the restroom for a moment," she said as she rose to her feet.

He stood up and blocked her exit. "Don't run from this. Just tell me the truth. What do you want?"

Chante sighed. What she wanted was the fantasy. She wanted them to exist in a vacuum and wanted to go back to simply having fun. She wanted to forget that she was running from her own problems.

"I just want to go to the bathroom," she

said as tears welled up in her eyes. "I'm sorry." Her whisper hung in the air as she tore away from him. Once she was alone in the bathroom, Chante shut herself up in a stall and cried silently, trying to wrap her mind around the fact that she was a mess and had made an even bigger mess by getting involved with Zach.

I have got to stop leading with my thighs, she thought as she wiped her eyes with a rough piece of toilet paper. *That wasn't the problem with Robert; he just embarrassed me, and I'm still suffering from it. Now this thing with Zach. I need to get back to who I am and stop acting like a man is going to make things better.*

Emerging from the stall, Chante forced herself to put on a face that said she was fine. She forced herself to believe she was fine playing in this game, but if she was honest with herself, she would admit that the life she'd run from — husband and kids — was something that she wanted. Perhaps she'd spent such a long time rebelling against her mother's expectations that she'd squandered the chance to have just what her heart desired.

Wiping her face again, she headed out of the bathroom and ran into Rochelle as she walked in. The two women eyed each other with contempt. "Chante," Rochelle said with a saccharin tone, "I hope I didn't cause you any problems."

"Not at all," Chante said with a smile that was just as fake as Rochelle's concern. "We are just as fine as we were before your interruption."

"I know what your problem is," she said. "You've always thought you were better than me."

Chante laughed. "You thought I was better than you, and you wanted to be better than me. Rochelle, we've been out of high school for a long time, and you're still acting as if we're running for student body president."

"Whatever."

"Grow up." Chante strutted away from her. When she reached Zach, her smile was genuine.

"Feeling better?" he asked as he rose to his feet.

Chante closed the space between them and wrapped her arms around his neck. She brought her lips to his and gently brushed them with her tongue. "Much."

Zach smiled as he slid his hands down her back. "I don't know what kind of hand soap you used in there, but I like the effect it had on you."

"I say we order our food and then go break a law and have sex on Folly Beach," she whispered.

"Whoa!" Zach took a step back from Chante. "You know if we get caught, you have a lot more to lose than I do."

"Then I guess you better be creative." She winked at him, then took her seat.

"Oh, just me?" he quipped.

"I've actually thought about this for a long time, so yes, just you."

Zach wished he could make their food magically appear because he was tired of talking. Placing his hand on top of Chante's, he stroked her smooth skin with his thumb. "Seriously, I need to know what happened in the bathroom."

Her smile faded a bit as she stared into his eyes. "I've always allowed what other people think of me to dictate how I live my life. Everything was about proving someone wrong, proving that I could do everything that someone else could do, only better, and then there's my mother. It just hit me when I saw a grown woman still carrying a high school grudge that my life is mine. And it's time to live it for me."

"Hallelujah. See, that's why you walked into the bar looking so uptight. I knew it was inside you all along," he said.

Chante snorted. "You sure stared hard enough to see everything inside."

Leaning back in his seat, Zach folded his arms across his chest. "We just aren't going to let that go, are we?"

She shook her head, and before she could tell him why, the waiter returned with their entrées. The delicious aroma of the food rendered them both speechless for a moment. It was now time to eat.

Nic burst into Taiwon's office, catching the attorney off guard as he hung up the phone. "What in the hell," Taiwon gritted.

"Where is she?" Nic demanded.

"How did you get up here, and why do you think I . . . ?"

"We had a deal, Myrick! You were supposed to get Chante Britt back here and I'd keep your secret from your partners. Time is running out!"

Taiwon leaned back in his massive leather chair. "I can't force her to come back. Even after I dangled the partnership carrot in her face, Miss Britt is remaining hidden away where she is. So if you want to act on your threats, then go ahead. I'm getting sick of your bullshit and seeing your face."

"Don't think I won't act," Nic said. "You have two more days."

Taiwon rose to his feet and stood toe-to-toe with Nic. Glaring at the politico, he grabbed him by his lapels and slammed him against the door. "I don't work for you, and I don't give a damn about Chante and your candidate. My concern is this law firm; not having her here while this idiot tries to run for mayor is the best thing for us. Do you think this fool has a chance to win when everyone knows he seeks the comfort of hookers?" Taiwon pushed Nic to the floor. "Get the hell out of my office."

"You're going to regret this!" Nic said as he scrambled to his feet and stumbled out of Taiwon's office. As he went down in the elevator, Nic started to wonder if he should abandon Robert's ship. It wasn't as if he believed in him; it was just losing to Teresa, of all people, that left a bad taste in his mouth.

Besides, he'd helped worse people than Robert get elected. He planned to show that relic bitch that he was still in charge. And the only way to do that was to win this seat for Robert. She'd see that his influence still shaped this city, and that no matter who she thought she was, he still had the power.

As he headed out of the building, he knew he had to find Chante Britt by any means and force her to stand by Robert until he was elected mayor of Charlotte.

"Well, if it isn't Dominic Hall," a female voice said. Gritting his teeth, Nic turned around and faced the very woman he wanted to destroy.

"Stalking me, Teresa?"

"No, but I knew you'd be sniffing around here looking for Chante Britt because of this madness you and Robert are trying to accomplish. Mayor of Charlotte? Really?" She laughed and shook her head.

"He will win."

"Keep dreaming," she said as she walked into the law office.

What is she up to? Nic thought as he turned and followed her inside.

CHAPTER 12

Chante was in total bliss as Zach licked and kissed her womanly core. She stroked his head as his tongue lashed her throbbing bud. Clenching the beach towel, she muffled her screams as he sucked her slowly. Their eyes locked as she lifted her thighs to his shoulders. She arched her back a bit, pushing her sweetness deeper into his mouth. "Yes," she said quietly, happy for the sand dune that hid their tryst. One more lash of his tongue and Chante exploded. He smiled as she leaned back on the towel with a look of satisfaction on her face.

Zach covered her body with his and lifted one of her legs, wrapping it around his waist. "You're so sweet," he said.

"Mmm, you know how to make a woman feel good."

He thrust forward, allowing her to feel his arousal. "I can make you feel better, but I don't know how much more we want to press our luck with sex on the beach in the middle of the day."

Reality trumped her desire because as much as she wanted him to take her right then, the risk of getting caught was just too much. "Okay," she moaned, "let's go inside."

Zach leapt to his feet and, in an even swifter motion, lifted Chante into his arms. Before heading for the hotel, he covered her mouth with his and kissed her slow, deep, and long. Chante moaned as his hands roamed her back. Pulling her lips away from his, Chante gazed at Zach for a beat. "You have to stop."

"What if I don't want to?"

"Then we're going to get arrested," she quipped.

"Jail is the last place we need to be." He nearly ran up the steps leading to the hotel. Dashing through the lobby and to the elevator, he pressed the UP button several times in succession, as if his urgency for Chante would make the car come faster. She laughed at him as he pressed the button again.

"The elevator is on the twelfth floor. You're going to have to wait."

Zach looked to his left. "Or take the stairs." Chante was about to tell him that he could put her down, but he headed for the staircase and took the steps two at a time. When they reached the fourth floor, where his room was, Zach stopped. "All right, we have to go to my room," he panted.

"I was wondering when He-Man would lose his strength," she giggled. He placed Chante on her feet and opened the door leading to the hotel suites. She patted him on his shoulder.

"I think I'll walk from here," she said.

"I like the way you move," he said as he stared at her shapely backside. Chante put a little extra twist in her hips, and as he thought about her riding him and his hands on those hips, he was harder than Charleston cobblestone.

He couldn't open the door to the room fast enough. Once he did, Chante sauntered inside and stripped out of her suit. Zach drank in her image, then stepped out of his trunks. Closing the space between them, he pulled her against his chest. The feel of her smooth skin made his heart beat like a bass drum. "So soft," he whispered as he leaned into her and kissed her neck. He could feel her tremble against him. Zach slipped his hands between her thighs, seeking her wetness. And she was so wet. As he slid his finger between her wet folds of flesh, Chante moaned and ground against it as her flesh thickened with desire and yearning.

He threw his head back as she got wetter and wetter at his touch. "Zach," she cried out as waves of pleasure washed over her senses. "Need. You."

"Not as much as I need you," he said. His fingers toyed with her feminine core, and she could feel herself puckering at his touch. He'd primed her for his hardness, and Chante couldn't wait to feel him deep inside her. He brushed his lips across hers as he pressed his finger deeper inside her. Chante cried out in pleasure, on the brink of her release. Throwing her head back, she moaned as he made ripples of wanton desire wave over her.

"Please!" she moaned.

Unable to prolong her pleasure, Zach rubbed the tip of his erection against her wetness, and it took everything inside him not to plunge into her. But somehow he found the willpower not to enter without protecting them, no matter how hard he was.

Gently pushing Chante back on the bed, he spread her thighs apart. With his right hand, he stroked her wetness as he reached for a condom with his other hand.

"Zach!" she exclaimed as his strokes

deepened. Shivering, she felt as if she was about to explode from need and desire. Sheathed and ready, Zach removed his hand and positioned himself on top of her. Chante wrapped her legs around his waist, pulling him closer. "Need you," she moaned.

Zach thrust forward, diving into her. She gripped his neck as she ground against him. He reveled in her grip on his erection, following her rhythm as she tightened her thighs around him.

"Chante, Chante," he whispered like a mantra. "You feel so good."

"Umm, you feel even better." She thrust forward, and he gripped her hips as he rolled over on his back.

"Ride me, babe," he commanded.

Holding on to his shoulders, she heeded his call, slowly bouncing up and down as he stroked her bottom. She arched her back, and he matched her stroke for stroke. Fast. Slow. Up. Down. Chante shivered as the first waves of her orgasm hit her. Feeling her tighten herself around him, Zach slowed his movements, wanting to hold back his own climax as he watched her give in to hers.

But when she took him deeper into her valley and gave him a slow roll, he couldn't help but explode. "Oh Chante, damn, baby!" he cried as she collapsed against his chest.

"Wow," she whispered as she buried her face in his chest. "That was so worth the wait."

Zach kissed her on the forehead. "Tell me about it. But we're not waiting that long again."

Laughing, she wrapped her arms around him. "This has been a crazy week," she said. "Thanks for being a part of it."

"The week isn't over yet," he said with a wink.

Chante sighed as she thought about the reason she ran to Charleston in the first place. "Being here has given me so much clarity. I have to thank you for that."

"Really?"

She nodded. "My ex was making my life a living hell. Rochelle was right about him; he cheated on me with a hooker. At the time he was running for state senate, and when it came out, I was beyond embarrassed. My best friend tried to warn me, but I was blinded by the very thing I claimed I didn't want."

"Which was?" he asked.

"The status of being married and having my mother's approval." The admission shook her to the core. She hadn't even told Liza how she really felt about Robert and why she'd accepted his marriage proposal so quickly.

"But I thought you didn't care what your mother thought and the plan was to live your life for you."

She stroked his cheek. "That was the liquor talking. As much as we try to act like we don't care what our mothers think, we do. Part of me will always want my mother to be proud of me."

Zach kissed her cheek. "If she can't be proud of the woman that you are, then there comes a time when you stop turning yourself inside out to make her feel good about your life. I'm sure law school wasn't easy. I'm sure finding a job at a huge law firm in the South, as a woman, was a struggle."

Chante nodded. Everything he said was true, and if her mother didn't see that, would Chante ever gain her mother's approval? "Why don't we take a shower and go get some ice cream, bourbon, and brownies?"

Zach looked up and down her naked body and let out a low whistle. "How do you eat all of that and still look like this?" He ran his hand across her sculptured abs.

"That's why I don't come to Charleston

often. And I've been running a lot lately to counteract my wine drinking."

"Whoa, you have been going through hell," he said.

She gripped his arm. "I'm suspended from that law firm that I worked so hard to be a part of because Robert's sins were my fault and I became a distraction."

"Damn."

Slipping out of his arms, Chante rose from the bed. "So about that shower?"

Zach was up on his feet in a flash. "Let's do it."

Robert glared at Nic after he finished reading the latest polls for the mayor's race. He was way behind, and the election was about two months away. "I thought you said you had this handled," Robert demanded as he tossed the papers in Nic's face. "This is not what we planned."

"Is it my fault that you couldn't charm Chante into standing by your side or that you paid a woman for sex? That's all people think about when they see you, and the fact that we have one former mayor in prison . . ."

"I was never charged! My record is clear. You're supposed to be the man who can get results! I haven't seen any."

"You selfish bastard. I've been working my ass off to get you elected, and what have you done? You've been sleeping with staffers and pissing them off. Your girl, Gabby, told me about what's going on with the two of you and how you said she wasn't good enough to meet your parents or go to a political party. Have you forgotten that your mother was a crackhead, and God knows who your father is?"

Robert launched out of his seat and punched Nic in the face, knocking him to the floor. "Don't you ever mention my mother again!"

Holding his jaw, Nic slowly rose to his feet. "You're on your own. Good luck trying to win this seat now!"

"Fuck you, Nic. Now get the hell out of here!"

As Nic slammed out of the office, Robert knew he was on his own, and if he was going to be mayor of Charlotte, he had to step up his game. First on the agenda was finding Chante.

Then a light bulb went off in his head. Chante used to talk about her grandmother a lot, and her grandmother lived in Charleston. If he could find where she lived, he'd probably find Chante there playing the victim. Victim! He was the true victim because of her and that bitch Liza. If Liza had kept her damn mouth shut, he and Chante would be married and he'd be the one in the General Assembly. It was his seat and Liza stole it from him. He was going to take back what was his, the route to power. Picking up his phone, he dialed Liza's number.

"Liza Franklin."

"Where is Chante? And you've given up your identity for a man?" Robert laughed.

"Why do you keep calling me, you pompous jackass?"

"Because you owe me, and you should've kept your promise to me."

"Oh please, I'm sick and tired of this and you. Don't call me again, or I will file a report for harassment."

"I don't understand why you turned your back on me," he said.

"Why I turned my back on you? This is so funny to me. You and Nic tried to destroy my reputation and spread the rumor that I was a call girl. Is it my fault that people saw what a fraud you were before Election Day? I don't think so! Stop calling me, and leave Chante alone."

When the dial tone sounded in his ear, Robert seethed with anger. All those years she claimed to have his back, and she lied!

Typical woman. Just like his mother. Just like any tramp who'd ever claimed to give a damn about him. That's why Chante was going to pay what she owed. She was going to give one interview that would put him in the mayor's seat. If the public believed she had forgiven him, then they would as well.

And if she was in Charleston, he'd find her and have a camera crew in tow. Maybe after he explained to her how his being mayor of Charlotte would help her get back on a good footing with her law firm, she'd go along with what he needed.

Typing her grandmother's name into the Google search bar, Robert knew it was time to head south.

Zach would've paid money to watch Chante eat her ice cream cone. The way her tongue moved around the cold cream made his crotch swell with memories of how she had licked and sucked him to climax. Her lips were simply amazing.

"What?" she asked as she caught his eye.

"I'd tell you, but if someone heard me, they would be scandalized," he said, then kissed her on the tip of her nose. "I just know how magical those lips and tongue are, and I'm jealous of that cone right now."

"If you play your cards right, maybe I'll

treat you like this." She slowly licked the cream. "Later."

"Your wish is my command, darling," he said with a mock bow. Zach turned to his banana split and wondered how open Chante would be to him drizzling chocolate all over her body and licking it off.

"How's your banana split?" she asked.

"Pretty good," he said. "I see why Charleston is a foodie's dream. We haven't been to a bad restaurant yet."

"What brought you to Charleston? You don't seem like a foodie, and I've been taking up a lot of your time, so I don't know what kind of business you've been doing."

Zach offered a smile. She'd been honest about his ex, maybe it was time for him to tell her the truth about his.

"Well," he said, "I'm probably going to start looking into some real estate opportunities soon, but I needed a break first. My ex has been in the news because of some illegal activities. A lot of people in New York are trying to link me to her misdeeds."

"What did she do?" Chante asked as she lowered her waffle cone.

Zach shoveled a spoonful of ice cream into his mouth. He wanted to tell her everything, wanted to be open with her. But he was still having a hard time wrapping his mind around the fact that he had been married to a pimp.

"Fraud, tax evasion," he said, then stopped speaking. "It's pretty complicated."

"Wow. So how is that affecting your business?"

"Badly."

"I'm sorry."

Zach touched her hand. "Don't worry about it. I'll bounce back."

She smiled. "I don't doubt that one bit." Chante leaned in and kissed him on the cheek. Neither of them noticed the long lens pointed at them.

CHAPTER 13

"Who is that woman?" the photographer asked.

"We'll run her face through Google photo search," the ambitious director replied. "I can't believe Harrington is in a new relationship so quickly. He must be trying to revamp his image."

"Ever think he's fallen in love?" the photographer asked as he snapped images.

"I don't care. I just want to get a newsworthy story that will get me back in front of the CNN editors. This travel-video shit is for the birds. We're going to be the first people to get Zachary Harrington on camera!"

The photographer kept shooting the kissing couple. This would be a coup and make both him and the director famous.

Chante pulled back from Zach and looked into his eyes with a smile on her lips. "You taste so good. I wonder if we can take some of this chocolate with us."

Zach grinned. "You read my mind."

Leaning in closer, she whispered, "I know where I want to cover you with chocolate and lick it off."

Zach raised his eyebrow and smirked, "Your sweet tooth is that big, huh?"

Smacking him on the shoulder, she couldn't help but laugh. The truth was the truth, though.

He looked down at his half-eaten banana split. "Give me one second," he said as he rose to his feet and headed to the counter. Chante held back her laughter as she watched him get his tray filled with chocolate sauce.

When he returned to the table, he showed her the container. "I say, let's get out of here before this thing springs a leak."

As they headed out the door, Chante just happened to look over her shoulder, and she spotted the photographer. "What in the . . . Why is that man taking pictures of us?"

Zach looked at the photographer. "I don't know, why don't we just . . ."

Before he could say get out of there, the two men rushed over to them. "Mr. Harrington!" the director called out as Zach ushered Chante into the car.

"Mr. Harrington, are you in Charleston to avoid being connected to the 'Harlem Madame'?"

"Stay away from me," Zach growled as he hopped into the car. He sped out of the parking lot and drove faster than Chante ever had.

"What was that all about?" she asked as she gripped her seat belt.

"Nothing."

"The 'Harlem Madame'? That's your ex?"

Slowing the speed of the car, he nodded. "I had no idea what she was doing, but no one seems to care about that."

Chante let out a frustrated sigh. "So you lied to me."

"I didn't lie . . ."

"Don't give me that shit. I'm so sick of men lying! You made it seem as if she was facing financial charges when you knew good and damned well that your ex is a pimp."

"Which has nothing to do with me!"

Chante dropped her head in her hands. She wasn't ready for this. She wasn't going to deal with this. "I'm just supposed to believe your wife ran a call-girl ring and you were clueless? Zach, you're smarter than that."

"So you knew your fiancé was buying sex on the side?"

She narrowed her eyes at him. "Stop the car!"

"Chante, I'm sorry."

"Stop. The. Damn. Car."

"I . . ."

"If you're trying to hurt me to cover your guilt, it's not working. I poured my heart out to you, and you sat there silent. Don't sit here and try . . . You know what. Let me out of this car or I'm going to jump out."

"I'm not stopping this car, and I'm not going to sit here and justify why I didn't want to tell you my ex was selling sex. And you're not going to jump out of this car because I'll drive a hundred miles an hour to stop you."

Chante rolled her eyes. "Fine, but when we get back to the resort, I don't want to see you again. I'm done with men and their sex scandals."

"This isn't my sex scandal!" Zach banged his hand on the steering wheel. "Okay, I'm tired of being held responsible for someone else's bad choices. Natalie did what she did because she wanted to. I was in the dark, and I'm not going to keep apologizing for her bad acts."

"How were you in the dark? She was your wife."

"In name only. Our marriage had been over for years, and I'd been too blind to see that I needed to file the divorce papers."

"Because you loved her?" Chante asked.

"No. Because I didn't want the bad press. At one time, Natalie and I had been the face of my company, which is why so many people think I had some knowledge or involvement in her call-girl ring."

Chante could see where he was coming from. She had no idea about all the things Robert had been involved with. Still, she'd been honest with him about Robert, and he'd kept the most scandalous part of his ex-wife's drama under wraps. She teetered between understanding and anger.

When she finally decided to speak, she asked, "What are you going to do? Obviously you wanted to keep a low profile, but you have people on your tail now."

"I'm done running," he said in a low voice. "I didn't do anything wrong, but I'm acting as if I did. Sure, I wanted to come to Charleston and try to do some business with people who knew nothing of what was happening with my ex's case. This just showed me that in the age of twenty-four-hour news cycles, there is nowhere to run."

She glanced at him and sighed. How long would she be able to stay hidden from her own drama?

"Maybe we shouldn't go back to the resort," she suggested.

"I said I'm . . ."

"We're not running, but there is no need to walk into a media circus right this minute. We can go to my grandmother's place. It might be under construction, but I'm sure we can find a room to hide out in for a day or so. Then maybe people will think you've gone back to New York and you can finish your vacation — alone."

"Alone?"

"I've got my own issues to deal with, and I don't want to add your baggage to my luggage rack. Thanks for the fun times, but when this is over, we're going to go our separate ways. Take a right at this intersection," she said, then stared out the window.

Chante directed him to her grandmother's house, and she didn't say anything as he pulled up the winding driveway. "So it's the silent treatment now?" he asked as they exited the car.

"I just don't have anything to say right now." She pointed to a small cottage in the backyard. "Let's hope she hasn't decided to renovate this too."

"A little dollhouse?"

"Hush," she said. "This was our dream house. We'd do arts and crafts out here. I would've stayed here, but my grammy set up reservations at the resort."

"Then I guess if I ever get the chance to meet her, I should thank her."

"That's not going to happen. I meant what I said, when this dies down, you go your way and I'm going to go mine," she said as she reached underneath the welcome mat and grabbed the spare key.

When she opened the door, Chante was happy to see the cottage hadn't changed — much. The yellow walls were a bit faded but still bright. The white French provincial furniture was just as elegant as it had been when she'd seen it with her young eyes, especially the baby-blue settee in the right corner. She marched over to the chair and sat down with a smile on her face.

"I've always loved this chair," she said.

"What's so special about it?" Zach crossed over to her and waited to be offered a seat. After a beat, she nodded for him to sit down. "It is soft."

Chante turned and faced him. "When did you find out what your ex was doing?

Zach tossed his head back and sighed. He hated thinking about those moments when the FBI burst into his office. Looking at the questions in Chante's eyes, he realized that he owed her the truth. "I was in my office, about to close a deal with a Japanese company. It was going to be a multi-million-dollar contract that would have put my company over the top. This would've led to more business from them because they were buying up a lot of property in Manhattan. FBI agents, with guns drawn, bursting into my office killed that deal. It cost me a lot of money, and to make matters worse, they took my computers, files, and everything. So I was basically shut down for nearly a month before they figured out that I had nothing to do with Natalie's business. Between the media and all the stories that were swirling around New York about her and our marriage, I couldn't escape the rumors."

"Wow," Chante said, realizing that her incident on *Charlotte Today* paled in comparison to Zach's experience.

She couldn't imagine how she would've reacted if she'd been implicated in a crime Robert committed. She'd probably be in jail, not hiding in Charleston. "Why were you a suspect in the first place?"

Shrugging, he stroked his forehead. "At the end of the day, Natalie blames me for everything that went wrong in our marriage and her life. Business has always been important to me, and she knew that. Did I neglect her? Yes, but I was always faithful to her. She couldn't say the same."

"And I guess she wasn't a woman who decided to take responsibility for her own actions, huh?" she said with a snort. "Sounds a lot like Robert."

"Both of us fell for the wrong people, and we're still suffering from it," he said, then drew her into his arms. Chante wanted to push away from him. She didn't need another sex scandal in her life.

"Zach, I know this may not be your fault, but I've had my fill of sex scandals. Look at us, hiding out in a cottage because of someone else's bull."

"Then let's stop hiding."

She was about to say yes, but the thought of her mother seeing them on the news wasn't something she wanted to deal with. Then she looked into Zach's eyes. He was right: they had done nothing wrong — other than fall for the wrong people.

"You know what, why don't we go to Savannah for the rest of the day? We can have dinner at Alligator Soul and make a fire on the beach."

Zach smiled. "I thought you didn't want

anything else to do with me?"

"Maybe I'm just bored?" She grinned, then leaned in and gave him a kiss on the cheek.

"I'll take it."

"You stay here and I'll drive your car back to the hotel, since the photographers saw your rental."

Zach winked at her. "Sounds like a good plan. You've done this before, huh?"

"No, but I have a good friend who specializes in such things." She rose to her feet, and Zach wrapped his arms around her waist.

"I have a better idea," he said as he toyed with the waistband of her shorts. "Let's spend the night right here and head to Savannah in the morning." He unbuttoned her shorts and pulled them down. When he saw that she wasn't wearing any panties, his mouth watered with desire and anticipation. He slipped his finger between her wet folds of flesh and, with his other hand, pushed her shorts around her ankles. "I know what I want to eat."

Before Chante could say anything, his lips covered her puckering core as his tongue sought out her throbbing bud of desire. Chante cried out when he found her sensitive spot, and her knees shivered as his

205

mouth devoured her.

"Come for me," he moaned as her juices filled his mouth. Chante thrust her hips against him as his tongue lashed her throbbing bud. She was so wet, so hot, and when he licked her clit, Chante's knees went weak.

"Zach!" She fell against him, out of breath. Her body shivered as the waves of her orgasm washed over her body.

"What did I do to deserve that?" she asked once she caught her breath.

"You didn't jump out of the car." He winked at her, then pulled her shorts up. "Don't worry, there's more to come when we get to Savannah."

"How about when I come back with my car?" she asked with a wink of her own.

"Wouldn't your grandmother be scandalized by such behavior in such a pretty little dollhouse?"

"She's probably wondering why I've never done anything like this before," Chante replied, then walked out the door.

Robert watched CNN with rapt attention as he saw Chante and Zachary Harrington running to a Mustang in Charleston. "So that *is* where she's hiding," he muttered. "The game has changed." Picking up his phone, Robert placed a call to the one reporter he knew would answer his call, Persone Wallace, the editor of *QC After Dark*.

"Robert," Persone said, "good to hear from you. When are you and Chante making your announcement?"

"I'm meeting her in Charleston, and I think you should come down there with me. That way you will get the exclusive on our reunion."

"I think you're full of shit, Robert."

"I can show you better than I can tell you. Chante and I are back together, and when I'm mayor, she'll be standing by my side."

"I don't believe that woman has forgiven you."

"Why would I lie?" he asked.

Persone snorted. "Because," he began, "you've been lying since I met you. Liza Franklin nearly bankrupted me because you said she was a call girl. I can't mention her or any of her clients on my blog. That is the only reason you're getting so much space. That heffa represents everybody important in Charlotte."

"Stop your whining! This is about to be the biggest story in Charlotte. And here's an added bonus for you. Have you heard of the 'Harlem Madame'?"

"Have I?" Persone said excitedly. "That is a cluster . . ."

"What if you can get an interview with her ex-husband?"

"How?"

"Let's just say I know where he is, and I'm sure when we show up, he's going to have a lot to say."

"If you can deliver all of this, then I'll be one of the first people in line on election day to cast my vote for you."

"Meet me at my office around seven tomorrow morning, and we'll head to Charleston," Robert said smugly. "Then we will both stage an epic comeback the likes of which the Queen City has never seen before."

After hanging up with Persone, Robert smiled. If Chante didn't play ball, she'd be ruined because of her new friend. Either way, he'd get some press and possibly some sympathy because he was the one being cheated on this time.

CHAPTER 14

Chante expected to get back to the resort, quietly park Zach's Mustang, head to her room, get her keys, and leave.

However, what happened wasn't that simple. Three media trucks were in the parking lot — one local station, a CNN truck, and one with a crew from a Charlotte station. Hoping to back out of the lot without being seen, she slammed the car in reverse, nearly hitting another car. When she slammed on the brakes and the tires squealed, Chante brought all the attention she was trying to avoid down on her like a ton of bricks.

"Miss Britt, Miss Britt," a reporter, whom she recognized as being from Charlotte's NBC Six, called out as she rushed over to the car. "What is your relationship to Zachary Harrington? Are you representing him and his wife?"

Chante knew she couldn't just sit in the

car as the cameramen and reporters surrounded the Mustang. She also knew she wasn't going to say a damned word to any of them.

Opening the door, Chante pushed past the media crush and dashed inside the hotel. A security guard crossed over to Chante. "Ma'am, are you all right?"

"Yes, but please tell me there is another way out of here."

He nodded. "We're trying to keep our guests isolated from this nonsense. Seems as if some noteworthy people have been staying here and the media got wind of it."

Chante smiled and didn't say a word. The security guard told her there was a back exit from the parking garage where she could avoid the media if she had parked her car in the guest lot. Luckily, she had. Chante hadn't wanted to run the risk of getting her Jag dented.

"May I ask you a question?" the security guard said.

"Yes, I'm one of those noteworthy people," she replied.

"What did you do?"

"Told the wrong man I would marry him. I've got to get out of here."

"Let me help you," he said. "When you do whatever you came in here for, meet me on the basement level."

Years of watching Investigation Discovery and reading mysteries made Chante pause about meeting this strange man in the basement. "I don't . . ."

"You can trust me," he said. "I value my job, and obviously people would come looking for you."

Chante laughed, then headed for the bank of elevators. After she made it to her floor, she glanced around the corner to make sure she hadn't been followed. She was thankful the reporters didn't know what floor she was on. Heading into her room, she grabbed her keys and a change of clothes, then crossed the hall to the elevators, praying she wouldn't end up a headline for another reason. When she reached the basement, the security guard was waiting for her with a smile and no visible ax.

"Follow me," he said, then started walking toward an exit. Chante had never been so happy to hear silence.

"Where are we?"

"In the back of the parking deck." He looked down at her shoes. "I hope you don't mind walking up a few flights of stairs."

She kicked her high-heeled sandals off and stuck them in her bag, then changed into a pair of flip-flops. "Let's do it."

The guard kept his word and led her to what Chante thought of as the secret exit. She drove out onto a back road and was happy that she knew the area. Chante was definitely going to ask her grandmother why Sheldon Richardson built this little secret exit.

Right now, she simply wanted to give him a hug and a kiss for doing it. As she drove, Chante closely watched the cars behind her, making sure she wasn't being followed. Thankfully, she made it back to her grandmother's house without being spotted by a reporter. She pulled her car behind the cottage and then headed inside. She was surprised to find Zach sprawled across the blue settee, sleeping. Quietly closing the door, she crossed over to him and kneeled down beside the chair.

He looked so peaceful, and she wondered how long had it been since he'd had a moment of peace. The anger she'd felt when he'd told her the truth about his ex had dulled considerably. Touching his cheek, she wanted to tell him about the scene at the hotel, but more than anything else, she wanted to kiss his full lips.

So she did. Soft. Slow. His eyes fluttered open as he parted his lips, and their tongues mated. Zach eased back from her.

"I thought I was dreaming," he said. "Then I felt your clothes."

"Ha," she said, then stood up and stripped out of her clothes. "It was something like this?"

Zach's eyes sparkled with desire. "Just like that." He rose to his feet and drew her into his arms. "What took you so long to get back?" Before she could answer, Zach lowered his head and took her nipple into his mouth. Sucking, nibbling, and licking. She moaned and held the back of his head, urging him to keep going. And he did, his tongue circling her diamond-hard bud.

"Mmm," she moaned. He sucked harder as he stroked her tight abs. Chante shivered as his hand slipped between her thighs. His fingers brushed against her folds, and her breathing became staggered as he slid his finger inside her.

"You're so wet and ready," he said when he released her nipple.

"Yes," she breathed. "Need. You."

Zach pressed his finger deeper. Chante moaned with desire and anticipation. Deeper. Deeper. Chante felt as if she was about to explode. Zach felt her flowing like a waterfall, and he knew that he had to be inside her.

He pulled out of her and licked her essence from his finger. "So sweet," he said, then quickly took his clothes off. They were both heady with need and desire, and when Zach dove into Chante's wetness, neither of them thought of protection. She wrapped her legs around his waist as they thrust into each other. The bite of her nails against his shoulder added fuel to his fiery want for her. Zach thrust harder, and Chante accepted the blissful release of her orgasm. And as much as he wanted to pull out, knowing that he had to protect them, she felt too damned good, and he couldn't stop the explosion.

Chante blinked as the reality of what they'd done sank in. "Oh my God," she exclaimed, then pushed against his chest. "That was so irresponsible."

"I know and I'm . . ."

"Zach, this is on both of us. I mean, I'm on birth control, and I have a clean bill of health, but . . ."

"Let's not borrow trouble." He gave her naked body a slow once-over and had to stop himself from pulling her into his arms again. Chante cleared her throat.

"I'm going to take a shower and see if I can find some blankets or something."

"Chante, are you all right?"

She gave him a stiff smile and nodded

before heading into the bathroom. Once she closed the door, Chante shook her head and paced the small room for a minute or two. *How could I be so stupid? I guess I'm really losing my mind these days. What I need to do is go back to Charlotte and return to the status quo.*

"Are you sure you're okay in there?" Zach asked. "Or is there no water?"

"Umm, just give me a few more minutes. I'll be sure to leave you some hot water." Hopping in the shower, Chante promised to be more careful with Zach and, more importantly, to get her life back on track. It was time to stop running from Robert, her mother, and the partners at the law firm. She needed to channel her inner Elsie Mae and get her power back. It was time to stop making mistakes and make moves. After her shower, she wrapped up in one of the towels in the bathroom and headed back into the sitting room, where Zach was waiting.

"All good?" he asked.

"I'm about to be. This situation that we're in right now isn't our fault."

"Listen, I . . ."

"Not talking about that," she said holding her hand up. "I came to Charleston for many of the same reasons that you did. I'm tired of running."

Zach rubbed his chin. "You're right. And what good has running done me? However, going to Savannah isn't running. That's just continuing our good time." He winked at her. But honestly, he hadn't been ready to let her go yet. Wasn't ready to return to the media questions and the coldness of the city, when he had such warmth and freedom in Chante's arms.

She looked at the clock on the wall near an old-school, nineteen-inch TV; it was a little after eight. "I don't know about you, but I'm hungry."

Looking at Chante in that towel, which barely skimmed her thighs, he wanted to eat; however, it wasn't food that was whetting his appetite. But it had been a while since they had had a meal. He needed food almost as much as he needed to be inside her.

"What are our options?"

"We're going to my parents' house. This is step one in taking my life back, and she's too southern not to feed us." Chante laughed, and her towel slipped from her body. Zach's mouth watered at the sight of her skin, glittering with moisture. She quickly picked up the towel and covered herself.

"I'm going to get dressed. The shower is

all yours," she said.

Zach slowly rose to his feet. "We should've saved water and showered together." When he walked into the bathroom, Chante released a sigh. That man made her body tingle all over, just with his lusty glances. Part of her regretted that this would all be coming to an end soon.

She had to be honest: there was no future between her and Zach. She needed to wrap her mind around that and accept it. Charleston had been fun, but real life waited. Zach wasn't a part of her real life.

Dressing in a white maxi dress and a pair of gladiator sandals, Chante thought about her real future. When she returned to Charlotte, she was going to resign from Myrick, Lawson and Walker and start her own firm.

And she was going to handle divorces now. Love was a big joke, and if she could help the heartbroken get what they deserved, then she was doing a service, not being a money-hungry attorney.

When a phone rang, shattering the silence, Chante almost leapt out of her skin. She saw it was Zach's phone. Picking it up, she crossed over to the bathroom and knocked on the door.

"Your phone is ringing," she said and heard the water shut off.

"Do you mind bringing it to me?" he asked. Chante opened the door and handed him the phone. Seeing him step out of the steamy shower, it was her turn to salivate. Turning her head, she nearly stumbled as she walked out of the bathroom.

"I-I, um, I'm going to call my dad," she said, then closed the door. Chante fumbled around in her purse, looking for her cell phone. When she found it, she heard Zach cursing from the bathroom.

"She did what? I'm not coming back to New York for that bull . . . I'm done."

Chante heard a bang. Rushing to the bathroom, she pulled the door open and saw that Zach had put his fist through the thin wall.

"What in the hell?!"

He dropped his head, "I'm sorry," he said. "I'll make sure to pay for the damage."

"What happened?" Chante glanced at his bleeding hand and reached for a washcloth to wrap around it. "Zach?"

"That was my assistant. Natalie just held a press conference and said my sister, Zoe, was her partner in the call-girl ring. So my sister was just arrested in Indiana."

"Oh my God. What are you going to do?"

"I can't do what I want to do, which is find Natalie and strangle her. She knows what she's doing, and I'm not going to let her get away with coming after my family. And she'd better hope that I get to her before Zoe does."

"Then I guess you're going to New York and not Savannah in the morning."

"You're right," he said. Then he shook his head. "I'm sorry. But this I can't ignore."

She nodded and wiped his hand. "I guess it's time for us to stop running and take our lives back. We're going back to the hotel, and I know a secret way in so we can at least have a modicum of privacy before leaving."

He stroked her cheek with his good hand. "Do me a favor," he said.

"What's that?"

"Don't forget about me and what we had these past few days. When I clear this up, I'm coming to get you."

"You don't have to say that. I understand what this was all about — a vacation fling and a lot of fun. But we both have a lot of baggage that can't really be overcome right now. I won't forget you, but I don't expect anything more."

Zach nodded but didn't reply. A beat passed, and he smiled. "I'm going to get dressed, and we can get out of here. Thanks for bringing me here. I get the feeling that it takes a special person to get this close to you."

She smiled and wanted to tell him how special he was. But what would be the point? Who knew when they'd have their lives together or what would happen when they went back to their respective parts of the world?

Suppose he met someone who moved him and allowed him to get over his ex-wife, someone closer to him?

"Lamont Thomas," she said.

"What?" Zach asked, his brows furrowed.

"The only other guy who has ever been to the cottage with me. We were in the tenth grade, and he said he loved me. I thought we'd be high school sweethearts and end up married. I thought he would love the ambience here and we'd just kiss. So after we ate some of my grandmother's desserts, I thought I'd bring him out here. Unfortunately, he thought I brought him out here to have sex," she said, then stopped talking.

"Ouch. Did anything happen?"

"I kicked him in the nuts, and he called me a bitch. Then I punched him in the face and broke his nose. In retrospect, he wasn't that special."

"So you've basically compared me to the teenaged boy who wanted to sample your cookies because you were grooming him to be your first love? I feel some kind of way about that."

Chante shook her head. "You should feel great. My ex-fiancé doesn't even know about this place. What I was trying to say was that you are special, and I will never forget this day."

Zach drew Chante into his arms and gave her a gentle kiss on the chin. "Neither will I."

She wanted to say more, wanted to tell him that he was unforgettable. But she just couldn't let those words leave her throat. "Let's get out of here."

"I might need to get dressed first," he said with a smirk.

"All right," she said as she returned to the settee and searched for her cell phone.

CHAPTER 15

Robert didn't tell Persone Wallace that he had no idea where he was going when they entered the Charleston city limits. But he'd been following a News Fourteen van and figured they'd seen the same reports about Chante and Harrington. He almost snorted as he thought about Chante judging him so harshly about sleeping with that girl, and here she was, dealing with a man who had documented links to a call-girl ring.

Her moral high ground was gone. Pulling into the hotel parking lot, Robert turned to Persone. "Didn't I tell you?"

"Just because the press is here doesn't mean . . ."

"That's Chante's car!"

Persone watched Chante and Zachary Harrington pull up underneath the canopy of the hotel and get whisked away by two security guards. "Well, I'll be damned," Persone said. "Looks like you were right." He hopped out of the car with Robert in tow. Persone pulled out his iPad Mini and took a few shots of Chante and Zachary walking into the hotel. It wasn't lost on him that Zachary's hand was on Chante's bottom.

"I thought you said you two were getting back together?" Persone asked.

Robert glared at the couple. He wasn't jealous, but he was angry. How dare she judge him when she was hooking up with a pimp?

"Bitch," he mumbled. "I bet . . . You know what, she is just trying to get attention. Once we see each other, we'll be back on track."

Persone dashed toward the front door of the hotel but was stopped by security.

"Do you have a reservation?" one of the guards asked.

"I don't. I need a room, though," Persone said. "My brother and I are here to see our sick mother at the Medical University of South Carolina."

The guard folded his arms across his chest. "Aren't you pretty far from the hospital?"

"There were no vacancies closer."

"And there are none here. Sorry." The guard gave Persone a gentle push. "Good luck finding a room near your mom."

"So that's how you're going to do me?"

"I know why you're here, and sitting up here pretending that your mother is sick is low, even for a reporter." The guard walked away, and Robert headed inside. He was a little less conspicuous in his three-piece suit and carrying a briefcase.

Walking up to the front desk, he smiled at the clerk, then said, "I'm Robert Montgomery, and my fiancée is expecting me."

"And what's her name?" the comely woman asked with a smile.

"Chante Britt."

"Do you want me to call her and let her know you're waiting for her?" she asked.

"Well, I want to surprise her, and I was hoping you could direct me to her room."

The woman shook her head. "I'm sorry, but I can't give out a guest's room number."

"But I want to surprise her. Please, help me out."

She shook her head again. "Sorry, sir. But hotel policy doesn't allow me to do that."

"Fine," Robert said, tempering his anger. "I'll wait for her in the lobby."

"That's a good option," the woman replied before heading into an office behind the front desk. Robert took a seat on one of the sofas facing the elevators and hoped that Chante would come downstairs sooner rather than later.

Chante sighed as she walked into Zach's suite. Inhaling, she tried to commit his masculine scent to memory, since she figured this would be the last time she'd see him. He nodded, then plopped down on the bed.

"I can't believe Natalie did this."

"Maybe she was trying to get your attention."

"She's going to regret getting it this way."

Chante stroked his shoulder. "Keep in mind, I don't practice criminal law." Her smile softened his mood for a minute, and he wanted nothing more than to take her into his arms and pretend nothing was going on.

"I promise I won't need a criminal attorney," he said with a laugh. "Hopefully Zoe won't either."

"I don't understand how or why she was arrested based on the word of a suspect in a major crime."

"Neither do I. But then again, if she had judges in her pocket, who knows who else she has in that black book."

Chante didn't want to ask, but the lawyer in her wondered if his sister had indeed been involved in his ex's criminal enterprise and whether the evidence that led to her arrest was accurate.

"I'm sorry I dragged you into this when you were just looking to get away from your own issues," Zach said as he walked over to the closet and pulled out his suitcase.

"It's all right. We had fun, and that's what we said we were going to do." When Chante's phone rang, she regretted turning it on in the car. Looking down at the screen, she saw it was her mother — again.

Noting the look on her face, Zach asked, "Do you need to get that?"

Chante hit IGNORE. "Nope. Have you booked your flight yet?"

"Yeah, I did it from the Delta app on the drive over. The flight leaves at six, and I can drop the Mustang off there."

"Aww, the Mustang."

"I think you liked that car more than you liked me," he quipped as he stuffed his clothes in the suitcase.

"No way. That car is sweet, but it can't compare to you at all."

He stopped packing and pulled Chante into his arms. With his lips inches from hers, he stroked her cheek and wished he could pack her up and take her to New York with him. "Chante," he whispered.

She covered his lips with hers, holding

back declarations of any emotions they may have been feeling. Right now, she couldn't handle it. Watching him pack almost had her in tears. As she kissed him, she reminded herself that this was the last time she'd ever see him.

Until Zach pulled back from her and wiped away a tear with his thumb, Chante hadn't realized she'd been crying. "Are you all right?"

"Yeah, yeah," she said. "I'm just . . ."

"It's okay. Everything is going to work out for both of us," he said, then planted a gentle kiss on her lips.

"I know, but I feel as if we're suffering because of what other people did to us, and that isn't fair. As soon as we leave this room, the media is going to be on us like a pack of wolves on a wounded lamb. What did we do to deserve this?" Chante paced back and forth, her anger building with each step.

Zach placed his hands on her shoulders, stopping her from wearing a hole in the carpet. "Chante, we didn't do anything other than put our trust in the wrong people. You thought that jackass was really in love with you, and I married a woman who was a pimp. Unfortunately, when you see someone's true colors, it can be too late. Bell Biv DeVoe was right."

"Huh?"

"Never trust a big butt and a smile."

As much as she didn't want to, Chante burst out into laughter. "You're nuts, you know that? I'm going to miss you."

He stroked the side of her neck. "Not for long. I'll be back."

She didn't say anything, because she wasn't sure what he'd find if he came back for her. "We never got a chance to eat, and since we're here, we should order room service before you get ready to fly out."

Zach nodded; then his cell phone rang. He pulled it from his pocket and shook his head. "Here comes the boom. It's Zoe."

"I'm going to order dinner and give you some space."

Zach answered the phone and could barely get hello out of his mouth before his sister started ranting.

"That idiot you brought into the family thinking that she'd be a good mother to my nieces and nephews is going to come up missing! Not only did she cost me money, she blew a case I was working on. Oh, and here's the damned kicker: while I'm under investigation by the F-B-fucking-I, my PI license is suspended."

"Zoe, calm down."

"Calm down, my ass! I told you I didn't

trust her and not to marry her. Did you listen? No. Now you know what it was all about. She wanted access to top-level men for her call-girl ring."

"How do you know this?"

She snorted. "You really think I'm going to get called in for questioning and not look at files and get questions answered myself?"

Zach smiled. "I guess I forgot who I was talking to."

"Yeah, you did, Zach. From what I've uncovered, Natalie has been at this for a while. And you're not her first husband. She did this in Orlando about three years ago, but she had the case tossed because there was video of one of the judges with an under-aged call girl. However, the FBI has been on her tail, and she won't be getting out of this case."

"All right, but why is she coming after us?"

"Because she is a psychotic bi— . . . Think about it, Zach, this is a woman who thought she was Teflon. She's scorned and angry. So she wants to get anyone she can. That means you and, by extension, me. We're going to get out in front of this, so that means you . . ."

"I'll be back in New York in the morning."

"Why did you leave today?"

Zach glanced at Chante as she hung up the phone on the nightstand near the bed. "We'll talk about that when I see you tomorrow."

"I hope this woman is better than the last one!"

"Good night, Zoe." Zach hung up and then turned his phone off. He crossed over to Chante and wrapped his arms around her shoulders. "So what did you order for us?"

"That seafood quiche you brought to my room. It was rather delicious. I'm thinking there must be oysters in it."

Zach raised his right eyebrow. "And why's that?"

"Because after eating it, I really wanted you." She took his hand and placed it between her thighs. "To touch me right here."

Smiling, he stroked her. "And what did you want me do with my hand? This?" He pressed his finger against her throbbing bud, making her moan in delight. "Or this?" Pushing the crotch of her panties aside, he thrust his finger in and out, sending shivers of delight up and down her spine.

"That right there," she said as she gripped his wrist and pressed his finger deeper inside her.

"Umm," he said. "You're so wet."

"That's what you do to me." Chante moaned as his finger went deeper and deeper.

"There's something else I want to do to you." He removed his hand, then lifted her in his arms in a quick motion and laid her on the bed, then pulled her shorts and panties off. "This is not the last time," he said as he kicked out of his pants. As he dove into her wetness, they melted into one another, grinding and thrusting against each other with zeal. Chante clamped her thighs around Zach's waist as they bounced up and down.

"Zach, Zach!" she repeated like a religious mantra as she came.

As he felt her wetness dripping on him, Zach couldn't hold back his explosive release. "Damn, baby," he groaned, "you got me weak."

"I don't think I can move!" She closed her eyes, and all she could think about was how she felt in his arms and how this memory needed to be imbedded in her mind.

"Chante," he said.

"Hmm?"

"Come to New York with me."

Her breath caught in her chest. "I-I can't."

"Why not?"

"Because it's time for me to stop running. I have to go back to Charlotte and straighten my mess out."

"I feel like we're the inspiration for Erykah Badu's 'Bag Lady.'"

She laughed and reached for her shorts when they heard a knock at the door. Room service couldn't have come at a better time. Not only was Chante ravenous, but she didn't want to continue the conversation.

Zach pulled his pants on and padded over to the door to get their dinner. While Zach tipped the room-service attendant, Chante dressed and tried to wrap her mind around what she had to do when she returned to Charlotte. First, she was going to quit her job; then she would confront Robert and tell him to leave her the hell alone, or she'd team up with Liza and run him out of Charlotte like she did Alvin, Liza's cheating ex, who learned the hard way not to mess with Liza Palmer. Then she'd have to remove Zachary Harrington from her brain.

"Seafood quiche," he said as he returned to the bed with the covered trays.

"This is the best thing I've had in a long time," she said as she took one of trays from his hand. He joined her on the bed and removed the cover from his plate. Zach cut into the cheesy dish and took a huge bite.

"Oh, this is good," he said when he swallowed. "I definitely taste the oysters."

Winking at him, she took a bite of her quiche. "Good choice to impress me."

"A glass of Pinot noir would have really set this off, but I need to have a clear head in the morning."

Chante set her fork on the side of her plate. "So how are you and your family going to handle this?"

Sighing, he pushed his food aside. "Well, Zoe is mad as hell, and she's uncovered that Natalie has done this before and has also been under FBI surveillance for a while."

"How did she trick you?"

Zach rolled his eyes. "How do you think?"

She shook her head and sighed. "I guess you'd better get to sleep, and I should probably go pack my things."

"Don't leave yet," he said, then wrapped his arms around her. "I just want a few more hours with you before we have to return to the real world."

She leaned against his chest and sighed. The real world was waiting outside the door, and as much as they wanted to pretend they could avoid it, Chante knew that was not an option.

"What is your plan when you get back to

Charlotte?" Zach asked as he brushed his lips across her neck.

"Operation Take My Life Back," she said, suppressing a moan. Zach began to massage her shoulders while kissing her neck. "I'm going to quit the firm and start my own."

"Good for you," he said when he tore his lips away from her neck. "That's really a smart thing for you to do, Chante."

"I know, and I'm sure it will make things a lot easier for my current firm. Not that I care, but the sooner we cut ties, the better it will be."

"I'm sure that Taiwan guy will be happy."

"If there is a happy contest, I'm going to win it. You don't understand how long and hard I worked to get these men to see that I deserved to have my name on that door. Had I been smarter, I would've just walked away years ago."

"That's right. You don't need anyone's permission to be happy or successful."

Looking into his eyes, she smiled. "Zach," she whispered, "I wish we'd met each other first. Life would have been a lot simpler. We'd be here probably having an argument with my mother, but not hiding from the media." She rolled over on her stomach and looked up at Zach.

He leaned in and kissed her on her forehead. "I'm not going to give up on us," Zach said. "I believe we're going to see each other again."

Chante sighed. She couldn't sit here and pretend that she and Zach had a future. But when she was about to say as much to him, she had the instant impulse to kiss him. As she covered his mouth with hers and felt his tongue dancing with hers, Chante almost decided she wanted more from him — wanted to wait for him and see if they had a legitimate chance at a future.

But she couldn't. Fear kept her from charging forward with her heart on her sleeve.

Downstairs Robert Montgomery looked at his watch, then the elevator doors. When they opened and a well-heeled couple stepped off, he groaned. "Where in the hell is she?" Rising to his feet, Robert headed for the door, then stopped. He could get Chante to come out of hiding. All he had to do was get in front of a camera and let Liza find out about it. Then she'd call Chante and tell her how her life was being ruined. That's one thing Liza was good for, sticking her nose where it didn't belong. He wouldn't even be in this situation if Liza had stayed in her lane.

Pulling up his Twitter account on his smartphone, Robert grinned as he thought about how people would react to his tweet, especially after seeing Chante with another man on CNN.

Now he was the victim, and he was going to play it to the hilt. *Turnabout is fair play,* he thought as he typed, I've 4given Chante and she's 4given me. We're good. #FirstcoupleofCharlotte.

His phone began to light up after the tweet was posted. Even Persone fought his way into the hotel to find Robert. "Really?" he asked when he grabbed Robert's elbow.

"Perception is reality, and I know that this is going to send her flying downstairs. You just make sure you're ready to take the picture of our reunion."

"You're nuts," Persone said. "If she comes down here and slaps the shit out of you, I'm snapping that picture too. Is she worth all this trouble?"

Robert wasn't trying to win Chante back, and the trouble wasn't his to deal with. It would be hers. He wanted her to face the same humiliation that he had after she and Liza had exposed him. The fact that Chante was dealing with a man like Zachary Harrington would knock that shine off the so-called halo she thought she wore. All those people who thought Chante was the victim would now see her as the scandalous tramp he'd make her seem on social media.

"This isn't about winning her back. I could care less about Chante and winning her back. That bitch embarrassed me, and I'm going to return the favor."

"That's cold, man," Persone said with a laugh. "I wish I could quote you on that."

"When I'm mayor of Charlotte, you can." Robert looked down at his phone and saw that his tweet had been retweeted more than a hundred times.

"If," Persone mumbled as he shook his head at Robert. He knew that Robert was damaged goods, but he made for great copy and a lot of page views. That was the only reason he indulged his insanity.

And he had to be three shades of insane if he thought he had a snowball's chance in hell of being the next mayor of Charlotte. Still, it was fun to watch him try.

"I see your former friend has seen your tweet. Check out what Liza just posted." Persone held his phone out to Robert. When he read Liza's tweet, he fumed.

" 'The city of Charlotte deserves a leader who isn't delusional. Team Clemmons.' That bitch!"

Persone tapped Robert's elbow when he saw a security guard coming in their direction. "Chill, man. You're lucky they've let you stay here as long as they have."

"What right does she have to continue inserting herself in my political career? She won; she needs to let it go."

"Are you sure there wasn't something going on with you and Liza? You're still really mad at her, and she wasn't your fiancée."

"Shut up."

"It's a question that a lot of people want to know. What was the real deal with you and Senator Franklin's wife?"

"There is no story there. Liza was supposed to be a woman I could trust, someone who had my back, and she's no better than my damn mother."

Persone nodded, knowing there was a story there, but he'd uncover that later. Right now, it looked as if Robert was on the edge of unraveling. That story was going to be huge.

Robert fired off a tweet back to Liza, " 'You should sweep around your own front door. #Stayinyourlane.' "

"Really, dude?" Persone asked when he read the tweet. "You're really going to get into a Twitter battle with Liza Palmer?"

"I'm not battling anyone. I know how

these women work, and this is all I need to get Chante to come flying out in a tizzy."

"You better hope this doesn't blow up in your face," Persone said.

"It's not my face that I'm worried about," he said.

CHAPTER 16

Chante wished she'd ignored her phone. She wished she'd used the last few minutes with Zach to kiss him and make beautiful memories. Instead, she answered the phone and listened to Liza tell her what was going on in the real world.

"Chante, I hate to even tell you this, but Robert is out here doing it again," Liza said.

"Doing what?" Chante asked with a sigh. "He is the last thing . . ."

"He's on Twitter talking about how he's forgiven you and you've forgiven him. And what is up with you and Zachary Harrington?"

"How did . . . Wait, did Robert tweet I've forgiven him? Is he insane?"

"He is trying to make it seem as if you two are back together."

"Son of a bitch!"

Zach glanced at Chante, then stroked her shoulder. "What's going on?"

She held up her finger and walked over to the balcony doors. "What am I missing?" Chante asked Liza.

"Pictures of you and Zachary Harrington popped up on CNN and MSNBC. Then the Charlotte media hopped on it. Have you been watching anything?"

"No, just the media trucks camped out in the hotel parking lot. Zach is leaving in the morning to straighten things out in New York."

"All right, good for him. But what are you going to do?"

Chante sighed. "I'm going back to Charlotte to start my own law firm."

"That is so awesome! I'm going to meet you there and get the story focused on you, not that lying-ass Robert."

Chante laughed. "I'm glad you're on my side," she said.

"I think you should've done this years ago, personally. So if I can help you make this a success, I'm all for it."

"And Jackson's all right with you leaving him to get into this fray?"

"Well," Liza began, "my husband is threatening to delete my Twitter account because he said it's childish to argue over the Internet."

"You're arguing on social media?"

"All I did was tweet '#Team Clemmons' and Robert went off."

Liza's laughter made Chante laugh as well. "You are too much."

"But I'm done because I don't want to be a distraction to your new law firm or the fact that Jackson is trying to get some bills passed in Raleigh."

"And no more *Charlotte Today* interviews," Chante quipped.

"There you go," Liza said.

"I'm over it, but it still stings a little bit. Mostly because I allowed this jackass to make a mockery of our sisterhood and friendship, but I digress. When are you coming to Charlotte?"

"Jackson and I will be there in the morning. When are you leaving?"

Chante looked over her shoulder and smiled at Zach, who had been watching her with concern etched on his face. "In the morning," she said with a sigh.

"You sound like you don't want to leave," Liza noted.

"I'll talk to you tomorrow, all right?" Chante said. When she hung up the phone, Chante turned to Zach. "This has been a crazy night."

"Tell me about it," he said as he crossed over to her and drew her into his arms. "I'm glad you were here with me."

"Zach, thanks for this week and . . ."

"You don't have to thank me for having the time of my life." He brushed his lips across hers. "Chante Britt, you are going to take over the world, and I can't wait to see it happen."

She kissed him slowly and smiled. "And maybe you can help me find some property for new law offices."

"Do you want to be linked with this notorious Yankee?" Zach quipped. "I'm sure your mother has seen the news coverage and is pretty horrified by now."

"I've ignored quite a few calls from her, and I can only image what the voice-mail messages say."

"And this Robert person, your ex, is causing trouble for you on social media?"

Chante nodded. "But I think he forgot who my best friend is. Liza Franklin is a social media maven. She's going to destroy his little plan."

"Remind me to stay on your good side. Sounds like you and your people don't play."

Chante winked at him. "Don't push us against the wall, because when we come out swinging, it is not always pretty."

"I'd feel sorry for Robert, but I think he

probably deserves what's coming his way."

"Without a doubt." Chante looked at her watch. "I'm going to pack, and you need to try and get some sleep since your flight is so early."

"I'd sleep better with you in my arms," Zach said. "So why don't you pack and come back down here so I can get a good night's sleep."

"You know if I get in this bed with you tonight, we're not going to do much sleeping," she said.

"Oh yes we will. Eventually."

Chante smiled again. "All right. I'll be back in about twenty minutes," she said.

"I'm timing you," Zach said as she walked out the door.

Chante figured that since she was checking out early, she'd head downstairs and return the room key after she gathered her things from her suite. That way when she was ready to go, all she'd have to do was leave. And since her car was parked in the guest deck, she could avoid the media. But maybe they'd be gone by morning. This story had to be losing traction by now, at least when it came to her. She had nothing to do with Zach's life in New York or his wife's crimes. And if his sister had uncovered all that stuff about his ex, hopefully the narrative would be moving in a different direction.

"And this too shall pass," she whispered as she walked into her suite. While gathering her things, Chante felt excited about going back to Charlotte and reclaiming her life. Nothing was going to stand in her way, and she felt sorry for anyone who tried. After packing, Chante headed down to the lobby to return her key. When the elevator doors opened and she locked eyes with Robert, her knees went weak. *What in the hell is he doing here?* she thought angrily as she stepped off the elevator. Robert crossed over to her with a smile on his lips.

"Chante, darling, I see you're ready to come home to me," he said. She looked to her left and saw a man holding up an iPhone.

"Oh hell no," she muttered. "Robert, get away from me!"

"You don't have to be concerned about your little break with this Harrington guy. I know that was your way of getting back at me for my shortcomings. We're even, now, baby."

"Don't call me baby, and we are not even. We're not even an us! I need you to stop telling people we're together. I loathe you. You are the worst kind of man in the world.

A liar. A fraud. You want power, and you don't care how you get it. You don't care who you hurt or how dirty you have to play. I'm not in the game with you. I'm pretty sure the people of Charlotte don't want another scam artist as the mayor of their city. But you are going to keep my name out of your mouth! You've done enough to turn my life upside-down, and it's time for you to stop."

"I turned your life upside-down?" Robert asked with a smirk. "And what do you think you and Liza did to me?"

"Showed people who you really are. Robert, this is tiring, and I'm done."

He reached out and grabbed her arm. "We're not done."

She looked down at his hand and counted to three. Then she slapped his hand away. "Touch me again . . ." she growled.

Robert smirked at her and took a step back. "So you think a man who's linked to a call-girl ring is a better fit for you? I could've given you everything. All men cheat. I'm sure your mother knows about your father's mistresses."

Chante hauled off and slapped him. "Shut up. All men aren't sorry liars like you. So why don't you go to hell?"

Robert held his jaw. "You know that's assault."

She narrowed her eyes at him. "And you being here is stalking. What in the hell do you want from me?"

"I want you to be humiliated," he gritted. "You and Liza systematically destroyed my life. I should be senator, not running for mayor! I asked you to marry me because you had an image that would work for what I was trying to do. You had one job!"

"Are you kidding me? I thought you loved me, but I was a political tool. So all of what you're saying is stupid and idiotic. My job was not to stand by you after you slept with a hooker."

"Maybe if you weren't so boring in bed, I wouldn't have needed to sleep with a hooker!"

Chante burst out into laughter. "Boring in bed, honey, look in the mirror."

"Damn," Persone exclaimed. Chante and Robert faced him, remembering they were being watched.

"Shut that camera off," Robert ordered.

"No, keep it rolling," Chante said. "You want a show. You want us to be linked together, and you want people to think I'm endorsing you. Let's give the world a show."

"You and Liza humiliated me!"

"You're doing a good job of that all by yourself. I pity you. You want power so badly that you've lost your mind. I guess you're trying to make up for the fact that no woman has ever given a damn about you. Not even your mother."

Robert stepped up to her and balled up his fist. Before he made another move, a security guard appeared out of nowhere and grabbed Robert.

"You're out of here, dude," he growled. Chante didn't feel anything as she watched him being dragged out of the hotel.

"Chante," Persone said. "What's the real deal with you and Zachary Harrington?"

She narrowed her eyes at him. "Get out of my face." Turning back to the elevator, Chante couldn't help but wonder what her spat with Robert would do to her chances of opening her own firm. Of course, the video would go viral. This was the kind of stuff people loved to tweet and post on Facebook.

Would the legal community hold this against her? "It doesn't matter," she muttered as the elevator doors opened. Stepping on, Chante knew that this wasn't going to be easy, but she hadn't expected a public fight with Robert to make things even more difficult. She could almost hear her grandmother say that she didn't have to worry about what other people think.

"And that's just what I'm going to do," she said with a smile.

When she reached Zach's suite, she was surprised to see him headed out the door. "Where are you off to in such a hurry?" she asked.

"I was about to come looking for you. Everything all right?"

"It will be. Had a small run-in downstairs."

"With the media? I thought the hotel was keeping those vultures away?"

Chante offered him a lopsided grin. "It technically wasn't the media. Seems as if Robert found his way here and was sitting in the lobby waiting for me."

Zach stroked Chante's cheek and looked her over to see if she had been injured. "Did he hurt you, because I will . . ."

"Slow down, cowboy," she said. "If anyone is hurt, it's Robert. He brought his own personal reporter with him, and the whole thing was caught on video. Knowing that guy, he's probably already uploaded it."

Zach shook his head. "I guess he underestimated how you were going to react to his ambush."

"Maybe the old me would've just taken it,

but I'm done playing the victim while other people use me for their own gain. It's just like how those partners used me for all these years while I tried to prove my worth to them. I'm enough. I'm enough, and I don't have to prove anything to anyone."

"I wish I had a drink so we could toast right now!" Zach kissed her on the forehead. "Come on, let's go to bed."

She smiled. "Sounds great."

The next morning, Teresa Flores woke up to headlines of Robert's breakdown. She couldn't help but smile. She imagined Nic pulling his hair out because he'd finally met a psychopath he couldn't mold into a viable candidate. Grabbing her smartphone, she called Taiwon.

"This is Taiwon," he said when he answered.

"Taiwon, your troubles are almost over, but you owe me big-time."

"What are you talking about?"

"Robert Montgomery's political dreams died a horrible death this morning. Nic has nothing to hold over your head anymore."

"Is that so? Why do I owe you anything, though?"

Teresa took a deep breath. "You men are so funny. Chante Britt doesn't deserve anything that's happening to her."

"Here we go with Chante again. What do you people find so special about her?"

"She is a brilliant woman, and she has worked for your firm for years. Until this crap with Montgomery, she had a stellar reputation and made millions for you and the other *men* who run that firm. Stop exploiting her talents and making her suffer for what a man she thought she loved did. Make her a partner, and everything Nic had on you disappears."

"And if I say no? Hell, what if she says no?"

"She can say no. You say no, and you're going to see your secrets go viral. Just do the right thing." Teresa hung up the phone and headed into the kitchen to make herself a cup of coffee. She was going to need a jolt before she gloated to Nic.

CHAPTER 17

Zach closed his eyes as the plane took off, silently replaying the last few minutes with Chante.

He'd brushed his fingers across Chante's cheek as she slept. Peaceful. She looked so peaceful and beautiful. Holding her made him feel calm, and he wanted to forget what he'd be facing in a few hours. Leaning into Chante, he gave her a gentle kiss on the cheek. Her eyes fluttered open like the wings of a butterfly taking flight.

"Hello, beautiful," he said.

"Umm, what time is it?"

"A little after four. I was going to let you sleep, but I couldn't resist kissing you."

"So little self-control," she quipped.

"I guess real life is right around the corner."

She nodded and eased closer to him. "Will you call me when you get settled in New York?"

"Of course. You're going to have to give me your number, though. I'm sure calling the hotel isn't going to help me." Zach winked at her, then reached for his phone.

Chante rattled off her cell-phone number, and he saved it in his address book. "Do you promise to FaceTime me in the nude?" he asked as he returned the phone to the nightstand.

"Maybe," she replied, "but only if you do the same. Remind me what I'm missing."

He took her hand and placed it on his growing erection. "Are you talking about this?"

"Among other things," she said as she stroked his cheek with her other hand. Zach brought his lips down on top of Chante's with a quick motion, but his kiss was slow and deliberate. She shifted in his arms, her wetness topping his hardness. It was a total struggle for Zach not to dive in. But they'd been reckless too many times, and he needed to protect her.

For a split second, as he reached for a condom, he wondered what Chante would look like filled with his seed. Would their son look like her and their daughter look like him? Wait, why was he thinking about making a baby with a woman who'd made it clear that she was reclaiming her life in Charlotte and his business was in New York. His redemption would happen there as well. New York was a part of him, and he didn't see that changing. Then he glanced at Chante. North Carolina might not be that bad . . .

"What's with that look?" she asked, then licked his bottom lip.

"You're beautiful. And you already know I like staring at you." Zach quickly slipped the condom on his erection and pulled Chante on top of him. "Ride me, baby."

She happily obliged, pulling him in and staring into his eyes. Deep. Intense. She threw her head back and moaned while his fingers teased her nipples.

"Zach, oh, Zach," she cried out as he thrust deeper and deeper into her. She tightened her thighs around him, and Zach felt an explosion building in his belly. He wanted to hold back and watch Chante give in to pleasure. He loved the way she smiled as she came and licked her full lips when a second orgasm hit her.

But when she ground against him and licked his earlobe, Zach couldn't hold his climax back anymore. They collapsed against each other and took a singular satisfied breath.

"My God, woman, that was amazing," Zach said, then kissed her on the cheek.

"You're amazing," she replied. "But if we don't get out of this bed, you're going to miss your flight."

"That might not be such a bad thing if I get to spend the rest of the day just like this," he said as he stroked her bottom . . .

"Sir," the flight attendant said as she tapped him on his shoulder. "You need to fasten your seat belt."

Zach nodded and followed her instructions. As much as he wanted to get lost in sweet memories of Chante, he had to get his mind together to face Natalie, the FBI, and Zoe's anger.

"Vacation is about to be over," he muttered as he glanced out the window and watched the clouds.

Chante didn't bother going into the lobby when she was ready to head back to Charlotte. She just took the elevator to the guest parking lot, where her Jag was parked.

She was going to her mother's house first, because she wasn't going to avoid her anymore. After loading her things into her car, Chante headed for Summerville, and she was happy to see that the media trucks were gone from the parking lot as she passed by. Either there was some other scandal going on or the reporters were just following up on the video of her fight with

Robert. Chante knew it was wishful thinking to believe that it hadn't hit the Internet. But since she had turned her phone off and hadn't taken a glimpse at the morning news, she had no idea.

She was headed to Summerville to let her parents know that she was going back to Charlotte, and to see how much of the media coverage they'd seen. Part of her wanted to avoid her mother at all costs, but the main reason she wanted to see Allison this morning was to tell her mother that she was tired — of trying to prove herself to her mother and of failing to meet the sky-high standards that Allison set for her. And she was tired of turning herself inside out for approval she wasn't going to get.

It was going to end today.

When she pulled into her parents' driveway, Chante didn't feel as if she was seeking her mother's approval for a change. She was here to begin the journey to taking her life back. Finding her mother on the porch with a cup of coffee and a copy of *The Post and Courier,* she almost smiled. When she was a little girl, she and Allison would spend Saturday mornings reading the paper and talking about what was important in life, and how Allison hoped that Chante would come back to Charleston after she graduated from college, get married, and have a big family.

Chante shook off the memories and crossed over to her mother. "Good morning, Mom," she said.

Allison dropped the paper and glared at her daughter. "I was hoping you'd leave without bringing more embarrassment to us."

"Really? And just how did I embarrass you, Mom?" Chante asked, slapping her hand on her hips.

Allison rose to her feet and shook her head. "Don't you come here and act as if you've been honest with us about the people in your life. A man who's linked to a sex ring in New York, and then you have a ghetto-fabulous argument with your ex-fiancé for the world to see. Chante, who are you, and where did all of this come from?"

"I didn't know who I was, Mom. I thought I had to be someone's wife for you to acknowledge the things I'd accomplished. Do you realize that you've never looked at me and said you were proud of me? I graduated at the top of my class as an undergrad and from law school. But that wasn't enough for you."

"No!" Allison shouted. "You're not going to blame this on me!"

"You're right, I'm not blaming anything on you. I'm not going to ask you why it wasn't enough for me to be smart. I'm not going to ask you why you thought that what I did with my life wasn't enough because I didn't have someone else's last name added to mine. I wonder if you think I should've stayed with Robert even though he paid a woman for sex?"

Allison laughed and took a step back from Chante. "You are so silly. Don't you think I wished I could've impressed my mother? I'm not as smart as you think you are, but I know better than to air my dirty laundry in the media. How do you think your father and I are going to face our friends when this footage of our daughter is played on TV and the Internet?"

"Yes, Mom, how will you show your face? Through everything that I've faced over this past year, your concern has been about everything but me."

"What are you talking about?" Allison asked incredulously.

"Seriously?" Chante asked. "You're going to ask me that? All that I've ever done has been to prove to you that I was enough. From graduating at the top of my class to getting a position with one of the top law firms in Charlotte, I wanted you to see that

I was enough, and you never did. So I did what I thought would've finally proved to you that I was good enough. I accepted a ring from a man I knew didn't love me. How did that work out?"

"Don't you dare blame me for that!" Allison bellowed.

"Oh no?" Chante retorted. "You couldn't accept my achievements as an attorney because I wasn't married, so the first ring I got, I took. I thought that ring would make my mother happy. I thought bringing a husband home would finally make you proud of me, and it blew up in my face."

"Shut up. Don't sit here and pretend I'm the reason you've done this." Allison tossed the newspaper at Chante. "You made this bed, now lie in it, alone."

"I'm fine with that," Chante replied. "And for the record, he was never my fiancé. If that makes you feel better about showing your face at your bridge club, tell them your horrible daughter played a joke on you."

Allison narrowed her eyes at Chante. "Why are you so against tradition?"

"Maybe it's time to start a new tradition, or maybe I'm more like my grandmother than you want to believe."

"Chante, I just wanted the best for you,

and a southern woman needs a good husband."

"I'm going to prove you wrong, Mom. You and Dad are a great couple, but I'm done trying to prove that I'm good enough when I know that I'm better. If you want to spin some yarn to your friends about what an embarrassment I am to the Britt name, feel free. But I am so done worrying about what you think and figuring out how I can meet your approval. Have a good day." Chante walked off the porch, ignoring her mother's cries. She was going to be her own woman, and the world had better get ready for it.

"We're now descending into JFK International Airport," the pilot said. His voice awakened Zach, and he wiped his mouth. Now that he was about to be in New York, he had to get his mind focused on the task at hand, letting everyone know that he and Natalie had no ties.

Of course, he had to calm his twin down as well. Zoe was mad as hell, and she had every right to be. After getting arrested, everything she'd built during her career was in jeopardy. And as much as he didn't want to think about it, it was Zach's fault. Had he listened to Zoe, this might not be happening. She'd wanted to do a background check on Natalie, but he'd been in love and wanted a wedding. He'd told his sister to back off, and now the aftermath was too much to bear.

"Damn it," he muttered as he walked to the baggage claim. Despite all he'd done to insulate the company from the negative press, his family was still suffering. Zach felt as if he had failed his family by not being in New York. What if he had stayed instead of going to South Carolina?

"You would've never met Chante," he muttered as he picked up his baggage. Pulling his smartphone out of his pocket, Zach called his driver to make sure he was going to pick him up. He hoped there wasn't a team of cameras and reporters waiting for him as well. It was too damned early to deal with this drama, to answer questions that should've been put to rest months ago.

If only he could get his hands on Natalie. She could've just let their marriage go and moved on with her miserable life, but she wanted to bring him down to her level. Get him dirty because she was a criminal. He was angry and embarrassed that he'd allowed himself to fall for her. Now his sister and his family name were being dragged through the mud because he'd married the wrong damned woman.

"Mr. Harrington," his driver said when he answered the phone, "I'm about five minutes out from the airport."

"Great," Zach mumbled, "I'll be outside in a few minutes."

"Sorry that I'm late, sir. Traffic is . . ."

"Hey, it happens. Just hurry," Zach said as he made his way out of the airport. It must have been his lucky day because there wasn't a photographer in sight. Just as he was about to put his phone away, it rang. When he saw the name on the screen, he smiled.

"Hello, beautiful," he said.

"Are you in New York?" Chante asked.

"Yes. I'm standing outside of the terminal at JFK, waiting for my driver."

"No Mustang rental?" Her laughter made him remember her kisses and the sweetness of the area between her thighs.

"Not this time. Besides, you're not here to speed around in it. Wouldn't be the same without you."

"Sweet talker," she quipped. "I don't think I'd want to drive in New York. Charlotte is bad enough."

"Have you made it back yet?" Zach held his hand up as he saw his driver pull up.

"Not yet. I'm just leaving my parents' house. I finally told my mother I've had enough of her judgment."

"You go, Chante."

"I hope you can still say that when the fallout from that video hits," she said with a sigh.

"Don't even worry about that. You're smart enough to overcome all of that."

"From your mouth to God's ear," she said.

"Baby, I have all the faith in the world in you."

"Thank you."

"My driver is here, so I'm going to call you this evening and check on you."

"Sounds good. I hope everything goes well for you."

"So do I. We'll talk soon." When Chante said good-bye, Zach missed her like crazy. As he climbed into the black Lincoln that had stopped in front of him, he knew he had to focus on the task at hand, clearing his family's name once and for all.

"How are you, Mr. Harrington?" his driver asked.

"I've been better. Let's get to my office and get this day over with."

"Yes, sir."

It was midafternoon when Chante drove past the Charlotte city limits sign. She sighed with relief as she turned onto her street and saw there were no media trucks parked on her block. Sitting in the driveway, she dialed Liza's number to find out if her friend had arrived in Charlotte yet.

"Hello?"

"Liza," Chante said, "have you made it to Charlotte yet?"

"Have I? Honey, I'm already at Amelie's sitting in a corner waiting for you," she replied.

"Let me unload my car, and I'll be right there."

"Good, because we have a lot of work to do. Although I have to say that on a personal level, I love the video."

Chante groaned. "And," Liza continued, "that's what Robert gets for having that stupid blogger Persone Wallace follow him around. All he wants are page views, and I know he got a lot from people watching Robert's meltdown. Still, since you're my client, and he and I have a legal agreement about him covering my clients, I'm going to get the video taken down."

"The damage is already done. You and I know what goes up on the Internet is there forever."

"Just get here. We're going to game-plan this."

"All right." Chante hung up and got out

of the car. She was happy that the video had exposed Robert's madness, but she was smart enough to know there would be plenty of people who'd blame her for reacting to him.

"Forget them," she muttered as she unlocked her front door. Maybe it was time to rebrand herself, and that was what she and Liza were going to work on.

CHAPTER 18

Chante walked into Amelie's and quickly spotted Liza sitting at their usual table. Waving at her friend, she walked over and smiled when she saw two caramel salted brownies on the table.

"You are so awesome," she said as Liza rose to her feet and gave her a hug.

"Tell me something I don't know," Liza replied with a wink. "So before we get started, what's the real deal with you and Zachary Harrington?"

Chante felt a blush burn her cheeks. "Zach is a really nice guy. He made Charleston a lot of fun because Miss Elsie Mae is going around the world with her boo."

"Wait, your grandmother is on a trip with a man?"

"Guess who she's with," Chante said.

"Mr. Tanner?"

"How did you know?" Chante asked incredulously.

"I remember when we went to visit your grandmother that summer and he was there. You had to be blind not to see the sizzle between them."

Chante sucked her teeth. "Then call me Ray Charles. I figured they were just friends."

"Friends with benefits."

"Eww, Liza, come on! It's bad enough that she gave me a few too many details in the note she left for me."

"I hope when I'm older, I'm as fabulous as Miss Elsie Mae, and that Jackson and I are making our children and grandchild uncomfortable."

"I feel sorry for your unborn children already," Chante quipped.

"Whatever, Chante. So how did you and Zach meet?"

Chante told Liza how she went to her grandmother's house and it was gutted.

"She left a note with instructions for me to stay at the Charleston Harbor Bed and Breakfast. It's a wonderful place. Zach was staying there, and we ended up at the bar together."

"Pause," Liza said. "You picked up a guy at the bar? You?"

Chante rolled her eyes. "No, I didn't. As a matter of fact, I threw a drink in his face."

Liza broke out into laughter. "Of course you did. Why did you throw a drink at the man?"

Chante shrugged. "Because he kissed me."

Tilting her head to the side, Liza shook her head. "Okay. You meet a stranger, he kisses you, you throw a drink in his face, and y'all still end up kicking it together?"

"I blame the seafood quiche. It had oysters in it." Chante laughed as she thought about the meal she and Zach shared before they left Charleston. "As it turned out, his kisses were amazing. We even told my mother that we were engaged when she caught us kissing at Grammy's shop."

Liza shook her head. "I think I like this Zach person. I just hope all of this stuff going on with him isn't true."

"It's not," Chante said.

Liza raised her right eyebrow. "You're defending him, huh? How serious are you about him?"

"I-I wouldn't go that far. I mean, I barely know the man. After what happened with Robert, I'm not jumping into anything."

"Now, you have to stop that. What happened with Robert was the anomaly. And I feel responsible. I should've never introduced you two."

"Just because you introduced us doesn't

mean you have responsibility for anything that happened."

"Still, I don't like to be fooled, and I should have known that he would do anything to win that seat, including using both of us."

Chante shook her head. "We were both fooled. But I have an idea."

"Shoot."

"I don't want to be the Chante Britt that everyone knows anymore."

"What do you mean?"

"I think you'd call it rebranding. There are so many women in this city who suffer because of things the men in their lives do. I want to be the attorney who helps those women reclaim their lives."

"That is an awesome idea," Liza replied with excitement. "And you can make it more than just a Charlotte thing. Think of all of the women who are married to powerful men who mess up and she gets dragged through the mud? You'll be busy and rich."

"This isn't about money," Chante said. "What I went through with Robert taught me a lot, and I didn't like the lesson."

"It's not fair. I mean, you lost your position at your law firm, and he went on TV to bring you back into his mess."

"Tell me about it."

"Here's what we're going to do: we're going to do a video where you tell the world what you just said to me, and we make it go viral. All we have to do is juxtapose it against what happened in Charleston."

Chante closed her eyes. "Do we have to focus on the negativity?"

"We can't ignore it. It's out there."

Sighing, Chante knew her friend was right, but she didn't want that video of her and Robert to become a part of who she was turning herself into. But there was no denying that it would be one of the first things people saw about her.

"I guess you're right," she said.

Liza bit into her brownie. "I'm always right in this sort of situation."

Chante rolled her eyes. "Don't hold this over my head because I said you were right."

"Now, would I do something like that?" Liza laughed.

"Let me point to the fact that I got drunk sophomore year and threw up in your precious Mustang. You referred to that for years."

"I loved that car!" Liza exclaimed. "And it was only two months old."

"You talked about it for ten years."

"Again, I loved that car."

Chante smiled, thinking about the Mustang she'd been zipping around Charleston in and her handsome road dog.

"What's that look?" Liza asked.

"Zach rented a Mustang, and we drove it around the city and . . ."

"You really like him, Chante."

She wasn't going to admit anything. "We need to talk business," Chante said.

Liza nodded. "I know you aren't big on falling in love, but don't let one bad experience sour you. Look at me and Jackson."

"Everyone doesn't get a fairy-tale ending, Liza, and I'm all right with that."

"You don't have to be," Liza said, then threw her hands up. "I'm done. Let's talk business. I'm going to get with Duane Carter and Teresa so that we can get the video done professionally."

"I need office space," Chante said. "I don't want to do the whole start-up thing from my kitchen table, you know."

Liza patted the table excitedly. "I know a great space."

"Where?"

"My old office. It's in a terrific location, and I'm moving my stuff to Raleigh anyway."

"Really?" Chante asked.

Liza nodded. "And since you're just getting started, I'm going to rent that space to you for a dollar a month."

"I can't let you do that," she said as tears of gratitude sprang into her eyes.

"You have no choice in the matter. Chante, I'm so proud of you, and this is just my small way of showing support. You're my sister, girl."

Chante leaned over and hugged Liza tightly. "This means a lot to me, Liza. Thank you for forgiving me and . . ."

"Don't even go there. We're going to blaze a path in Charlotte that will make anything that happened in the past a distant memory. And we're going to need a really great name for your firm," Liza said.

"What's wrong with Chante Britt, Attorney-at-Law?"

Liza yawned. "That's boring! How many Blah-Blahs at law are there in Charlotte? You need something with as much oomph as you walked in here with. You have a fire now. Let it burn."

"You sound like a bad motivational speaker."

"Whatever," Liza said as she took a small bite of her brownie. "We have to be different."

"We?"

"Well, you. No, *we* is right. We are in this together because this is step one toward

Liza and Chante taking over the world."

Chante laughed, remembering their plan following graduation from UNC. Of course they had different goals then. Chante had wanted to be a criminal defense attorney and free the wrongfully convicted across the country. She had planned to take the bar in all fifty states, and Liza planned to write for *Essence.* There she'd chronicle Chante's cases. She figured that she'd write a book and make the *New York Times* best-seller list and become Oprah's new best friend.

"What happened to those young girls who wanted to take over the world?" Chante asked.

Liza shook her head. "We got tricked. Thought we had to follow the crowd and work for someone else."

"True. And we put what we wanted to really do on hold."

"We're on the right track now," Liza said.

"Yes, we are."

"Now, we just need a name for this firm . . ." Liza stopped speaking when her cell phone rang. "This is Teresa. Give me a second to take this." As Liza stepped outside, Chante picked up her phone to check and see if Zach had sent her a text. Not seeing one, she felt a little disappointed, even though she knew he had a lot going on.

Chante couldn't deny it: she missed him.

Zach sat in his office listening to Zoe rail about the press. "They are distorting everything!" She tossed a copy of the *New York Post* on his desk. "And look at my picture."

"Oh, so that's what this is about? Your picture? It's a mug shot, not a glamour shot." Zach chuckled, but his twin was not amused.

"Don't be a jackass. This company was built on our family reputation. That bitch and the press are ruining it. And let's not forget the fact that my business is all about people trusting me!" Zoe narrowed her eyes at Zach. "Did you leave your balls in Charleston? I figured you'd be ready to throw down. This, after all, is your company now. How many . . . What's her name?"

"What?"

"Don't play with me, Zach. Tell me who she is so I can verify that she isn't a crazy pimp!"

Zach rolled his eyes. "Here's the thing: I've called a press conference for eleven. We're also bringing one of the FBI agents on the case to the podium with us. He's going to lay out Natalie's case and how neither you, nor I, nor this company is involved."

"And you're going to tell the world you

married her because you were blinded by her body?"

Zach shrugged. "Whatever. If it will make you feel better for me to tell the world that you were right, then I will."

"Thank you. So the new broad who has your nose wide open is Chante Britt, right?"

"If you know her name, why are you harassing me?" Zach snapped. Zoe ignored his attitude and showed him a video of him and Chante dashing into the hotel in Charleston.

"What is it with you and scandalous women? This is the type you love."

Love? He knew he wasn't there yet. But Chante was a woman he could love. Everything about her was exciting, beautiful, and amazing. "She's not scandalous."

"Oh no?" Zoe asked, then showed him another video of Chante and a man arguing in the lobby of the hotel. As he watched, he saw the man was Robert Montgomery, the ex Chante had told him about. He was definitely not the man he'd expected. Robert seemed unhinged, nothing like someone he'd expect Chante to be involved with. When he saw him get in Chante's face, he was angry.

Zoe noticed it and smiled. "Chill, brother. I have to say this one is smart and feisty if this video is any indication. And she doesn't have a sketchy background."

"If you knew all this, why did you pressure me about her name and all of that drama?"

"Because I can," she said with a wink.

"You know, if you moved back to New York, you could take a more active role in my love life. And I need a good — no, great — chief of security," he said.

Zoe smiled grimly. "I'm not going to even tell you why that will never happen. You need to understand that I'm not going to take a cushy job with this company to make you feel better. I have a business that can't run without me. So no thanks, brother."

"I hate it when you call me brother like that. And I also hate it when you think I'm only offering you a job because I don't like what you do. This is a family business, and I want you to be a part of that business, Zo."

"I hate it when you call me Zo. It's not endearing," she replied. "You should know, I'm going to be in New York for a few months once this thing blows over. I'll be working on a case, and I plan to pretend that I work here."

"What kind of case?"

"Nope, I'm not telling you anything."

"But you're going to use my company as a front? I need details," Zach said.

"Just stay out of my way," she said. "Don't play the big-brother role, I have a gun, and I'm very good with it. I can handle myself. It's you, on the other hand, I have to be concerned about."

"Excuse me?"

Zoe widened her eyes incredulously. "Who got us into this mess?"

"Whatever."

"Don't *whatever* me. I told you that Natalie chick was nothing but trouble."

"I know," he said. "I fucked up, but that has nothing to do with you using my company as a front for whatever case you're working on."

"Let's talk about this press conference and the FBI agent you're bringing."

"Smooth, real smooth. Agent Banks has been on my ass since Natalie's arrest. On the way to the office, I presented your evidence to him, and now he actually believes I wasn't involved in her call-girl ring."

Zoe shook her head. "He sounds like a real winner. I hate G-men. They think nothing is more important than the job."

"Sounds like you're kind of bitter, sis."

"Whatever," she mimicked. "So what am I doing at this press conference?"

Before Zach could reply, he received a text that made him smile.

I miss you. I hope everything is going well for you.

Zach responded. I can't stop thinking about you. When this blows over, I want you to show me around Charlotte.

CHAPTER 19

Chante and Liza walked into Teresa Flores's office, and Chante was immediately impressed with Teresa's commanding demeanor. She watched in awe as Teresa handled whomever she was talking to on the phone.

"Damn it, I don't care what you think I need to do. This is what I'm doing — I'm going to tell the city that this tax increase is an attack on the poor and those who have lived in those communities all of their lives. I'm not giving you my support, and if anyone does, it's going to be because they don't care about keeping their office." She slammed the phone down, and Chante wanted to give her a standing ovation.

"I see you're still keeping the city straight," Liza said with a smile. Teresa looked up at the women standing in her doorway.

Pointing her finger at them, she smiled broadly. "You know why I keep a landline?

People need to know when you hang up on them. They need to hear that slam."

"Good point," Chante said.

"Miss Britt, I'm glad to see you back in the Queen City. How are you?" Teresa rounded her desk and crossed over to Chante and shook her hand.

"For the first time in a long time, I'm good," Chante said with a smile.

"I'm glad to hear that. I don't know how you worked with those assholes at Myrick, Lawson and Walker. I would've started my own firm years ago. Especially since you were the main moneymaker for those bastards."

Chante sighed. "If I'm honest, I stayed because I was afraid, and I thought I needed someone else's approval."

"You're over that now?"

Chante nodded.

"Good," Teresa said, "because we don't have time for that shit."

Liza burst out laughing. "Teresa will always tell it like it is."

"I see that," Chante replied.

"Ladies, have a seat," Teresa said. "I'm really proud of what you're about to do. The Legal Center for Women. It has a great ring to it."

Liza nodded at Chante. "Told you."

Teresa leaned against the edge of her cluttered desk. "There are too many women in this city and state who suffer because of what their men have done. Look at what happened to Patricia Broadhead because that dope from the CIA spilled secrets while they lounged in bed. You'd think she'd been the one with the loose lips."

Liza and Chante nodded in agreement, remembering how the award-winning journalist had been run out of town on a rail after the affair she had with a former CIA operative went public. To Patricia's defense, she had had no idea he had been married, and when she'd chronicled their relationship in her romance column, all hell broke loose.

Liza would've taken her on as a client, but the controversy had been too hot for her to handle during Jackson's first term. And she hadn't wanted to be linked to a scandal so quickly after the mess Robert had pulled her into.

"Too bad Patricia has gone off the grid," Chante said. "She could've been my first client."

"Oh, you're not going to have any shortage of clients. As a matter of fact," Teresa said, then picked up a file from her desk, "here's your history-making first case.

Amanda Chavis, former wife of Judge Harlan Chavis."

"Yes, I remember him," Chante said. "He was removed from the bench after it was discovered he was getting kickbacks from the juvenile center in Minnesota where he was sending all those kids."

Teresa nodded.

"And through no fault of her own, Amanda lost her job, her business, and much of the money the government seized after Harlan was sentenced. Well, she's finally ready to fight back."

Chante smiled excitedly. "This is what I'm talking about. These are the cases I want to take on."

"She should win. With you on her side, I almost feel sorry for the Treasury Department."

"Yes," Liza said. "Shoot, I might write that book after all."

"Book?" Teresa asked. "When will you have time for that? I know you and the rookie are going to be elbow deep in diapers soon."

Chante turned to Liza. "Did you forget to tell me something?"

"No!" Liza exclaimed. "Someone must have forgotten to tell me something too!"

"Please," Teresa said as she waved her

hand, "I know you and Jackson are getting a lot of practice in."

A deep blush burned Liza's cheeks. "Anyway."

"It wouldn't be a bad thing for you and Jackson to bring some little ones into the world," Chante said.

"When the time is right, it will happen. But Jackson and I aren't there yet. He's making waves in Raleigh right now."

Teresa smiled. "I'm proud of the senator. He's making people nervous, and that is why I want people like him in office." She turned to Chante. "What did you ever see in Robert Montgomery?"

"I was hoodwinked," she replied, and the ladies laughed.

Teresa sat down at her desk and started typing on her computer. "It's time to get down to business," she said. "Are you two ready?"

"Yes, ma'am," Chante and Liza said in concert.

Zach tugged at the knot on his tie as he listened to Agent Banks explain to the media that the investigation into Natalie's alleged involvement in sex trafficking had nothing to do with the Harringtons.

"Our investigation has turned up evidence

that proves Zachary Harrington had no part in the alleged crime. Zoe Harrington has also been cleared of any connection with the sex ring. We've dropped all charges against Ms. Harrington," he said, then glanced at Zoe. She shot him a stone-faced look that made Zach wonder if there was something else going on with the two of them.

"We'll take a few questions," Banks said. "But we can't release any details of the case."

"Mr. Harrington," a reporter called out, "how did you not know what your wife was involved with?"

"People lie," he replied.

"But you were married to her for . . ."

Zoe stood in front of the podium. "Listen," she began, "this woman is a professional liar. It's not surprising that a sex peddler used love and her body to get what she wanted, which was access to some high-end men who buy sex. Unfortunately, women are crafty, and my brother found out the hard way as our family's business was drawn into this sordid mess. What's even more disheartening is that the FBI jumped to the wrong conclusions and created a circus for my family." Again, she speared Banks with an icy look. "And that's all we have to say."

Zoe walked off the podium, and Zach followed his sister.

"What was that all about?" Zach asked.

"I don't understand the purpose of a long press conference and answering questions so that the media will have ammunition to spin the story their way. I stated the facts, and that's that."

"Zoe, don't stand here and try to play me. I'm talking about the daggers you were shooting at Agent Banks."

"You're exaggerating," she said, then started walking toward the exit.

Zach grabbed her arm.

"You stay up in my business. Tell me the truth about you and Banks right now," he demanded.

"There's nothing to tell. We were both working a case, things were confused, and we . . ."

"You slept with him, didn't you?" he asked.

"What does that have to do with the price of tea in China? That man lied to me, and then he had the nerve to slap handcuffs on me."

"Was that the first time?" Zach quipped.

Zoe punched her brother and glared at him. "Don't make light of this. I didn't judge you . . . well, yeah I did. But my point is, I don't want to deal with all of this right now, and you need to make sure the media stays on message and we can get back to our lives."

"And what are you going to do about him?" Zach asked as he pointed to Agent Banks.

"I'm out of here," Zoe said. As Banks took a step toward her, Zoe bolted as if she'd been struck by lightning.

Zach gave Banks a cool once-over. "What's going on with you and my sister?"

"That's classified information."

"Don't play with me. This isn't a case; this is my family."

"And as you can see, your sister wants nothing to do with me. Case closed."

"It better be. Zoe plays hard, but she isn't. Hurt her and I won't give a damn about you being a G-man. I will kick your ass."

"You do realize that you just threatened a government agent?"

"I don't care. She's my sister and . . ."

"Your sister broke my nose. I think she can handle herself."

Zach held back a laugh and shook his head. "That's good to know," he said, then walked away.

When Zach made it back to his office, he pulled out his phone and dialed Chante's number. When her voice mail picked up, he was disappointed. Turning to his desktop computer, he logged on to US Airways and booked a flight to Charlotte. He wanted to see his woman. Pausing, he stared off into the distance. He couldn't believe he was sitting here thinking about Chante as if she was his. How could he be sure she hadn't gone back to Charlotte and gotten into a situation that pushed him out of her life?

"I'm tripping," he said as he looked down at his phone again. "She had her own situation to handle, and she might be busy."

He just prayed she'd have time for him when he arrived in the Queen City. Before he could print out his boarding pass, Zoe burst into his office.

"You just can't mind your own business, can you?"

"What are you talking about?"

Zoe folded her arms across her chest. "Really? Did you think Carver wasn't going to call me and tell me you threatened him?"

"I didn't threaten him, I made a promise."

Zoe threw her hands up. "This is why I would never come back here and work with you. I'm not a little girl who needs her big brother — by five minutes, mind you — to protect me."

"I'm not trying to protect you, but I'm

287

not going to sit by and watch someone I love get hurt."

"You know that I can shoot the boogie man these days, right?"

Zach shook his head. "Whatever, Zoe. All I know is, that man has been on my ass during this whole investigation and knowing that you two had something going on . . ."

"It. Was. Work. Let it go and get your business on track."

"I got this."

She glanced at his computer screen. "What's going to Charlotte going to fix in New York? You need to take a woman break because you suck at picking the right one."

"First of all . . ."

"Just hush," Zoe said.

Zach was about to hit PRINT on his computer when the phone rang. "This is Zach," he said.

"Mr. Harrington, this is Lila Jacobson from Kinder and Bryant."

"Yes, Miss Jacobson, I've been trying to get a meeting with your CEO for a few weeks," Zach said.

"Well, he's been busy. However, he does have an opening tomorrow at nine a.m. That is, if you're still interested in doing business with us."

"I'll check my calendar and have my assistant give you a call." Zach couldn't help but smile. Obviously word had gotten around about him and his company being cleared in this mess with Natalie.

"I guess it's time for you to get back to work," Zoe said.

Zach rolled his eyes. "You're right." Picking up his smartphone, he called Kia and told her they were back in business. Unfortunately, Charlotte would have to wait.

Chante looked around Liza's old office and smiled. She could see the potential in this place. On the left wall, she'd set up a floor-to-ceiling bookcase for her law books. She'd definitely change the colors of the walls. The softness of the lavender didn't quite mesh with her idea of a law office. She wanted people to walk in and feel power, feel as if they were going to win their case.

"So," Liza said, breaking into Chante's thoughts, "what do you think?"

"Great potential. I hope you don't mind if I do some redecorating."

She shrugged. "That's not a bad idea. I know one thing, this desk is going with me."

"Good," Chante quipped, "because I didn't like it anyway."

"You got jokes, I see."

"I want this place to scream power and

289

winning."

"Yep. You definitely want a winning image. Perception is reality."

Chante nodded. "I need a great interior designer. I'm sure you know one."

Smiling, Liza nodded. "Of course. I'll call Damien Brown right now."

"Let's leave something to do tomorrow," Chante said.

"I'll have to give you his number now because Jackson and I are going to do some appearances in the district."

"Look at you. 'Appearances in the district' — you sound just like a politician's wife."

"Well, I am. I just happen to be married to an atypical politician. I'm actually looking forward to visiting the people who voted for him and the people he's working for." Liza's smile was infectious, and Chante was happy to see her friend so excited about her life with Jackson.

"There is no way Robert would've taken this much time with the people of the district. I'm just glad people can see the real him on the Internet now."

"And people will see that you are just the right woman to get justice for them. I was really proud of how you handled him. I was like, that's my girl. And had it been anyone else, I would've retweeted the link."

"I'm glad you didn't."

Before Chante could reply, the door opened and a woman walked in. "Is Liza Palmer here?"

"Yes, I'm Liza Palmer. How can I help you?"

"I want to make sure Robert doesn't turn on me," she said.

"And who are you?"

"I was working on Robert's mayoral campaign, and we were having sex. After seeing . . ." She looked at Chante. "You. You were the one on the video."

Chante nodded. "So you were working with Robert. Were you being paid for your services?"

"Excuse me?"

"The work you did on his campaign? Were you paid or a volunteer?"

"I was paid until he decided that *you* were the woman he needed to have on his arm once he got elected. Then I was locked out. Fired."

"Was it because of performance?" Chante asked.

"Or lack of performance," Liza muttered.

"Why are you here?" Chante questioned. "What do you think we — I mean, Liza — can do for you?"

The woman gritted her teeth. "Listen, I

just want to protect myself. I want to make sure that I'm going to be protected when he goes all HAM again."

"And how was I supposed to protect you?" Liza asked.

She pointed at Chante. "You saved her. I remember the way you rehabbed her image, and I thought . . ."

"Wait," Liza said, "I'm not in that business anymore. What I did for Chante was on the strength of our friendship. I don't know you."

"Maybe we should help her," Chante said. "Robert has been abusing and violating women for years."

"And if you take on her case you're going to look like a bitter ex."

"Case?" the woman asked. "I don't want to go to court."

"Then what do you want?" Chante asked.

The woman sighed. "I just wanted to know what to put on Facebook so no one would know that he humiliated me. I loved that man."

"What?"

"I said I loved him. I wanted to be with him, and I was so hurt when he said that I wasn't good enough."

"So if he broke up with you, why would you want to protect yourself? I'm sure he isn't thinking about you," Liza said.

Chante squeezed the bridge of her nose. "Liza! We can't just write her off."

"Forget it," the woman said and started toward the door.

"Stop," Chante said. "I want to help you, but I need to get some information first."

"Listen, I'm not trying to hurt him like y'all did. I still believe in him."

"Girl, bye," Liza muttered. Chante shot her friend a look that told her to shut up.

"What's your name?" Chante asked.

"Gabby."

"Have a seat, Gabby," Chante said as she took a seat behind Liza's old desk. "Liza, will you be a dear and get us some coffee?"

Raising her eyebrow, Liza nodded. Once she left the room, Chante took a look at Gabby. She was young and seemed very naïve — easily the kind of woman Robert could fool into thinking that he really cared about her. "Gabby," she began, "I'm not trying to tell you how to live your life or who you should love. But Robert is toxic."

"You don't know him like I do. He's changed."

"How so? I mean, he's the same guy who followed me to Charleston and threatened me because I'm not making his life easy."

"He just wants to help the city of Charlotte and . . ."

"No, Gabby, he wants to help himself. Don't let him use you, like I did."

She leaned back in her seat. "What should I do?"

"Learn to value yourself, Gabby. You say you believe in Robert, and there was a time when I did as well. But let me ask you this: what has he done to earn your belief, your trust, or your love?"

Gabby stared at Chante as if she was pondering her question. "You think I'm crazy, don't you?"

"Gabby, I think you've been hurt, and you're looking for someone to fix it. But you're looking in the wrong place."

"What would you know about that? I bet you had everything handed to you. You had choices I've only dreamed of."

"How old are you?"

"Huh?"

"You seem really young to be giving up on yourself for a man that isn't above using a woman to get what he wants. That's not love, Gabby. That isn't someone you can trust."

"But if he saw me the way he sees you, then maybe he would give me a better life. He would introduce me to the right people and . . ."

"You can do that yourself. Why do you think a man will open doors for you?"

"Not just any man," she said. "Robert is somebody."

"Robert is a liar, and he sold you a bill of goods he can't deliver. Gabby, don't do this to yourself. I tell you what, I'm going to help you."

"Why would you do that?"

"Because I don't want to see you living your life thinking that being someone's wife is the only way you can make your life better."

Gabby shook her head. "I still don't see why you would want to help me."

"Believe it or not, I know where you're coming from. My mother thinks everything I've accomplished is nothing because I don't have a ring on my finger. And maybe that's why I believed in Robert and why I thought I needed to marry him."

"You didn't love him?"

Chante sighed. "I thought I did. But I wanted to be his wife so that my mother would finally see some value in my life. I went to law school, graduated at the top of my class, and got a job with one of the top law firms in Charlotte. You know what my mother wants to know? When am I going to get married?"

"Are you serious?"

Chante nodded. Gabby blinked and shook her head.

"If I'd gone to law school, my mother would've thought I was the second coming. What's wrong with your mama?"

"She's one of those people who thinks a woman is incomplete without a man. I'm not living like that anymore. Gabby, you can have it all, but you have to believe it."

The young woman dropped her head. "That's the problem, I don't believe it."

"And that's why I want to help you. I'm offering you a job here, working for me."

Lifting her head, Gabby smiled. "Thank you. I'm not going to let you down."

"There's just one thing I need from you," Chante said.

"What's that?"

"You're going to have to stop seeing Robert. I don't want him around my practice, and you need to establish yourself."

"What if . . . ?"

"No what-ifs. If you want to work for me, then you're going to have to leave Robert in the rearview mirror."

Gabby dropped her head, then looked up at Chante. "All right."

"Good. Be here tomorrow at nine." Chante and Gabby rose to their feet, and

Chante extended her hand to Gabby. "Welcome to the Legal Center for Women."

Gabby shook Chante's hand and smiled. "Thank you so much."

As Gabby left the office, Liza returned with three coffees. "I thought I was getting coffee for three people?" Liza asked. "What happened?"

"I offered her a job."

"What? Are you crazy? How do you know Robert didn't send her here to spy on you?"

Chante took a cup of coffee from the drink tray. "Because she reminds me of who my mother was trying to make me. She thought Robert was going to lead her to the promised land."

"Poor child. She really thought that he loved her?"

Chante nodded. "Been there, done that. That's why I offered her a job. She's young, and she needs a chance."

"And you have to be the one to give it to her?"

Chante nodded. "It seems as if my mother's attitude is something that occurs in all walks of life. Someone told Gabby that she had to be married to get ahead."

"And she thought Robert was the answer?" Liza broke into laughter. "Poor baby. I see why you want to take her under your wing, but you need to focus on Amanda Chavis's case."

Chante sighed. She wished she could focus on kissing Zach, making love to him in the middle of the day, and tasting his essence.

"I can do both. I'm going to call Amanda right now."

Liza perched on the edge of the desk. "I don't trust that girl."

"What has she done to make you distrust her?"

Sucking her teeth, Liza cocked her head to the side. "She slept with Robert, didn't she?"

Chante swatted Liza on the arm. "So did I. What's your point?"

"You didn't know any better. She has proof. And if she loves him as much as she says she does, how do you know this isn't a trick?"

Chante sighed. "It could be, or she could've been subjected to the same nonsense my mother is still pushing off on me. Maybe we're kindred spirits."

"Or maybe Robert is trying to ruin your business before it gets off the ground."

"I'm sure that's not the case, and even if it was, Robert doesn't have the good sense to ruin anything without destroying himself."

Liza nodded, then took a sip of her coffee. "You're right about that. Still, don't you think this is a big coincidence?"

"Not really. She came here looking for you. And unless you and Teresa sent out some kind of smoke signal, no one knows about my firm."

"That is true, but I still wouldn't trust her."

Chante picked up the phone. "I'm going to get to work. You need to stop being so hard on people."

Liza rolled her eyes and drained her coffee cup. "I'm going to find my husband and let him be hard on me. You watch your back with that girl," she said as she headed out the door.

CHAPTER 20

Over the past two weeks, Zach's business had picked up tenfold. And the news of Natalie's arrest didn't take the shine off the company's revitalization, even if the media did bring up his link to her every time there was an update about her crime.

There were a few contracts that had been missed out on because of the controversy. What he'd found ironic had been the fact that the CEO of one company had been arrested for solicitation after he'd cried that morality kept them from doing business with Zach. Zach had e-mailed Kia and told her to send Mr. Yoshema a potted plant with a card that said, *I feel your pain.*

Kia replied and told him how childish that was and she wasn't going to do it.

With things back on track with business, Zach noticed that he hadn't heard from Chante. Though Zoe's idea of focusing on his business made sense, every morning he woke up with Chante on his brain, and he had to see her. The only problem was, he didn't know if she wanted to see him.

Lately, his calls had gone unanswered, and her text messages were usually a one-word reply. Busy.

He wondered if she'd forgotten about him and moved on with someone other than Robert Montgomery. She'd have to be some kind of fool to go back to Robert after what he'd done to her. But he knew a woman like Chante could have her pick of any man she wanted, and absence didn't always make the heart grow fonder.

"Whatever," he muttered as he placed his smartphone on his desk. He wasn't going to sit there and stare at his phone like a lovesick teenager. Instead, he decided to call Chante.

"This is Chante Britt," she said when she answered the phone.

"Finally, I reach the lady."

"Zach, how are you?"

"A lot better now that I'm hearing your voice," he said. "The question is, how are you?"

"Busy."

"Somehow, I knew that was going to be

your response. What's been keeping you so busy?"

"Well," she said with a sigh, "I have my law firm up and running. My first case has the potential to make history."

"Wow. I guess I don't feel so bad about all of the text messages you didn't answer. Can you talk about it?"

"I, um, I have to go. But I will call you tonight."

"How about you see me tonight?"

"Huh?"

"We'll talk later, lovely." After hanging up, Zach logged on to his US Airways account and booked tickets to Charlotte. Tonight he'd see the woman who'd been haunting his dreams.

Chante sat at her desk with a smile on her face after talking to Zach. Just the sound of his voice made her wet. And as much as she wanted to hop on the next flight to New York, she and Amanda were making headway in their case. Over the past few weeks, working with Amanda showed her how lucky she'd been to find out who Robert was before he put a ring on her finger. She could've been living Amanda's life instead of acting as her advocate.

When Amanda and Harlan had gotten

married, she'd had a thriving business in the posh South End of Charlotte and was doing public relations for some of the biggest companies in the Southeast. She and Harlan had met at a legal mixer, which, ironically, Chante had attended. Their relationship had been an affair at first because Harlan and his first wife, Harriett, hadn't finalized their divorce.

Chante had to reconcile her feelings about infidelity before she'd given her all to Amanda's case. After all, she'd been cheated on, and it hurt to find out that the man she'd thought she was going to marry had been unfaithful, even if she and Robert hadn't been married.

But Amanda made her see that you sometimes fall in love with a lie, and Harlan had told her that the marriage between him and his wife was over. What she hadn't known when the affair started was that Harlan was using her connections to win the judge seat. When she'd discovered the truth, she was in love with the man and thought she could deal with being the only one in the marriage who was in love. By the time Amanda realized that her happily ever after wasn't going to happen, she wanted out of the marriage. But Harlan wouldn't sign the divorce papers, and when she said she'd do it without his signature, he reminded her that he was the law and no one in town would take her case.

By the time she'd found a lawyer from Raleigh who'd represent her, Harlan had been arrested, and she was pulled into the storm around him. At the end of the day, Chante learned that Amanda was a phenomenal woman who'd gotten a raw deal because of the man she'd married.

"Chante, this whole ordeal has been draining and unfair. I'm the one who came into this marriage with an established career."

"I know," Chante said. "You shouldn't suffer because of his misdeeds."

"Tell me about it," she said with a disgusted eye roll. "I wasn't handing down those sentences, nor was I sleeping with the director of that center. Eighty-eight thousand dollars. He ruined my life for eighty-eight thousand dollars and some loose booty." Chante wanted to say something profound and inspiring, but she was at a loss. Instead, she nodded.

"I'm sorry," Amanda said. "I wasn't going to get emotional about all of this. This is about my money."

"But it's emotional as well." Chante sighed, thinking about how she had waited around for Robert to apologize to her after everything broke during the campaign. It wasn't as if she'd thought his apology would have been sincere or changed anything, but still, it would've been an acknowledgment of her hurt feelings.

"The state has offered a settlement — eighty percent of the money they seized from you — and I turned it down."

Amanda nodded. "Thank you. It's as if they are determined to make me pay for Harlan's crime. Going off the grid didn't help me as much as I thought it would have. My business is gone, my reputation is in ruins, and people act as if I should be in a cell beside him."

"That's why we're about to change the narrative, tell your truth, and get your money back."

Amanda leaned back in her seat. "But I'm about to open myself up to a lot of scrutiny. After all, I had an affair with a married man."

"A man who you married."

"Do you think people are going to care about that? Maybe we should settle?"

"No!" Chante crossed over to Amanda's chair and looked into her eyes. "If you want to recapture who you are, you have to tell your story. You might be able to help someone else in a situation like yours."

"I'm not sure I want to be a life lesson."

"Oh, I understand. I've been on the other side of this situation. But nothing made me feel better than when I took my life back. Those videos and the media camping out at my front door actually gave me a chance to look at what I'd lost."

"How?"

Chante smiled. "My grandmother is the one person I can always depend on to surprise me. I went to Charleston to get away from the judgment and the madness that had become my life. Then something unexpected happened."

"Your grandmother passed?"

"No, thank God! She's actually on a cruise around the world with a man she should've been with years ago. But that's not the point. She wrote me a letter that made me realize I hadn't been living, because I was scared of what my mother thought and what the legal community thought, and because of my confusion over why I hadn't gotten that partnership. All I needed to do was control my destiny."

"You make it sound so easy."

"It isn't. I'm scared. For the first time in my life, I'm in a position where I have to depend on me, and failure is not an option.

I have to make things right for you. That's part of my mission."

"That's a lot of pressure to put on yourself."

"I prefer my pressure to someone else's. And I know I won't fail myself or you. But you have to know that this will be hard."

"I can take it. I've allowed people to create stories about me, and I've done nothing wrong."

"And it's time for all of your judges to realize that. Don't settle. Fight and show the world how you are going to take back your life."

"Better yet, I'm going to pull a Chante and create an even better life."

Chante slapped high five with Amanda.

"Now, let's get ready to put you on the right path for . . ."

The intercom buzzed, interrupting Chante. "Yes, Gabby?"

"There is a Zach Harrington here to see you, and he wanted me to tell you that he'll wait as long as it takes."

"Please tell Mr. Harrington that I'm finishing up with a client and I won't keep him waiting that long."

"Did I mention that he's fine as . . ."

"Thank you, Gabby," Chante said and clicked the intercom off. She turned to

Amanda with a sheepish smile. "Sorry about that."

"No need to apologize because you have a fine man waiting for you."

Chante felt her cheeks burning with embarrassment. Wait. How did Zach find her, and what was he doing in Charlotte?

After Amanda and Chante agreed to go to trial and had set an appointment with the state's attorney's office, she was ready to see Zach. Fluffing her hair, she buzzed Gabby and told her to send Zach in.

When the door opened and he walked in, Chante's breath caught in her chest. "Hi," she said as she crossed over to him, "what are you doing here?"

"I missed you," he said as he drew her into his arms. "But now I'm starting to see why my calls went unanswered. This setup is amazing."

She smiled proudly. "I knew I had do something because there was no way that I was going back to the firm I was with before."

Kissing her gently on the forehead, he smiled. "I'm proud of you. I must say, some of the people at your old firm aren't happy. I went there first."

Chante dropped her head. "Who did you run into?"

"That guy Taiwon."

"Bastard," she whispered. "Anyway, what brings you to Charlotte?"

"Chante Britt. Like I said, I missed you."

She melted in his arms. "How are things in New York?"

"Great," he said. "My company and I have been cleared officially of any involvement in Natalie's sex crimes, and business is good again. I just have to figure out what's going on with my sister and the FBI agent."

"Huh?"

"Zoe, with her headstrong ways, and Agent Banks have something going on. I've never seen her flustered before."

"Wow."

"Enough about her. Let's have dinner tonight."

"Of course," she said. "I have some things I need to finish up here, and then I'm all yours."

"I love the sound of that. I'm staying at the Westin, so do you want to meet me there around seven?"

"Sounds good," she said as they made their way to the door.

"But before I go," he said in a deep whisper, "there's something I have to do." He brought his mouth down on top of hers, capturing her lips in a hot, knee-weakening kiss. Soft moans turned into impassioned groans as Zach slipped his hand between her thighs. Immediately, Chante wished she'd worn a skirt instead of her favorite slim-tailored black pants. Still, her body throbbed and her lips puckered with want and need.

Just as she was about to unbutton her pants and lay back on top of her desk, Gabby buzzed her. "Chante, your appointment is here."

"Damn it," Chante muttered as she and Zach broke the kiss. She stalked over to her desk and pressed the intercom button. "Give me five minutes, please."

"Yes, ma'am."

Chante smiled at Zach. "Duty calls."

"Yeah, you have to handle your business. I guess I can wait." Zach winked at her, then headed out the door. Chante took a deep breath and fanned herself, hoping her heart rate would soon return to normal.

"Gabby," she said into the intercom, "I'm ready."

As Zach walked to his vehicle on the parking deck, he prayed that Chante's meeting would be successful and short. Very short. Kissing her and feeling her in his arms made his desire for her skyrocket as though NASA had launched him into space. Seeing Chante in her element made him realize just how sexy she was. He hadn't expected to drool over her in a suit as much as he did when he saw her in a sundress. But damn. She looked good. Better than good. And she felt even better. Getting into his car, he decided that dinner was going to be in his suite — no waiters and no interruptions. He'd planned to take her to the famous Hometown Delights, but he'd have to sample that restaurant another time.

Tonight, all he wanted to taste was Chante. Arriving at the hotel, he called room service.

"How can I help you?" the attendant asked.

"Please tell me you have a seafood quiche," Zach said.

"I don't, but we have low-country-style shrimp and grits."

Smiling, Zach remembered how he didn't want to take a chance with grits that first night he'd taken Chante dinner. "You know, I really need a seafood quiche. I have a special lady visiting and that meal is kind of sentimental to us."

"Really? Well, being it's that special to you two, I don't want to have the chef try to make one and we mess it up. I'm going to call over to one of my favorite restaurants and see if they can help us out."

"If you make that happen, I will definitely make it worth your time."

"When are you expecting your dinner guest?"

"Seven. And what do you have in the way of desserts?"

"We have a great chocolate cake with extra frosting and a dark chocolate drizzle. And there is a caramel drizzle as well."

"I like that. I want to have a cake with both drizzles."

"Excellent choice, sir. I'll check on the seafood quiche and get back to you about what I can do."

"Thank you so much," Zach said. After hanging up, he called housekeeping.

"Mr. Harrington, is there a problem?" the woman who answered the phone asked.

"No, but I need some candles and rose petals."

"I'm sorry?"

"I have a special lady coming to visit me tonight, and I want to create a sexy mood. Can you help me out?"

The woman laughed, then said yes. "I have candles, but you're going to have to get your own roses. There's a florist on Fourth Street."

"That's awesome. Now, where is Fourth Street?"

She laughed again and gave him directions. Zach glanced at his watch. He had plenty of time to get everything together. As he headed for his car, his cell phone rang.

"Zoe," he muttered when he saw his sister's face appear on the screen. "What's up, sis?"

"Where are you, and are you sitting down?"

"Not sitting yet. What's going on?"

She blew into the phone. "Natalie is out of jail, and her case has been thrown out."

"What in the . . . How in hell did that happen?"

"Missing evidence or something like that."

"Bullshit. I bet she had a federal judge on her list too. This woman is like the Teflon Pimp."

"But it gets better. She's doing the *I'm the victim* media tour. And is talking about suing for defamation."

"Who's going to take that case?"

"Are you sitting yet?"

"Spill it, Zoe."

"Ever heard of the Legal Center for Women?"

"What? Wait, that's Chante's firm."

"A source told me that Natalie is in Charlotte meeting with your girlfriend."

Zach closed his eyes. This. Was. A. Nightmare. "I'm sure Chante won't take her case."

"I bet she will. New firm, all about empowering women. Can you imagine the press she'd get taking this case? I bet you're glad you didn't go traipsing after her in North Carolina."

"Zoe, I'm in Charlotte right now. And I probably narrowly missed seeing Natalie when I left Chante's office."

"I can't believe you. After everything you went through to restore the business, you're back on the chase. You're proof that women run the world and we just allow you men to live in it."

"What are you ranting about?"

"I think these women are setting you up."

Zach rolled his eyes. But what if she was right? "Where are you right now?"

"In the Bronx — why?"

"Not that I think you're right, but I'm going to see if there is something going on with Chante and Natalie. I'm going to need your help."

"This must be serious because you never want my help when it comes to a woman."

"I'll call you back." Zach hopped into his

car and headed for Chante's office. He silently prayed that Zoe was wrong.

CHAPTER 21

Chante sat across from Natalie Duvall Harrington and tried to remain professional. There was no way she'd take her case. But she did want to get a good look at the former Mrs. Zachary Harrington. She was pretty. Okay, the woman was gorgeous — with her auburn bob, hazel eyes, and café au lait skin — but full of shit.

"I've taken the fall for a lot of men," Natalie said. "I was the scapegoat, and powerful men are just going on with their lives while I'm being called the 'Harlem Madame.' "

"So the call-girl ring wasn't your idea, as the court documents say?"

She narrowed her eyes at Chante. "My ex-husband left me broke. I needed something to do. It's not as if I have experience in real estate or anything. I thought my marriage was going to be forever, and when it wasn't, I was depressed."

Leaning back in her chair, Chante folded

her hands underneath her chin. "So you were depressed and allowed someone to talk you into getting involved in an illegal enterprise?"

"When you say it like that it makes me seem crazy."

"Natalie, I sympathize with your situation, but I don't see a winnable case here. You got off on a technicality. Take that as a victory and move on."

"I know who you are, and I know why you're turning me down. You think you and Zach have some sort of future, don't you?"

"Get out of my office."

"Chante Britt, you're going to end up on the wrong side of heartache again. Zach isn't the man you think he is, and I can't wait until both of you fall off your high horses."

Chante rose to her feet. "Why are you here, because I know you didn't actually want me to represent you or help you rehab your image."

Natalie smiled. "I'd like to start over, and I need money to do so, because New York will no longer be home for me."

"Is this a shakedown? Seriously? You came to a lawyer to blackmail her? Tell me why I shouldn't call the police right now and have your ass hauled out of here."

Rising to her feet, Natalie crossed over to Chante. "You want your new venture to be successful. The bad press you'd get from calling the police and telling them I was here, yet you refused to help me, is going to tank your fledgling firm. How are women going to be able to trust you when you can't help me?"

"You're not the kind of woman who needs help. You're a liar who doesn't mind stepping on people to get what you want."

"Funny, you think the media will see that side of me? I have powers of persuasion that rival the truth at every turn. How do you think I convinced the FBI that your boo was involved with the call-girl ring? That boring motherfucker wouldn't even bet on the ponies. Maybe you two are made for each other. You seem boring as hell too, but you have some cash that I need. Make it happen, or everything you're trying to build is going to sink like the *Titanic*." Natalie sashayed out of the office, and Chante stood there with her mouth wide open.

Was the woman serious? Chante hit the intercom button. "Gabby, the woman who just walked out of here? Never let her back in this office again."

"Yes, ma'am. Can I come in and talk to you?"

"Sure. I think it's about time for us to shut down for the day anyway."

Gabby walked into Chante's office and took a seat across from her boss's desk. "I heard from Robert this morning. He said he wants to work things out with us, and he's dropping out of the race for mayor."

"What do you think of all of that?" Chante asked.

Sighing, tears welled up in Gabby's eyes. "I feel like he's settling, and I'm not his first choice. Chante, I'm not you. I'm not as smart as you are, and . . ."

"Stop. Stop it. You are enough. And you're right: you shouldn't be anyone's second choice, and you damned sure don't have to be like me."

"Over these last few weeks, I've seen what you've done here without anyone's help. I want to be that kind of woman. Not someone's second choice or a stand-in for the life he thought he could have with someone else. Why can't I find a man to love me and my potential?"

"How do you feel about you?"

"What do you mean?" she asked with a confused look on her face.

"You have to love you before you can expect someone else to love you back. Until you are the most important person in your world, you can't think that you're going to be that person to someone else."

"What if this is all I am? I mean, this job is wonderful, but I'm a receptionist. I'm not making a difference here."

"Yes, you are! I couldn't run this place without you. Think about this: if you want to do more, then you have to plan for your future. Have you thought about going back to school?"

"Back to school? I guess I could do that. I think I want to be a lawyer like you."

Chante hid her smile. Who would've thought she'd be able to save somebody from Robert? Whether or not Gabby went to school, she was already showing that she was smarter than she'd seemed when she first walked in the door.

Glancing down at her watch, Chante wanted to bolt. She and Zach were having dinner at seven, and she wanted to get a pedicure, but she wasn't going to leave until she was sure Gabby wasn't going to do something destructive for herself.

"Where did you go to school?" Gabby asked.

"The University of North Carolina."

"Maybe I should apply there in the fall."

"That is a great idea. I'll write you a letter of recommendation."

Gabby rose to her feet and hugged Chante. "Thank you. Thank you so much."

Chante broke the embrace and smiled at Gabby. "I'm going to expect a lot from you. I'm going to check on you and make sure you're doing what you're supposed to do."

"I'm going to make us proud. And then I'm going to pass the bar."

"And I'm going to hire you."

"Do you mean it?"

"One thing you will learn about me is that I keep my word. Now you're going to have to keep your word to yourself."

Gabby nodded. "I'm going to do that. Because I'm promising myself that I'm going to be the best damned lawyer in the state. People are going to be clamoring to have me represent them in court."

"I'm going to hold you to that," Chante said. "Why don't you head home and get your applications together."

"All right. I'm finally going to do something that will make a difference. Thank you, Chante."

"You don't have to thank me. Just find yourself. And know that I'm in your corner."

The women embraced again, and Chante felt as if she had found her purpose. Saving Gabby and making her think about her future meant more to her than winning

Amanda's case or anything else she'd been working on.

"If you need anything, I'm here for you," Chante said.

"Thank you for giving me hope," Gabby said as she headed for the door.

"You can thank me when you get your degree," Chante said with a smile.

Zach parked his rental car and watched Natalie get into a black Ford Escape. He would've never pegged his ex for driving a compact car, but if she was trying to hide, then this vehicle made sense. Pulling behind her, Zach blocked her exit. Climbing out of his car, he tapped on Natalie's window.

"I don't believe this," she muttered as she rolled her window down. "Stalking me?"

"I think it's the other way around," he snapped. "Why are you here?"

Natalie opened the door and got out of the car. She gave Zach a cold stare. "I'm here because I want to start over. New York is no longer my home, thanks to you."

"Thanks to me? That's a laugh. I didn't run a sex ring selling barely legal women selling themselves."

"You don't care about those women. You were upset because your little business got brought into my case. I knew it would kill you. And having that witch of a sister of yours arrested was just the icing on the cake."

"You're so unhappy with your life that you wanted to ruin my family."

"Please," she grunted. "You and your perfect family. None of you ever made me feel welcome or that I was good enough to be a Harrington. I was just your little freak. Behind closed doors I was your world, but when it came to your family, you didn't put me first."

"You're kidding, right?" Zach laughed and shook his head. "When I married you, I tried to include you in everything. You were the one who had other things to do and acted standoffish when Zoe came around. And you were the one who walked out on me."

"Oh, you want me back?"

"Yeah, I want to be with a lying, conniving snake," he gritted. "You enjoy ruining people's lives, don't you?"

She rolled her eyes. "What about me? No one ever thinks about what I need and what I want!"

"You sound like a petulant child. Grow up."

"Go to hell. When I realized that marrying you was just another mistake, I used you to get what I needed so I could connect with some heavy hitters. I'm glad you left your computer open. And when she figures out who you are, she's going to leave you too."

"Chante's nothing like you. She doesn't use people because she's bored."

"Keep thinking that. We had a great conversation. I taught her some tricks to get what she wants from you." Natalie winked at him. "With this new law firm, she's going to need media attention, and you're just the clown to help her get it."

"Stay away from me and Chante."

"I want to disappear as much as you want me to. It's just going to cost you."

"You're out of your mind."

She folded her arms across her chest. "Are you telling me that three hundred thousand dollars isn't worth peace of mind?"

"Not at all. I wouldn't give you a dime."

"Then keep looking over your shoulder wondering when I'm going to show up and ruin your life with Little Miss Perfect."

"Natalie, you're an idiot. It won't be long before you're in jail again. That's all I'm going to be looking over my shoulder to see."

She sneered at him. "I've honed my skills. As you can see, I'm not in jail now, am I?"

"That will change if you don't get off my

property," Chante said as she crossed over to the scene in the parking lot.

Natalie smiled at Chante as if they were best girlfriends. "You don't have to keep up the act. I told Zachary everything."

"Really?" Chante asked, slapping her hand on her hip. "You know, I don't like trespassers. I think you should leave, Natalie."

She nodded at Chante. "I get it. You don't want him to know that we're working on a plan together. My lips are sealed."

"Your lips are lying. Leave or I will call the police."

"I make you two uncomfortable? Is that why everyone keeps talking about calling the police? I've committed no crime."

"When did blackmail become legal?" Chante asked.

"I asked you for a donation," she said.

Chante rolled her eyes. "Extortion is extortion."

Natalie looked from Zach to Chante and shook her head. "You two want to live a perfect and stress-free life. I want that for you too, but I need some cash. Some money to start over, or I can set up my new life right here. Seriously, Chante, how many sex scandals do you want to be involved in?"

"Bi . . . You know what, you're not even

worth the breath it would take to cuss you out."

"But how much is your happily ever after worth to you? You want be Cinderella. I can be your fairy godmother or the evil step-mom. The choice is yours."

"Leave!" Zach exclaimed. "No one is giving you a damned dime, and you will not threaten Chante."

Natalie threw her hands up. "Touchy, touchy, touchy. You must really be smitten." She dropped her hands and turned to Chante. "It won't last long, so take advantage while you can." Smiling, she started for her car. "And just so you know, I don't make threats. Ask Zoe. Will you move your car so that I can leave?"

Zach glared at her and then headed for his car. Chante took a step toward Natalie.

"I'm not going to let you or anyone else ruin what I have here. So if you're looking for money or some kind of payoff, you're barking up the wrong tree."

"That's what you say now. But when you can't get even the lowest client, you're going to regret trying to stand with this clown." Natalie hopped in her car as Zach backed away. Chante squeezed her nose, holding back her scream. This was not what she needed right now. But there was no way in hell that she was going to cave to extortion.

When Zach moved his car and Natalie zoomed out of the parking lot, Chante wondered how Zach knew that Natalie was at her office. Dropping her head in her hand, she wondered if this was a part of a bigger plan. "Damn it," she muttered as Zach got out of his car.

"How did you know she was here?" Chante asked as he approached her.

"Zoe told me. Why was she here?"

Chante folded her arms across her chest. "Is something going on that I need to know about? Is your sister having me followed and investigated? Zach, I don't need this stress while I'm trying to start a practice."

"Stress? I'm causing you stress?"

Chante placed her hands to her temples. "That's not what I'm saying," she said with a sigh. "I don't know how that woman found me, and I want nothing to do with her. But I'm not giving her a damn dime."

"Neither am I, and I'm not going to let her hurt you."

"I don't need your protection," Chante snapped. "I'm sick and tired of everyone looking at me as if I need a champion. I can take care of myself!"

Zach backed away from her and shook his

head. "Did I say that? I want to protect the woman I love — not because I think you can't!"

She looked down at the pavement. "I'm sorry," she whispered. "I'm sorry. I just . . . There is so much riding on my success or failure. I don't want to let anyone down, especially my clients. So many women have been victimized just because they're women. Sexual harassment claims, work discrimination, and bad divorces."

Closing the space between them, he took Chante's face in his hands. "I love how you have taken control of your life. Love how you want to be every woman's champion. I want that for you, but you aren't Superwoman, and you're going to need a shoulder to lean on."

"And you're giving me yours?" she asked with a smile.

"Both of them." Zach brought his mouth down on top of hers and kissed her slow and deep. Soft moans escaped her as Zach cupped her bottom. She pressed her body closer to his, feeling every muscle in his body harden. She wanted him right there. Pulling back, she looked at him and smiled.

"I know we were supposed to have dinner, but I want to skip straight to dessert," she said.

"Sounds good to me. But I have plans for you," he said, then scooped her up in his arms. "Let's get out of here."

Across the street, a photographer snapped pictures of Chante and Zach's passionate embrace and the license plate of the car they'd sped off in. "Got them," the man said into the phone. "I'll upload the pictures now."

CHAPTER 22

Zach nearly broke the sound barrier to get to the Westin. Chante couldn't help but laugh at him. "Slow down, Zach. We're not in a Mustang or in Charleston."

"But I'm in need. I need to be inside you," he said as he pulled into the parking deck. "And I don't think I can wait to get into my room." Leaning over, Zach lowered the back of Chante's seat. "I want you right now."

She placed the palm of her hand against his chest. "Slow down, cowboy. There are way too many cameras around. I'm sure the walk to your room is only going to make it better." She opened the door, and he smirked.

"You're no fun," he quipped.

"Umm-huh," she said as she exited the car. "I'm going to show you fun."

Zach got out of the car and caught up with Chante as she headed for the elevator. "I know you will, sexy." Kissing her on the

330

back of her neck, Zach wrapped his arm around her waist. "I'm really proud of you."

"Thank you." She pressed the button for the elevator. When they stepped on, Zach pressed her against the wall and smiled at her. "You're an amazing woman."

"Zach."

"No, listen. When I went to Charleston, all I wanted was a break from the madness going on in my life. And then you walked into the room. You took my breath away, even if you wanted to pretend you didn't feel that spark. Since I've been back in New York, I can't keep my mind off you."

"Zach."

"Chante, I love you."

She squeezed her eyes shut. "You don't have to say that. I know that . . ."

"I know I don't have to say anything I don't mean. And I don't go around telling women I love them if I don't mean it."

She wanted to tell him that she loved him too, but fear froze her tongue. She couldn't take the risk of telling him how she felt. What if she told him and it blew up in her face? "Zach," she whispered, "your life is in New York. Can we be honest for a minute? Neither one of us has plans to move."

"What does distance have to do with anything?"

"A lot. Who's to say that on a lonely night, you won't reach out to someone else? You're a man; you have needs."

"I'm a man who wants to love one woman. You're right: I have needs. I need you."

"Now, while I'm standing here in front of you."

"Baby, your baggage has nothing to do with me. You can't paint me with the same brush that you used with anyone who hurt you."

She rolled her eyes. "I'm not doing that," she said unconvincingly. "I don't want you to be tied to me when you can find someone in New York."

"If I was going to find someone in New York, then I would've done it already. Not to brag, but I can have any woman I want."

"Then why are you here?"

"Because the only woman I want is you. You just have to believe that."

The elevator doors opened into the lobby. "I want to," she whispered. "But I can't. Maybe I should call a cab and go home. I don't want to hurt you, but I'm just not ready for this." Chante dashed to the front desk, and Zach stood there in disbelief.

As she headed out the door, Zach followed her. "Chante," he called out. "I'm confused. What just happened?"

"I gave you an out. I gave you the chance to do you without feeling guilty about it."

"Or are you trying to ease your conscience?"

"What?"

"Do you want me to walk away so that you can keep up the illusion that you have about men who love you? That every man who walks into your life is somehow trying to take advantage of you? I'm not going to let you do that."

"Let me? Zach, I'm going to go."

"Yeah, you're going upstairs, and we're going to talk like two rational adults." He touched her elbow and guided her to the elevator. They rode to his room in silence. This was not the reunion he'd planned.

When they stepped off the elevator and he opened the door to his room, the flickering flames of the candles and the heart-shaped rose petals in the middle of the bed reminded him what this night was supposed to have been.

"Wow," Chante said. "You did all of this for us?"

"I had other plans for this evening, but right now I think we need to talk." He flipped the lights on and pointed toward the bed.

"What's left to say? I'm just not . . ."

"Chante, I think your problem is you're trying so hard to prove people wrong that you don't know how to live your life. You've tried to cut off the part of your heart that we all have. People need to be loved, and you're not any different."

"I'm realistic. At some point this isn't going to be enough. You're going to get tired of . . ."

"Now you can read my mind?"

"Zach, I'm scared," Chante admitted. "I just don't think I can handle getting disappointed again."

"Why do you expect the worst?"

Chante rose from the bed and paced back and forth. "Because that's what I've experienced."

"The past is the past. I'm offering you a future," he said as he crossed over to her.

"Zach," she said, then turned around and faced him. His eyes seemed to bore into her soul, made her believe that there would be a future for them and that happiness was within reach. But the voice of doubt whispered loudly in her ear. *This isn't going to work.* "How are we going to make this work?" she asked.

"Easy. Anything worth having is worth putting in the work, right?"

Chante nodded in agreement, then leaned

against his chest. "I guess I screwed up what was supposed to be a beautiful night." She looked around the room. "When did you have time to do all of this?"

"I had some help. And the night isn't ruined. We're here and . . ."

A knock at the door interrupted him.

"Room service."

"Dinner is here, so the night is saved," he said as he crossed over to the door. When he opened the door, flashbulbs went off, and a man started barking out questions.

"Mr. Harrington, what is your relationship with Chante Britt now that she's representing your ex-wife?"

"Get out of here!" Zach exclaimed as he pushed the man back and slammed the door.

"What in the hell!" Chante said. "I am not representing that woman!"

"I know you aren't. I guess this is Natalie causing trouble."

Chante's cell phone rang at the same time that Zach's did. She looked down and saw it was Liza calling. "What's up?" Chante said as she walked to one side of the room to take her call and Zach headed for the other side of the room.

"That's what I want to know. You're representing Natalie 'Harlem Madame'

Harrington and sleeping with her ex-husband?"

"I'm not representing her, and how does anyone know about my personal relationship with Zach?"

"I guess you haven't seen the pictures of you two in front of your office? Hot and heavy. It's gone viral."

"Oh. My. God. I can't believe this."

"Then don't watch the news."

"Why?"

"Trust me. Don't do it, okay?"

"You can't say that and expect me not to turn on the television." Chante walked over to the set and pressed the POWER button. Then she flipped to News Fourteen.

"Coming up," the anchor said, "a local attorney finds herself in the middle of a sex scandal — again. Next on News Channel Fourteen."

"Let me guess," Chante said. "They interviewed Robert."

"You know it, and you don't need to see it. What we need to do is make sure none of your real clients are affected by this."

Chante ran her hand across her forehead. As much as she didn't want to see the coverage of this latest rumor about her, she hung up so she could watch the report.

"Charlotte attorney Chante Britt isn't a

stranger to sex scandals. She was engaged to North Carolina senate candidate Robert Montgomery, who was allegedly sleeping with a prostitute while running for the seat won by Jackson Franklin. Montgomery attempted to run for mayor of Charlotte but dropped out of the race last week. Britt, who just started her own law firm and is handling the case of former judge Harlan Chavis's ex-wife, has allegedly taken on another controversial client — the 'Harlem Madame,' Natalie Harrington. Harrington was recently cleared of charges of running a call-girl ring in New York, as well as tax evasion. Harrington is trying to rehabilitate her image, and allegedly Britt is helping her. But photos surfaced of Britt and Zachary Harrington, Natalie's ex-husband, in a very compromising position."

A photograph of Chante and Zach kissing in the parking lot flashed on the screen. "Shit," Chante muttered. Zach looked over his shoulder at her, then told whoever he was talking to that he'd call them back.

"What's going on?" he asked.

"Now this is a thing," she said as her phone began ringing. "Chante Britt."

"Chante, this is Amanda. What is all of this on the news?"

"A bunch of lies," she replied.

"But this looks so bad," Amanda said. "I mean, your credibility is going to come into question, and I don't want to be mentioned every time . . ."

"Amanda, this will pass. Just let me talk to Liza about running some interference."

"I don't know if that's going to be enough. I think I want to drop my case and just take a settlement. I don't need or want this kind of publicity. Thank you for everything you've done, but I'm going to let Taiwon Myrick handle things from here on out."

"Amanda, don't do this. Hello?" The line was dead, and Chante was pissed. "This is some bullshit!"

"What's going on?" Zach asked.

"Amanda believes what she sees on TV. And she went to Taiwon Myrick, of all people, to settle her case. A case that I could win for her! Damn it!"

"If you need to talk to her, go ahead. I have to head to the airport and meet Zoe."

"Don't tell me your sister believes this mess too."

"That's not important. You go save your client." Zach leaned in and kissed Chante gently. "We'll get this straightened out."

She nodded, then pulled out her phone and called a car service to pick her up. Zach opened the door and peeked around the corner to see if there were any reporters or photographers roaming the halls. When he saw that the coast was clear, he and Chante headed downstairs.

"I could take you back to your office," he said when they made it to the lobby.

"Maybe we shouldn't be seen together," she said. "I don't want the media attention right now."

He nodded, then leaned in and kissed her cheek. "We're going to get past this," he said. "None of these rumors change anything."

She smiled, but it didn't reach her eyes. She knew how rumors could change everything. Just as she walked outside, the car she'd ordered pulled up, and she ducked inside it before the media could descend on her. She watched Zach dash to his car, and tears welled up in her eyes. She knew the future they'd planned for wasn't going to happen. A soft sob escaped her throat as she turned around and decided that she had to let Zachary Harrington go.

Charlotte Douglas International Airport wasn't as big as JFK, but it was busy as hell, Zach thought, as he slowly inched along, part of a long line of cars. He wondered about Zoe's purpose for coming to Charlotte. If she was going to hit him with a chorus of "I told you so," he'd drop her off at the first bus stop he came across and let her find her way around the city on her own.

Spotting his sister standing near the taxi stand, he put his blinkers on and blew the car horn at her. She crossed over to his car and hopped in. "You just can't stay out of trouble," she said.

"Hello to you too."

"I should've shot Natalie when I had the chance."

"And when was that?"

"The day you brought her home. What she's doing is beyond words."

"So you're here to do what?"

"Get her arrested." Zoe patted the black briefcase that rested on her lap. "I know she wants money, so I just need to . . ."

"She's already done her blackmail thing. Chante and I told her to go to hell. She went to the press."

"I know. Saw the coverage. She's a criminal, and she belongs in jail. I'm sure she doesn't have a southern judge in her little black book."

"How do you know that?"

"I have friends in high places."

"Like the FBI?"

"Don't start."

Zach shook his head as they stopped for the red light. "You stay in my business, but yours is off limits?"

"Yep, that sounds right," she said. "Light's green. Good thing we're not in New York; you'd be run off the road."

Zach drove through the light. "What's the plan?"

"We're going to find Nat the rat and pay her off, then watch the FBI haul her off to jail, where she belongs. I hope they send her to Angola."

"That's in a totally different state," he said.

"Doesn't matter. She could be a rodeo clown for the prison. Anyway, I looked into Chante Britt's involvement with her, and I have to say I was wrong about your new love. She's pretty brilliant."

"Tell me something I don't know."

"It's amazing what she plans to do with her law firm."

"That is, if she doesn't lose everything. She had a client call her and fire her tonight."

"Because of this mess that Natalie's doing?"

Zach nodded. "She loves ruining people's lives."

"It ends now. She's going to learn today!"

Zoe clasped her hands together. "This is the part of my job that I love."

"Pretending you're Batman?"

Zoe rolled her eyes at her brother. "You can thank me by keeping your sarcasm to yourself."

When they pulled up to another traffic light, Zach leaned over and kissed his sister on the cheek. "Thanks for having my back."

"Always! Now let's find this bag of trash and put her where she belongs."

CHAPTER 23

Chante wasn't surprised to see the media trucks parked outside her office. The driver pulled the car around back, and she hopped out of the car, trying to avoid the cameras. But the lenses were pointed in her direction, and flashes lit the night as she walked into her office.

Chante wondered how Liza had dealt with all of this when she went through that mess during the election. She walked into her office and kept the lights off, fearing that someone's long lens would catch her. Plopping down at her computer, she shook her head as she logged onto the machine and opened her Google Chrome homepage. "This is a nightmare," she thought aloud as she typed her name into the search field and watched the links populate the screen. Lies, innuendos, and just plain bullshit. Of course, *QC After Dark* had the most reprehensible story about her, replete with videos and stories about her relationship with Robert.

Picking up the phone, Chante dialed Liza's number, again hoping she wasn't interrupting anything with the newlyweds.

"I was expecting your call," Liza said when she answered the phone.

"Are you busy?"

"Yes, I'm writing a press release about this 'Harlem Madame' thing, and trying to get Teresa to calm down because she thinks Nic and Robert are behind this."

"No, this is all Natalie."

"What about Gabby?"

"Really, Liza? That girl . . ."

"Probably has something to do with this. I told you not to hire her, and look at this."

"Liza, Gabby isn't who you think she is."

"I don't trust her, and everything that's happening right now proves that she was still with Robert while she was telling you she admired you and wanted better for herself. All she was doing was setting you up."

"You've never met Natalie. She did this because she wants to destroy Zach. Talk about a woman scorned."

"Is he worth it?" Liza asked.

"Right now, I just want to save my firm."

"That's what I want to help you do. But I

still don't trust her."

"My problem isn't Robert or Gabby. This Natalie chick is nuts — but connected. What am I going to do, Liza?"

"Are you ready for some hard truths?" she asked.

"Not really, but I will listen — this time."

"You have to distance yourself from Zach. I know that might be hard for you to do, since you care about him. But the court of public opinion isn't that forgiving. So even if you love this man, publically you need to pretend you don't."

"But that isn't fair to Zach."

"Chante, far be it from me to give advice on love and falling in love with a man who looks bad on paper, but do you plan to move to New York to follow Zach?'

"I don't know. I love him. But I don't how I can make this work. Liza, I do love him — even if I can't tell him that."

"Well, if he doesn't know, then you shouldn't tell him and rehab your image. If you and Zach are meant to be, you'll find your way back later."

"When you and Jackson met, you were working to get Robert elected and wanted me to marry him, and you didn't hide how you felt for him."

"That's different," Liza said.

"No, it isn't. You were about to lose everything, Jackson could've lost everything, but you guys stuck it out, and look at you now."

"There wasn't a crazy ex in the mix determined to destroy me or Jackson. Nor was there a questionable employee . . ."

"Leave Gabby out of this."

"Fine, keep your blinders on, but there might be a hint of truth in Teresa's theory. At the end of the day, you need to step back and get your business together. Love can wait."

"I can't believe you said that," Chante said.

"I don't want you to get hurt, Chante. I don't want your business to suffer when you've already given up so much."

"This really feels like déjà vu. I gave you some really bad advice about Jackson and you ignored it."

"Let's be serious for a minute," Liza said. "There are a lot of people out here hoping that you fail. I don't want to see their smug faces because of this madness. Being a woman means we have to be perfect. We can't have sex and can't make bad decisions, and our hair better always be on point."

"That is true, and I'm tired of following

the rules. I've been following everybody's rules all my life, and I'm done."

"Any other time I'd be cheering for this new and improved Chante, but we have to think about your brand and the business."

"Liza, I love you, but it's not your business. And you know what? I'm not going to let these rumors derail me or my relationship. You know how good it feels to have someone love you, and I have that."

"All right, my sister," Liza said. "Check your e-mail."

"What?"

"I wanted to see where your head was at, and how you would deal with some pushback. Miss Elsie would be proud."

"You know what? You make me sick."

"Nah, I make you better. And guess what, you need to go find that man and make a statement to the media ASAP. That's actually a part of your media plan. And speaking of men, my sexy senator just walked in the door. I have to go."

"Thanks, Liza," Chante said with a smile on her face. She hung up and dialed Zach. When his phone went straight to voice mail, her heart quaked. Where was he? And what was he doing?

Zach sat in his rental car and watched his

sister hand Natalie the briefcase. *Okay, so where is the FBI?* he thought as he watched the women. When Zoe shoved Natalie, he almost hopped out of the car because he didn't want to see his sister being led away in handcuffs as well.

Then Natalie made a mistake: she tried to slap Zoe. Zach smiled as Zoe grabbed her wrist and bent it backward. Natalie fell to her knees, and then three agents appeared from the darkness and separated the women. Zach almost broke into applause when he saw Natalie get handcuffed. But he tempered his excitement as he saw Agent Carver Banks cross over to his sister and wrap his arms around her. Then they kissed. The man who'd harassed him to no end was kissing his sister. He needed answers, and as he opened the car door to get them, his phone vibrated in the console. Looking at the screen, he saw that he had a missed call from Chante.

Deciding that he was going to let Zoe handle her business, he called Chante instead.

"Hello," she said when she answered the phone.

"Hello, beautiful."

"Zach, where are you?"

"At the Doubletree by the airport. Zoe

and I found Natalie, and I'm happy to say she's being led away in handcuffs right now."

"Really? What happened?" she asked.

"Blackmail is illegal, and Zoe knows how to do her job," he said with a laugh.

"Wow," she said. "I guess we have something to celebrate."

"Yep, and the media just pulled up. Chante, I told you that we were going to get this worked out. The last thing I wanted was to cause you problems."

"I know."

"And I need you to know something else too," he said.

"What's that?"

"I love you."

"I love you too," she said. Her voice was light and reminded him of a sexy jazz song.

"What are you doing right now?" he asked.

"Trying to save Amanda from making the biggest mistake of her life — well, second biggest."

"You can do it. And when you save her, I want to finally have our dinner — or just dessert."

"That sounds so good," she said. "Zach, I can't thank you and Zoe for what you've done. Liza and I were talking about ways that we could get around these rumors, and neither one of us could come up with anything."

"Sometimes people don't believe the truth, but we're going to show them what happens when you try to come between two people in love." Zach looked up at Zoe and Banks. Did that man love his sister? Should he mind his business and let whatever they had develop? Nope. He needed answers.

"Chante," he said. "Meet me at the Westin in an hour."

"Sounds good. Because I need to be with you so bad," she said.

"Me too," he replied. "Really bad."

"See you soon," she said. When Chante hung up, Zach got out of the car and headed toward his sister and Agent Banks.

"You two look really cozy," he said, causing the duo to break their embrace.

"Zach," Zoe said, "chill out."

He focused a cold stare on Banks. "I already told you: if you hurt my sister, I'm going to hurt you."

"There you go threatening a federal agent again," Banks said with a smile.

"Not a threat . . ."

"Not your business," Zoe said. "And there's nothing going on here."

"Is that so?" Banks asked her. Zoe folded her arms across her chest.

"I'm not doing this right now. We work very well together, and that's about it."

Banks turned to Zach. "Excuse me, but your sister and I need to talk privately." Before Zach could say a word, Banks had scooped Zoe into his arms and dropped her into an unmarked car with dark-tinted windows. It happened so fast that Zoe didn't even have a chance to protest. Standing there with his mouth wide open, Zach knew he was going to have to find out what was going on with his sister and the G-man.

But right now, he was going to focus on Chante. Every inch of her. Heading back to his car, he drove to the hotel. This time there were no cameras or reporters following him. And if someone knocked on his room door, he wasn't going to open it.

When he arrived at the hotel, he sent Chante a text. I hope you're in the lobby.

Her reply came quick. Ready and waiting for you.

Zach parked his car and sprinted inside. Seeing Chante sitting in the lobby with a silk scarf tied around her head and wearing a pair of oversized sunglasses aroused him and made him laugh.

"Really?" he said when he approached her.

"Yes. I'm so tired of seeing my face on websites and TV. So I decided to channel my inner Louise from *Thelma and Louise.*"

"There's something mysterious and sexy about you being in here in the middle of the night looking like this," he said as he drew her into his arms. Then he noticed her pink trench coat. "Nice coat."

"Wait until you see what's underneath."

"Let's go." He took her hand and crossed over to the elevator. He impatiently pressed the up button.

"Zach," she said, "I have to tell you something."

He glanced at her as the elevator opened. "What's that?"

"And I'm not sure what we're going to do with all of this and all of this space between us. But I want to work for it. I want us to be happy."

He wrapped his arms around her waist, and they stepped into the elevator. "We will be happy. All of this craziness will pass sooner than you think."

"I can only hope, but I don't even want to think about that right now. We're just going to focus on you and me."

Zach nodded and grinned. "I'm all for that."

When they got into Zach's room, he was more than ready to unwrap Chante. Pressing her against the wall, he slowly untied the belt on her coat, then pushed it off her shoulders.

The sight of her amazing body made him hard. "So beautiful," he said as he ran the palm of his hand between her breasts. Then he took her shades off. "I love you."

"I love you too," she said, then pressed her lips against his.

Lifting her into his arms, Zach went over to the bed and laid her across it. She looked so alluring, so demure, and so sexy. Zach quickly undressed, but he wasn't going to rush anything else as he parted her legs and slipped his finger between her wet folds of flesh.

Chante moaned as he probed her hot body with his finger. It was as if he was on an expedition to discover what pleased her and how to make her revel in delight. Each touch made her hotter, wetter, and Zach could barely contain his desire to melt with her.

"Zach," she moaned as his tongue replaced his finger. He pressed her body closer to his lips so that he could taste every inch of her. Chante grasped the back of his neck as waves of pleasure washed over her. Zach traveled up her body, spending time around her navel, before reaching her breasts and suckling them until they swelled against his lips. He could have taken her easily. His hardness pressed against her thighs, and the heat radiating from her body made it difficult to control his desire. But Zach didn't want to rush. He wanted to take his time making love to the woman he loved. Knowing that she felt the same way heated his blood and made him want to bury himself inside her forever.

"Zach," she gasped as his tongue lashed her diamond-hard nipple. "Oh, Zach. I need you inside me."

"And you're going to have me. But you just taste so good," he said, then took her breast back into his mouth as she ground against him. Pulling back, he reached for a condom from the nightstand. Chante stroked his chest with her fingertips as he slid the sheath in place. He pulled her against his chest, and their lips met. Chante kissed him deeply, sucking his tongue as if it was a piece of delicious chocolate. Holding her closely, he flipped her over so that she was on her back. As they broke off their kiss, Zach dove between her legs, seeking her sweet wetness, feeling as if he'd gone straight to heaven as her warmth enveloped him. He licked and sucked her throbbing pearl until she screamed his name as she exploded.

"Zach, Zach," she cried, an orgasm washing over her. Peeling his mouth away from her, he plunged inside her. They fell into a sensual rhythm, matching each other thrust for thrust. Zach wrapped her thighs around him, and they rolled over so that she was on top.

"Chante, Chante, Chante," he moaned like a prayer as she rode him fast then slow, then faster and then slower. She leaned forward and nibbled on his earlobe, and Zach lost it. He climaxed and gripped her hips tightly as he spent himself. She fell into his embrace, and they drifted off to sleep.

Chante woke up with a smile on her face, until she looked at the clock on the nightstand. It was nearly nine a.m. As much as she wanted to stay in Zach's arms, she had a lot of work to do. She had to find Amanda and stop her from settling her case. Then she needed to clear her name. Liza had planned to help her do a media tour, including another appearance on *Charlotte Today.* She shivered, thinking about how she'd looked the last time she'd been on that show . . .

The questioning started.

"So, you and Robert Montgomery are engaged?" Ramona, the interviewer, asked.

"Were engaged," Chante said, then waved her left hand, which was ring-free. Liza had dusted some bronzer around the tan line so it looked as if she'd taken the ring off a long time ago.

"Did you know he'd been unfaithful and was entertaining hookers?"

"A good friend tried to warn me after the incident she'd witnessed with Dayshea Brown, but I didn't want to believe it. I'd been the stereotypical woman, accusing my single friend of being jealous of my relationship. But then I noticed a change in Robert, and things that he'd been saying didn't make sense. I'm a lawyer, I deal in logic. So I had to evaluate my relationship."

"Then why didn't you believe your friend when she first came to you?"

A wave of embarrassment had washed over her as Ramona asked that question. Why hadn't she listened to Liza when she already had a feeling that something had been going on with Robert? Their sex life had become nonexistent, and she no longer believed his excuse, that is was because of the stress of the election. Still, this wasn't something she wanted on display for the whole city to see. And that question wasn't on the list she and Liza had gone over. Still, she couldn't sit there looking like a deer in headlights.

"Well, I-I," Chante began, "I wasn't expecting that question. But if I'm totally honest, I didn't want to believe her. I thought I was in love, and I thought I was loved in return. She walked into my house when I was planning my wedding, telling me that my then fiancé was cheating on me. What would you have done, Ramona?"

When they'd gone to a commercial, it had taken everything within her not to snatch her mic off and run off the stage. Had Liza set her up to look like an idiot?

The last two questions were easy, and she couldn't wait to get off the stage. Following the interview, Chante stormed out of the studio — no selfies with Ramona. Liza had to run to keep up with her friend.

"Chante."

She whirled around. "What was that all about? Did you two sneak that question in, because it damned sure wasn't on the list! You said that I wouldn't look like a fool."

"I didn't know she was going to ask that. And you didn't look like a fool. The producer said . . ."

Chante folded her arms across her chest. "Oh no? Funny, everyone else was mentioned by name — but you."

"Just what are you accusing me of?" Liza

snapped.

"I know you, Liza. You put your reputation above everything else, no matter who you throw under the bus. No wonder you and Robert were so close. You two are just alike." . . .

"Good morning," Zach said as he stroked her back.

"Morning."

"What's wrong?"

She turned around and faced him. "Reality bites," Chante said. "I have a lot to do today, and I don't want to do any of it."

"I'd say don't do it, but I know how important it must be for you to get your reputation cleaned up. How can I help?"

She wrapped her arms around his neck and hugged him tightly. "Just hold me for a second."

And a second was about all the time they had before Chante's phone began ringing. Sighing, she broke her embrace with Zach and picked up the phone.

"This is Chante Britt," she said when she answered.

"Chante, where in the hell are you?" Liza asked.

"Hello, Liza, I was just thinking about you."

"You need to be thinking about the press

conference that we have in thirty minutes. Let me guess. You're with Zach?"

"Yes, I am."

"Kiss that man good-bye and get down here. And by the way, the lead story this morning is Natalie's arrest on blackmail charges."

She looked over at Zach and winked at him. "That's good news, right?"

"Actually, it is. Makes my job a whole lot easier," Liza said.

"All right, I'll see you in a little bit." Chante hung up the phone and turned to Zach. "Duty calls."

"Go knock 'em dead," he said. "And when you finish righting this ship, I have a surprise for you."

Chante's eyes sparkled. "What is it?"

"Keyword, babe: *surprise.*"

"I'm getting sick of surprises," she said as she rose from the bed. Zach followed her lead.

"This is one you're going enjoy, trust me," he said with a wink.

She put her coat on and tied the scarf around her head, but she wanted nothing more than to hop back into bed with Zach. Instead, she went to the door. "Wish me luck," she said.

He pulled her into his arms. "You don't

need luck," he said. "You have truth and justice on your side."

"Now I'm Superwoman?"

He nodded. "But you always have been." He kissed her, slipping his hand underneath her coat and cupping her bottom. Moaning, Chante pushed him back.

"If I don't walk away right now, I'm not going to make it to my press conference."

"See you later, darling," he said as he opened the door. As Chante headed for her car, she was glad that she had clothes in her office and a bathroom where she could take a quick shower.

As she arrived at her office, Chante was a bit pissed off. Yesterday, when there was a scandal brewing, the media was camped out in the parking lot; now there wasn't a blogger with an iPhone in sight. Then again, that may have been a good thing since she wasn't dressed appropriately at all.

"It's about time!" Liza said when Chante walked in the door. "And what do you have on?"

"A coat," Chante said, then headed for the bathroom.

"I'm going to have to try that one day," Liza said. "But you need to hurry up and look like Chante Britt, attorney-at-law. And Teresa's on her way with Amanda."

"Thank God," Chante said as she closed the door. Five minutes later, Chante stepped out of the bathroom dressed in a gray and teal pantsuit and a white blouse with a ruffled collar.

"Classic and lovely," Liza said. "Do you have red lipstick?"

"No," Chante said as she pulled out a bronze-toned lip gloss. Liza crossed over to her friend and shook her head.

"You're about to make a bold statement. You need bold lips." She handed Chante a tube of red lipstick. "These days, red is more about confidence than sex."

"Right," Chante said as she looked at the bright tube Liza held out to her. "I don't know about this color. Maybe it's a little too much?"

"This from the woman who was driving around town in a pink trench coat and no clothes underneath it? Put the lipstick on, and make sure you don't get any on your teeth. Trust me on this."

"Only because it's you," Chante said as she took the lipstick from Liza's hand. After smoothing it on her lips, she looked in the mirror and had to admit, the red lips gave her added confidence. "I hate it when you're right."

"Then you must always be hating," Liza joked.

"I know you're not under the delusion that you're always right."

Liza raised her right eyebrow. "Whatever."

"Knock, knock," a familiar male voice said from the doorway. Chante watched Liza light up like a Christmas tree when Senator Jackson Franklin walked into the room.

"Hi, Jackson," Chante said as Liza crossed over to her husband and hugged him.

"Babe, what are you doing here?" Liza asked.

"I missed my wife this morning, and I needed to make sure you and Chante were all right."

Liza kissed him. Chante turned her head and silently wondered if she and Zach would have a future like this. Of course, Raleigh was a lot closer to Charlotte than New York. And Liza's business was a lot more mobile than hers. *Stop it,* Chante thought. *You and Zach deserve to be happy, and you will have that happiness, somehow.*

"Guys," Chante said, "this isn't Liza's office anymore."

The amorous couple broke their kiss and started laughing. "Sorry about that," Jackson said. "Had a flashback."

"Stop it," Liza said as she swatted his

hand away. "Listen, we're about to have a press conference, and I'm sure you don't want to get caught up in all of this."

"No, I want to get caught up in my wife. And I'm sure Teresa is going to be here, and I need to talk to her."

"Oh, all right."

Jackson looked at Chante and smiled. "Besides, I'm here to support our sister."

"You married a prince, Liza," Chante said as she fluffed her curls.

A few moments later, members of the media began filing into the office. A couple of reporters tried to question Jackson being present in Chante's office, but Liza redirected them to the press release she'd handed out.

"We're here for a statement from Ms. Britt," Liza said.

There were a couple more rumbles about why Liza and Jackson were there, but when Chante stood in front of the reporters, everyone quieted down.

CHAPTER 24

"Ladies and gentlemen," Chante began, "thank you for being here. I have a brief statement, and then I'll answer a few questions. Over the last few days, I've been drawn into a situation that has put my business in jeopardy. Natalie Harrington has been arrested for a blackmail plot that involved me and her ex-husband, Zachary Harrington. Before Natalie came to my office, I only knew of her alleged involvement with a call-girl ring in New York. When I opened this law firm, my goal was and is to help women who have been wronged by systems that are supposed to protect them. Natalie isn't and has never been my client. What she was accused of doing was reprehensible, and she isn't the kind of client I'd represent. The women who were allegedly harmed by her crimes, I'd happily represent.

"People continue to focus on my past. I'm not perfect, and I've made mistakes, I've dealt with men who have brought me into their controversial story lines. Today I'm setting the record straight. I'm Chante Britt, and I won't be defined by what other people think about me. I want to empower women and let them know that it doesn't matter what other people think about them. What does matter is what they think about themselves. There is power in confidence, and so many women lack that confidence because society judges us differently. If a woman is successful, she's called derogatory names, while a man on that same level is lauded. So many women are judged by the mistakes their significant other makes, and some women can't recover from that. That's why I'm here, because I did recover from the mistakes made by the man I thought I was going to marry. And it wasn't easy. He also used our former relationship again when he wanted to further his career. What happened to me happens to a lot of women, and that's not fair. Now I'll open the floor to questions."

A reporter from the CBS station raised her hand. "Ms. Britt, what is the nature of your relationship with Zachary Harrington?"

"Not that it matters," Chante began, "but we have a personal relationship. That is why

I never would have been able to take Natalie's case, and she knew that."

"So," a reporter from the ABC station started, "you are no longer affiliated with Myrick, Lawson and Walker?"

"No, I'm not," she said.

"Why did you leave the firm?" another reporter asked.

"I wanted to start my own firm with a different philosophy."

Liza stood up and smiled at the reporters. "Thank you for being here, but that's all we have time for." A few of the other reporters blurted out questions about Robert and how the end of their relationship had sparked her change. Liza ushered Chante out and closed the door behind them.

"Whew," Chante said.

"You handled that really well," Jackson said. "Some of those questions were out of line, if you ask me."

"I agree," she said, then looked at Liza. "But I have a great coach."

"Well, not to toot my own horn, but this is what I'm best at," she said. Jackson stroked her hip.

"You're good at this, but you're best at . . ."

"Hey, I'm in the room," Chante quipped.

Jackson laughed. "I was going to say she's

best at taking care of the people she loves."

Liza kissed Jackson's cheek. "We'd better get over to the *Charlotte Today* studio."

Just as they were about to leave, Teresa and Amanda walked into the office. "Looks like the gang is all here," Teresa said with a smile as she crossed over and hugged Jackson. "Why aren't you in Raleigh?"

"My wife disappeared on me, and I needed to find her and check on my district."

"Umm, huh," Teresa said. "Let's go have coffee and let Amanda and Chante talk."

When Chante and Amanda were alone, she took a deep breath and offered Amanda a seat.

"I'm only here because Teresa asked me to come and hear you out. I still think settling will end this nightmare."

"Amanda," Chante said, "you shouldn't settle because you have a legitimate chance to win your claim. It isn't just about the money; it's about the principle. You agreed with me on that."

"But Taiwon said you have too much baggage to give my case the attention that it needs and settling would at least give me enough capital to start over someplace else."

"Why should you have to move?" Chante asked. "This is your city. You are a Charlotte socialite. Why would you leave?"

"Because I want people to look at me and see Amanda, not Harlan's ex. I don't want people to judge me for the rest of my life."

"So you're going to run?"

Amanda shook her head. "It's not running, it's . . ."

"Running. And you're better than that. I'm better than that. I thought about it. I could've gone back to Charleston and pretended as if none of that embarrassment with Robert ever happened. But I didn't, and I'm not going to let you do it either."

"You do have a point, but I don't know if I want the attention that will go along with a trial and . . ."

"This doesn't sound like you. This sounds like a man who wants to take his percentage of your settlement and move on."

Amanda tilted her head to the side and looked at Chante. "And what do you get out of this? Nobody does anything out of the kindness of their heart anymore."

"Winning this case would put my firm on the map, there is no doubt about that. But I also took this case because I've been in your shoes. I'm still in them."

Amanda nodded. "You do have a thing for scandalous men." She laughed, and Chante knew they were getting somewhere.

"Or maybe they have a thing for me."

"I saw the picture of you and Zachary Harrington. I'd lose my mind over him too," she said. "But why does it seem as if whenever a woman falls in love, she suffers? That guy is from New York and your roots are here. How are y'all going to have a future?"

Chante offered her a tense smile. "If it's meant to be, then it will happen. But this is about you. Do you want to fight, or do you want to settle?"

"Chante, I want to settle. But this is my number, and I want a formal apology," she said as she slid her a folder. Chante opened the folder, and a smile spread across her face.

"That's a great number. It covers everything that you lost and more."

"I'm not settling for anything less. Taiwon didn't understand that," Amanda said. "But the most important thing for me is to get my apology."

Chante nodded, then looked down at her watch. There was no way she was going to make it to the *Charlotte Today* studio, and she was fine with that. She'd given the media all they were going to get today. It was time to work.

Zach headed to the airport and dropped off

his rental car. He exchanged the sedan for a convertible Mustang. Part one of the surprise was taken care of.

The next thing he needed to do was to confirm the reservation at the Charleston Harbor Bed and Breakfast. He'd gotten a suite on the top floor where they would have a lot of privacy. The picture they'd e-mailed him showed a wraparound balcony with a privacy screen. He couldn't wait to make love to Chante on that balcony at sunset and sunrise.

After getting the car, he typed "Hometown Delights" into the GPS so that he could get some food. He'd heard so much about the restaurant, from the infamous stories about a couple of violent incidents there to the mouthwatering menu created by famed chef Devon Harris. He knew he couldn't leave Charlotte without trying the restaurant.

As he pulled into the parking lot, he called Chante to see how her day had gone. But her phone when straight to voice mail. He couldn't help but wonder if everything had worked out in her favor.

Walking into the restaurant, he wasn't surprised to see how busy it was. He hoped that meant the food was just that good.

"Welcome to Hometown Delights," the

hostess said. "Will this be dine in or carry out?"

"Carry out," Zach said.

"No problem. You can place your order at the bar," she said, then pointed him in that direction. Heading to the bar, Zach was taken with the ambience of the restaurant. Natural light shone over the lunch patrons, but he could tell that at night the lanterns in the middle of the tables would cast a deep glow and give the room a romantic tone. The bar area was wide and spacious, giving people who were on a date a chance to lean in close to each other and someone drowning his or her sorrows a chance to be alone.

"Welcome to Hometown Delights," a tall woman with shoulder-length auburn hair said. She had a smile that would light up the darkest room. She was fine but didn't hold a candle to Chante. "What can I get for you?"

"I heard you guys have the best chocolate cake in the city."

"The state, actually," she said with a smile.

"I need to get one of those . . . and," he said as he looked down at the menu, "two orders of the New Orleans Chicken, a side of sweet potato fries, and a bottle of your best merlot."

"That sounds good. Taking a road trip?"

She nodded toward the picnic basket he'd set on the edge of the bar.

"Heading to Charleston, but I couldn't leave without trying this place," he said.

"Well, as one of the owners of *this place,* I have to say thank you, and you made some great choices for road-traveling food," she said, then extended her hand to him. "Serena Billups."

"Nice to meet you, Serena. Zachary Harrington."

"I've heard of you," she said. "Nice to see you here."

He reached into his wallet and handed her his business card. "If you ever plan to expand in New York, let me know."

"And face the wrath of Solomon Crawford? I don't think so. If we expand into New York, it would probably be as a hotel restaurant. You know his wife is another one of the owners here."

"Hometown Delights is bigger than that," he said. "Think about it."

"I'll talk to my partners. Let me put your order in," she said as she sauntered away.

Zach pulled out his phone and dialed Chante again. Voice mail. "What in the hell is going on," he muttered as he shoved his phone back into his pocket.

■ ■ ■ ■

Chante sat across from Jacob Dillinger, the assistant state attorney general, with her poker face intact. "This is not acceptable," she said. "Mrs. Chavis was the primary moneymaker in the home, and for the last three years, the state of North Carolina held her money hostage. No interest was accrued on the money, and we know that if this were the other way around, she'd be hit with all kinds of penalties. So you're going to tell me that she doesn't deserve something extra?"

"You want the taxpayers of this state to suffer because you think your client deserves more?" he asked.

Chante crossed her legs. "Jacob, my client is a taxpayer, and you didn't mind making her suffer."

"I don't know about the public apology."

Chante rose to her feet. "Then I guess we will see you in court."

"Wait. No one wants a drawn-out legal case, but . . ."

"All you need to do is write an apology and release it to the media, and pay my client what you owe her with interest. But all of this is moot if you don't acknowledge that she was wronged by the system."

"We were doing our . . ."

Chante placed her hands on Jacob's desk. "Amanda Chavis wasn't the judge in any of those cases. She's never been on the bench, and she never benefited from the money that Harlan received and hid in offshore accounts. You discovered that in the investigation but still froze assets that Amanda had brought into the marriage. Assets that she needed to run a business that had nothing to do with the legal system and that had been established before she even knew who the hell Harlan Chavis was. You owe her money and an apology. We're not letting this go without both." Chante leaned back in her chair and shot Jacob a cold look.

"Fine," he said. "I just need to get my boss's approval, and we'll have this wrapped up by the end of the day."

"Why don't you call your boss now? I think Amanda has waited long enough for the state to acknowledge its wrongdoing."

"Give me a minute." As Jacob walked out of the office, Amanda turned to Chante.

"You're amazing," she said.

"I knew this was important to you, and I told you I was going to get results."

"So, if the state won't apologize, should I refuse the money?"

"We're taking the money, but I know you're going to get that apology because they are as wrong as two left shoes, and I'm sure they don't want the media coverage that would come from the trial or the campaign that Liza would create on social media."

Amanda was about to respond when Jacob walked back into the office. "Ms. Britt, Mrs. Chavis, we have a deal."

"When will the paperwork get here?" Chante asked.

"Two hours tops," Jacob said.

Chante smiled and crossed over to him with her hand extended. Jacob gave her a limp handshake, which led her to believe that his boss wasn't happy about the way things had gone. Oh well.

CHAPTER 25

Chante and Amanda were standing in front of the press again, with the state's attorney at their side. This time, the uncomfortable questions were being hurled at Jacob. Chante smiled as he struggled to answer why it had taken the state so long to return Amanda's money to her when she wasn't involved with Harlan Chavis's crimes.

"We had to conduct an investigation to make sure the illegal funds that former judge Chavis received weren't included in the accounts that belonged to Mrs. Chavis," Jacob said. "Chante Britt, her attorney, provided a forensic account of Mrs. Chavis's accounts and the money she'd brought into the marriage. The state has determined that all of the funds belonging to Mrs. Chavis weren't received illegally."

"Why did it take so long for Mrs. Chavis to be cleared of any wrongdoing?" a reporter asked.

"Things like this take time. It would've been irresponsible of us to rush our due diligence. The state of North Carolina wants to issue a public apology to Mrs. Amanda Chavis for any inconvenience she suffered during the course of the investigation, and we hope that today's decision will give her what she needs to reclaim her life. Thank you." Jacob stepped back from the podium, despite the questions the reporters called out.

"Do you want to address them?" Chante whispered to Amanda.

She shook her head. "I got what I wanted, and I don't owe anyone an explanation. Thank you, Chante," Amanda said as tears welled up in her eyes.

"Let's go," Chante said, and she took Amanda's elbow and headed away from the press. Once they were out of the spotlight of the media, Amanda hugged Chante tightly. "I'm glad I didn't listen to Taiwon. Chante, you're brilliant, and you will go far with your law firm. Now I'm going on vacation," she said.

"You should. I think I'm going to do the same thing," Chante replied. When Amanda left, Chante pulled her phone out of her briefcase and turned it on. She couldn't wait to call Zach and tell him the good news.

"I was beginning to think you'd forgotten all about me," Zach said.

"I could never do that. I just got the State of North Carolina to admit it was wrong, and I got my client all of her money back. It has been an amazing day. But it will be more amazing when I see you."

"Where are you now?"

"At my office."

"I'll meet you there, and you can get part one of your surprise," he said.

"Which is?"

"The keyword, again, is *surprise.* See you shortly." Chante smiled as she looked at her phone after Zach hung up. Her phone rang again, and she saw Liza's face on her screen. She knew her friend was going to be pissed off about her missing the *Charlotte Today* interview.

"Hey, girl," Chante said.

"Had I not seen you standing with Amanda and the state's attorney eating crow, I'd be so pissed with you right now."

"Well, I knew this would change the conversation today. I just proved that I get results."

"Good job. I'm proud of you, sis!"

"Thank you. Now I can get on with my life, and you can go to Raleigh and make a baby with the senator."

"There you go. Can my husband and I have a little more time together before we have our son?"

"Nope. I want to see you with a baby and throw you the biggest baby shower ever."

"You and Zach should make a baby then. I'm the better party planner, remember."

"Girl, please. We're not even close to being there."

"Whatever you say. Oh, Erica Bryant wants to interview you and Amanda."

"I don't think so. I want to stay off the media's radar for a while."

"Can't say that I blame you. I'm enjoying being back behind the scenes."

Chante was about to reply when Zach walked in carrying bags from Hometown Delight and a picnic basket. "Liza, I have to go."

"Tell Zach I said hello," she said. "I'd love to meet him one day."

"I'll let him know." Chante hung up the phone and crossed over to Zach. "Hello, sweetie."

"You look so professional," he said as he set the food on her desk. "And it's sexy as hell." Zack kissed her softly. "I missed you today."

"Well, I was out kicking ass and taking names," she said excitedly.

"Congratulations," he said. "That will teach those people who didn't make you partner."

"That's right," she said, then inhaled deeply. "That food smells amazing."

"I heard a lot of good things about this place. Let's eat, then hit the road."

Zach opened the bags and handed Chante one of the containers of New Orleans Chicken.

"Where are we going?"

"It's a surprise," he said.

"I really hate surprises. Just tell me."

Zach opened his food and took a bite of his chicken. "Nope," he said after swallowing. "This is good."

She pouted at him and grabbed a fork from the bag. "You're not playing fair."

"I'll tell you one thing," he said as he wiped his hands on a napkin. "We're riding a pony."

Chante smiled. "You rented a Mustang?"

"A convertible one."

"So you have to tell me where we're going because I'm driving."

"That's what GPS is for. The sooner we finish eating, the sooner we can leave. What's the next case on your docket?"

"I'm clear for the week."

"Good, because I might bring you back

next week."

"Back from where?"

Zach sat down across from her desk and shook his head. "You can keep asking, counselor, but I'm not saying a word."

"But I need to know what to pack," she said.

"That's taken care of," he said. "You can buy what you need when we get there. I got you."

Chante crossed over to him and took his food from his hands. "I'm going to let you get me right now." Covering his mouth with hers, she kissed him. Zach pulled her closer as their kiss deepened.

"You taste better than the chicken," he said when they broke the kiss. "I've wanted to do that all day."

"There's something else I wanted to do all day," she said, then rose to her feet. Chante slowly unbuttoned her blouse, then pushed it off her shoulders. Zach watched in rapt attention as she slowly stripped for him. Standing there in her pink lace panty-and-bra set made his desire rise like fog from a lake.

"You're so beautiful," he said.

"And you have too many clothes on." Chante reached down and unbuckled his slacks. Zach's erection sprang forward as she stroked him back and forth. Zach lifted his hips as she tugged at his pants so that she could push them down to his ankles. Zach kissed her breasts until her nipples perked up through the lace of her bra as she wrapped her legs around his waist. Moaning, she stroked the back of his head, urging him to continue. His erection pressed against her thighs, and heat radiated from every pore in her body. "I want you," she moaned.

"You got me, and you can have me any way you want," he said as he parted her legs. Zach could feel how ready she was even before he removed her lace panties. Slipping his index finger inside her, Zach sought out her throbbing bud. Chante arched her back. "Yes," she moaned.

"Damn, you feel so good," Zach said.

"Make me feel better," she said as she ground against his finger. "Need. You. Inside."

Zach brought his mouth down on top of Chante's as he pushed the crotch of her panties to the side. She moaned in delight as his tongue glided across hers and he plunged inside. She rode him slow, and he thrust deeper and deeper inside her. Chante gripped his shoulders as she felt her body come closer to climax.

"That's it, baby," he groaned. "Let it go. Come for me."

"Oh," she moaned, unable to hold back her climax. She exploded, and Zach's orgasm wasn't far behind. Chante closed her eyes and leaned against his chest. Feeling the heat of his seed oozing down her leg, she expelled a sigh. "We have to stop being so careless."

"I know. And I'm sorry," he said.

"We're both responsible, but we have to do better."

Zach kissed her chin. Part of him wondered again what a baby with Chante would look like. *Wait, now you're just being ridiculous,* he thought as he watched her cross the room. He did love that woman, though. From the tips of her toes to the top of her head.

"Zach, did you hear me?" she asked breaking into his thoughts.

"Huh?"

"Do you want to take a shower before we leave?"

"Sounds good. This office has everything, huh?"

She nodded as Zach crossed over to her. "The person who used to have this office practically lived here for a while."

"I hope you don't plan to be like the last

tenant," he said as he pressed her against the wall.

"Not if you plan to make it worth my while not to be." She winked at him, then opened the door to the bathroom.

Gabby pulled into the parking lot of Chante's office, hoping to catch her boss so that she could tell her how proud she was to be a part of her business. Smiling, she hopped out of her car and headed for the entrance.

"Gabby," Robert called out. Turning around, she was surprised to see him.

"What are you doing here?"

"That's a better question for me to ask you. I guess you're just like the rest of them."

"What are you talking about?"

"I thought you loved me," he said as he stepped closer to her. "But you teamed up with these bitches to bring me down." Robert grabbed her by the collar of her shirt. "You said you loved me."

"You said I wasn't good enough! Get your hands off me," she said as she pushed him. Robert hauled off and slapped her.

"You aren't! I had to give up everything because of her, and now you're working with her! What's the plan? How is Chante trying to ruin me now?"

Gabby held her cheek, shocked at how crazy Robert was acting. "You'd better get away from here before I call the police. You're sick! That's why she left you!"

He pushed Gabby, causing her to fall backward. "You're no better than her! When I needed you, you weren't there for me. Nobody ever thinks about what I need!" He stood over her and sneered. "You bitches are going pay today." Robert reached into his waistband and pulled out a gun. "You deserve to die."

Gabby screamed at the top of her lungs, and Robert slapped her across the face with the gun, knocking her unconscious.

"Did you hear that?" Chante asked as she slipped into a maxi dress. Zach nodded.

"Sounds like someone is in trouble," he said as he stepped into his pants. Chante crossed over to her desk and looked out the window.

"Oh my God, it's Gabby." She picked up her phone and started to dial 9-1-1 when the door to her office was kicked open. Robert burst inside with a crazed look in his eyes and pointed a gun at her.

"Put the phone down, bitch!"

"Robert, what are you doing here?"

Chante asked nervously.

"Saw you all over TV today. Still playing the victim and ruining people's lives. That ends today."

Zach took a step toward Robert, who then turned the gun on him. "This ain't about you," he said. "But I will shoot you if you try to be a hero."

"Look, man," Zach said, "you don't want to do this."

"Don't tell me what I want to do! She ruined my life, my career, and any chance that I have for a future." He turned back to Chante and pointed the gun at her chest. "You're just like my mother."

Chante threw her hands up. "Robert, I didn't . . ."

"Shut! Up!"

Zach stood still and looked around the room for a weapon he could use to disarm Robert. There was no way in hell that he'd stand there and let this man hurt Chante. He figured the lamp on the table near the door might work. He just needed to get over there without arousing Robert's suspicions.

He took a quick step as Robert kept ranting at Chante. "All you had to do was play your position. I would've been a great senator, but you let Liza get in your head. What man doesn't cheat? This isn't a fairy tale where some prince charming is going to be your everything. Especially to a cold bitch like you. You know why I was with someone else? Because you bored me. We were good on paper. You would've looked good on my arm at political events. You'd know what to say and who to talk to when I would need you to help me get things done. But no! You wanted to ruin me."

"I never wanted that. I just wanted you to leave me alone," she said. "Robert, please put the gun down. You don't have to do this."

"I do have to do this! You're never going to learn if I don't."

"Learn what?"

"Shut up!" He fired a shot that narrowly missed her shoulder. Zach leapt into action, grabbing the lamp and smashing it into Robert's head. Robert fell to the floor, and Zach kicked the gun from his hand. Chante grabbed the phone and called 9-1-1. Robert stirred and stretched his hand out for the gun. But Zach grabbed it and pointed at him.

"Give me one reason why I shouldn't blow your head off."

Robert spat at him. "She's going to ruin you too. You can't trust that bitch." Zach stopped himself from kicking Robert in the face.

"Don't say another word," Zach snapped. "Idiot."

Chante shivered as she leaned against the window. "The-the police are on their way."

"Are you all right?" Zach asked, not taking his eyes or the gun off Robert.

"Yeah," Chante said. When she heard the sirens, she released a sigh of relief. Within seconds, two officers burst in the office. "Drop the gun!" one of them yelled as he eyed the scene. Zach dropped the gun and put his hands up. When the officer crossed over to Zach, Chante yelled.

"No, he's not the one who tried to kill me! It's that fool on the ground," she said.

The other officer nodded and grabbed Robert, then slapped handcuffs on him.

"Are you two all right?" an officer asked as he collected the gun from the floor.

"Yes, but what about Gabby? She was in the parking lot, and I don't know what he did to her."

"Medics are out there with her now."

Zach crossed over to Chante and pulled her into his arms. She was trembling like a leaf in a hurricane. He kissed her on the forehead. "It's all right, babe, it's all right."

"Ma'am," one of the officers said, "I think

you should go to the hospital and get checked out."

Zach nodded in agreement. "You do need to get checked out," he said.

"Come with me," the officer said to Zach.

"Of course," he said. Zach and Chante waited until Robert was led out of the office before heading out themselves. A second ambulance pulled up, and the paramedics rushed over to Chante. She looked at the first set of paramedics who were attending to Gabby. When she saw movement from the stretcher, she expelled a sigh of relief.

As she was loaded onto the ambulance, Zach climbed in with her, holding her hand tightly.

"I'm guessing this isn't the surprise you were talking about," she said.

"Not at all."

CHAPTER 26

It didn't take long for word of the shooting to get out. When Chante arrived at the hospital, there were media trucks in the parking lot and Chante's phone was ringing nonstop. Zach was beginning to regret not putting a shirt on before hopping into the ambulance with Chante, but he'd been totally focused on her well-being.

"This is just great," she muttered as an intake nurse approached her with a wheel-chair. "I can walk."

"Hospital policy, ma'am," the woman said. "I have to wheel you in."

"All right."

Zach nodded at the nurse, then said, "Let me push her." The nurse pointed him toward the registration area.

"I should've never said I wanted to come to the hospital," Chante whispered. "I'm fine, and . . ."

"Chante," he said, "you were trembling

and could barely breathe. Even if you hadn't come in the ambulance, I would've brought you here to make sure you were all right."

Her cell phone rang before she could reply. Looking down and seeing it was Liza, Chante answered the call.

"Chante, where are you?" Liza asked frantically. "And please tell me this is a joke."

"I'm at Carolinas Medical Center."

"We're on our way."

"Liza!" The line went dead. Zach kneeled down beside Chante's chair.

"Your friend is coming, right?"

Chante nodded, then wrapped her arms around his neck. He felt her warm tears on his shoulder. Stroking her back, Zach kissed her cheek. "Chante, it's fine now. He's locked up, and you're going to be all right."

"I just can't believe this happened. He tried to kill me. I thought I was going to die in that office."

"I wasn't going to let that happen," he said. "If I had to stand in front of that bullet, I was ready."

"You saved my life," she sobbed. "If you hadn't been there . . ."

He pulled back and looked into her eyes. "But I was there, and I'm always going to be there. I love you."

"I love you too."

Zach kissed her gently and wiped her tears away with his thumb.

After registering, Chante and Zach sat in the emergency room waiting area until a doctor could give her the all clear. Before the doctor came to see them, Liza and Jackson burst into the room. Jackson pointed at Chante and tapped his wife on the shoulder. They crossed over to her and Zach.

"Chante," Liza said, "are you all right?"

Chante, who had her head on Zach's shoulder, looked up at her sorority sister and started crying again. The women hugged tightly.

"He looked so crazy, and I think he tried to kill Gabby."

"Are you serious? My God."

"He kept ranting about his mother and how we ruined his life."

Liza shook her head. "That sick bastard."

"Chante Britt," a nurse called out. "Chante Britt."

Zach rose to his feet and touched Chante's elbow. "Come on, babe. We'll be back," Zach said.

Liza smiled at Zach. "Thanks for taking care of my sister." He smiled and nodded at her.

Once Chante and Zach were in the exam

room, he held her hand. "Your surprise is going to be even better now. You're going to rest for at least two days, and I don't want to hear anything about it."

"This is one time when you won't get an argument from me. I'm not even going to ask what the surprise is anymore. I just can't get over all of this." Chante closed her eyes and saw Robert standing there with the gun. He didn't even look like the man she'd known. The expression in his eyes was crazed and scary. What did he think killing her would've done for him?

"Chante?" Zach asked. She opened her eyes and smiled when she saw the face of her savior, the man she loved.

"Yes?"

"You were breathing funny," he said.

She stroked his cheek. "I was just thinking about that moment in my office. I just don't . . ."

"Shh," he said. "Don't think about what could've happened, all right. The what-ifs don't matter." Leaning in and kissing her, Zach knew they were going to stay in their hideaway for at least two weeks when the doctor gave her a clean bill of health.

Finally, the doctor entered the exam room. "Hello, Mr. and Mrs. Britt," he said.

Neither of them bothered to correct him.

"How are you feeling, Mrs. Britt? Any shortness of breath?" He pulled out his stethoscope and checked her heart and lungs.

"Earlier she was having some choppy breathing," Zach said. The doctor nodded.

"That's expected. I can prescribe a sedative if you're going to have an issue sleeping tonight."

"No," she said. "I don't want a sedative."

The doctor nodded. "There is only one thing I want you to do, and that's talk to a counselor. I can get a list of names for you and even set up an appointment."

Chante nodded. "I'd like that, thank you."

The doctor touched her shoulder and walked out of the room. She turned to Zach and noticed for the first time that he didn't have a shirt on.

"I can't believe you've been running around this place with no shirt on," she said with a smile.

"The shirt didn't matter, I had to make sure you were all right," he replied. "I just hate that I'm meeting your friends like this."

A nurse walked into the exam room with discharge papers and a T-shirt, which Zach was very thankful for.

When the couple returned to the waiting area, Liza and Jackson approached them.

"We've got to figure out how to get out of here while avoiding the media," Liza said.

"I hate cameras, and I don't want to talk to anyone about what happened," Chante said.

"I'm sure we have to give the police a statement before we leave town," Zach said.

"And where are you going?" Liza asked. "By the way, I'm Liza Franklin, and this is my husband, Jackson."

"Nice to meet you. I'm Zach Harrington."

"You were there?" Liza asked as she blinked back tears. "I feel so responsible for this."

"Liza," Jackson said as if they'd been having the conversation. "You didn't do this."

"He's right," Chante said. "Who knew Robert was psychotic?"

Liza ran her hand across her forehead. "I never thought he was dangerous, and if he'd hurt you, I think . . ."

"I see why you and Chante are so close," Zach said. "You two are just alike. Listen, he didn't hurt her. And we're not going to focus on what could've been when we need to focus on what is right in front of us."

"Amen, brother," Jackson said. "Do you guys need a ride to the police station, or are you going back to Chante's office?"

Chante shivered as she thought about going back to that office. A place that was supposed to be her salvation, her difference maker. Now she wanted nothing to do with it. At least not today.

"Just take me home first," Chante said. "I can't . . ."

"All right, I'll stay with you," Liza said. "And Zach can pick up your car or anything you need from the office."

"Yes," Zach said as he kissed her cheek. "And if the police are there, I'll let them know you aren't ready to give a statement."

"No," Chante said, "I want to get that over with as soon as possible. Just have them meet me at my house."

Zach nodded. "Whatever you want."

As they got into Jackson's SUV, Chante squeezed Zach's hand. "Thank you," she whispered. "I'm sure this isn't what you expected when you came down here."

"Doesn't matter," he said. "I'm glad I'm here for you. I love you."

"Love you too," she said, then leaned against his shoulder and closed her eyes.

Robert sat in the interrogation room at the headquarters of the Charlotte-Mecklenburg Police Department. How did he let those bitches bring him down like this? He'd never been on this side of the table. Most of his clients didn't even get arrested. Now here he was, looking like a common criminal. Leaning back in the cold steel chair, he wished he hadn't missed when he'd fired at Chante. The only thing that would've made it better would've been for Liza to be on the other end of the bullet. This was all their fault.

His career was over, both law and politics. Part of him regretted hurting Gabby. She was just a dumb little girl. But she should've known better than to team up with Chante, of all people!

The door to the interrogation room opened, and a burly detective walked in with two cups of coffee.

"Mr. Montgomery, would you like some coffee?" he asked.

"I'd like to get out of here," Robert said. "This is all a big misunderstanding."

The detective snorted and opened the file folder that lay on the table. "A misunderstanding? Looks like we're talking aggravated assault, kidnapping, and assault with a deadly weapon. That's a hell of a misunderstanding. How did we get here? I mean, not too long ago, I was voting for you to be my senator. Now you're sitting here facing some serious charges."

"I'm not saying a word until I get a lawyer."

"So you won't be representing yourself?" The big detective smirked.

"Those women set me up. Ruined everything I worked for, and I'm the one in handcuffs. That makes no sense."

"Who are these *women* you're referring to?"

"I have the right to remain silent, and that's what I'm about to do."

"Fine. But if there was some provocation or you were defending yourself, you should tell me, and we can work on making this case more of a misdemeanor than a felony."

"I know these tricks, and you must think I didn't pass the bar. I've asked for an attorney. You can't question me anymore."

The detective pushed the cup of coffee over to Robert. "Enjoy your coffee, Mr. Montgomery. It's Starbucks, and it will probably be a long time before you have any coffee as good as this." He rose to his feet and left Robert alone in the interrogation room.

When Liza and Chante arrived at Chante's house, she felt as if she was taking her first real breath since Robert burst into her office. Plopping down on the sofa, she brought her knees up to her chest.

"I'm going to make some tea," Liza said when she looked at her friend.

"How about opening that bottle of Chardonnay in the bottom of the refrigerator," Chante said.

"My girl," Liza replied. "Because I don't know a damned thing about making tea." Liza headed for the kitchen and grabbed the wine, two glasses, and corkscrew. She returned to the living room and set the bottle and glasses in the middle of the coffee table.

"How could we have been so wrong about Robert?" Chante asked as she grabbed the bottle and opened it.

"Maybe he's mentally sick and hid it all these years. I don't know, but when I heard about the shooting at your office, I was beyond scared."

"Liza, he looked like a madman when he came in there. And poor Gabby. I thought he'd killed her." Chante filled the wineglasses.

"Just tell me that he didn't walk in on you and Zach doing . . ."

"No! Thank God. We'd just gotten out of the shower and were about to head off on this surprise trip he'd planned. Then we heard the scream. As soon as I picked up the phone . . ." Chante's voice trailed off, and her hand trembled, sloshing wine on the sofa. Liza held her friend's hand and took the glass from her. "Calm down. Maybe you don't need this."

"Liza, I'm fine," Chante said. "I just thank God that Zach was there. When Robert shot at me, you would've thought I was with Superman. He smashed him in the head with that ugly lamp of yours."

"My Tiffany lamp?"

"Yes. I was going to donate it to Goodwill. I guess it's a good thing I didn't."

Liza thumped her friend on the arm. "Anyway. Well, at least he took that creep down in style."

"Robert thinks we ruined his life, Liza. Has that man ever accepted responsibility for anything?"

"Robert has always had issues with women, and I know it's because of his mother. But his past doesn't give him an excuse to act like a fool. And he damned sure can't be rolling around Charlotte shooting at people. I guess we're lucky he wasn't a better shot."

Chante reached for her glass of wine with a steadier hand and took a sip. "And that's why I'm sitting here a ball of nerves. I could've died today."

"But you didn't, and that's what you should be thankful for. That and Zachary Harrington. He's fine. Not as fine as my husband, but honey, you hit the jackpot with him."

"Really? Weren't you the one telling me to have a secret relationship with this jackpot?"

"After a man saves your life, you have to tell the world about him. You need to take his last name and all of that."

Chante laughed. "You're going too far."

"Anyway," Liza said, "I think he's a keeper."

"I know he is, but I'm still wondering how we're going to make this long-distance relationship work."

Liza sipped her wine. "You two will figure it out. Hell, after what happened today, I get the feeling that he's going to be by your side for a long time."

Chante set her glass aside and smiled at Liza. "I like the way that sounds."

A few seconds later, there was a knock at the front door. "I'll get it," Liza said. "Hopefully, it's the guys."

Chante hoped so as well. When she heard the click of cameras and Liza cursing, she knew that the media was running with this story. "This is some bull," Chante muttered as she crossed over to the window. The street was lined with media trucks. She saw a Mustang zoom down the street, followed by Jackson's SUV.

"You all need to get off the property and give Miss Britt privacy," Chante heard Liza say, then slam the door. "Damned vultures," Liza said when she returned to the living room.

"I hope Zach and Jackson can make it inside without a problem. I saw them pull up while you were shooing the media away."

Liza looked out the window. "They aren't leaving," she said. "And it looks like the police are coming in with Jackson and Zach."

Chante sighed. She wanted to give her statement and get the hell out of Dodge. "Good, maybe Zach and I can be far away from here before midnight."

"Getting away is a good idea," Liza said. "But you know that when you come back, the reporters are still going to have questions."

"Then I guess you're going to have to write a nice statement for me requesting privacy." Chante took a sip of her wine.

"You're lucky I love you or I'd send you a bill." Liza winked at Chante and picked up her wineglass.

"I know. But you also know I can't afford

you right now," she replied. Liza crossed over to the door when she heard a knock. Chante was so excited to hear Zach's voice. Putting her wine down, she crossed over to him and hugged him tightly.

"The detectives want to talk to you," Zach said. "But if you're not up to it . . ."

"No, I would tell my own client to give a statement while it's still fresh."

"Zoe said if you need her to help you with the case, she's willing to do whatever you need."

"Tell your sister thanks, but I'm hoping I won't need any help and the DA will get it right — if it even goes to trial."

Zach kissed her forehead. "We're not going to worry about that."

"Excuse me, Miss Britt. I'm Detective Marcus Thomas."

Chante extended her hand to him. "Please call me Chante," she said.

"I'd like to take your statement. Mr. Harrington gave us his at your office, and I understand that you two are going out of town for a little while."

Chante nodded and led the detective into the living room. She almost regretted the half-empty bottle of wine she and Liza had left on the middle of the table.

"I didn't drink all of this by myself," she

said when she noticed the detective looking at the wine bottle.

"After the day you had, it would be understandable."

Zach wrapped his arm around Chante's shoulder as Detective Thomas began asking her about what happened inside her office. As she told her story, Zach could feel her tense up. He gently stroked her arm as she spoke, and his touch seemed to calm her.

"One last question," Detective Thomas said.

"What's that?"

"When's the wedding?"

Chante looked from the detective to Zach. "What?"

"I see a lot of couples in my line of work, and I have to say, you two have some amazing chemistry."

"Put Montgomery away and you'll be on the VIP guest list," Zach said.

"Miss Britt, thank you for your time," Detective Thomas said as he rose to his feet. "And if there are still a bunch of reporters out there, then I will threaten to arrest them if they don't leave."

"Thank you," Chante said. Zach rose to his feet and escorted the detective to the door. Then he turned to Chante.

"Go pack," he said.

She gave him a mock salute, then headed for the kitchen, where Jackson and Liza had been hanging out.

"Everything all right?" Jackson asked as he sipped a cup of coffee.

"Yes, we can finally leave now," Chante said. "I just hope no one has a clue as to where we're going."

"While you were talking with the detective, your grandmother called, and she is really mad at you. I told her you would call her, and she said she's going to take you over her knee," Liza said, then handed Chante her phone.

Chante burst out laughing. "And I thought she was still on her cruise."

"Are you going to see your mom?" Liza asked.

Sighing, she shook her head. Typical, her Grammy cared more about her than her mother did. Chante wouldn't be surprised if her mother was trying to figure out how to keep this story from the neighbors for fear of embarrassment.

"I'll think about that later. Zach told me to pack a bag, and I wanted to thank you both for being here for me."

"Chante, you're family," Jackson said. "And your dude Zach is cool. He really cares about you. And he's a much better man than me because I think I would've pistol-whipped Robert until the police got there."

"Ooh, don't talk like that," Liza said. "You know when you go all Batman that gets me hot."

"Oh, Lord," Chante, said then rolled her eyes.

"Do we need to put a fire out before heading back to Raleigh?" he asked with a seductive tone to his voice. Liza nodded. Chante shook her head.

"Just lock up when you leave! Liza still has a key." Chante went upstairs and packed two bags. When Zach walked into her bedroom with a smile on his face, she was so ready to go.

"I see Liza and Jackson have made themselves at home," he said with a chuckle.

"Still in the honeymoon phase, I guess. If you're ready to go, so am I. My grammy's threatening to spank me."

"Now, you know that's my job," he quipped.

"You are so bad," she replied. "Let's go."

The ride to Charleston was quite uneventful, and Zach was thrilled. Chante slept most of the way. He imagined that her adrenaline rush had worn off and she needed the rest. It was a good thing Chante had loaded her grandmother's address into the GPS before she went to sleep. Zach wanted her to rest as long and as much as she could. When he pulled into her grandmother's driveway, the place looked totally different from when they'd hidden out in the cottage before. The renovations were complete, and the house looked as if it belonged on the cover of a home and garden magazine.

"Chante," he said as he put the car in park, "we're here."

Her eyes fluttered open, and she looked up at the house. "It feels good to be home," she said as she stretched her arms above her head. "Why did you let me sleep so long?"

"Because you needed to?" he said with a shoulder shrug. The porch light flickered on, and Chante opened the passenger door as an older woman stepped onto the porch. Zach was barely out of the car by the time Chante was up the steps and embracing the woman.

"Girl, do you know how worried I've been about you? And the news made it seem as if you were dead. I thought I was going to have to slip your mama a sleeping pill. And who is Zachary Harrington?"

Zach cleared his throat. "That would be me," he said.

The older woman let Chante go and then wrapped her arms around him and gave him a tight hug. "You saved my baby." She took a step back. "And you're so handsome. Very handsome. This is the kind of man you have babies with."

"Grammy!" Chante exclaimed. "Zach, you have to forgive my grammy, Elsie Mae. She is something else."

"Chante Britt, you know I speak my mind, and I don't care. Come on, let's go inside before we become dinner for the mosquitoes."

"I like her," Zach whispered to Chante.

"I knew you would."

Elsie led them into a grand sitting room, where there was a teapot and a snifter of brandy sitting on the table. "Elsie?" a man said as he walked into the room.

"Theo, I told you my grandbaby was on the way."

"Hi, Mr. Theo, how are you?" Chante said.

He crossed over to Chante and gave her a tight hug. "Just fine, darling. I'm glad you got here because this woman was worried about you."

"Yes, I was, but I didn't know she had her own personal hero. Theo, this is Zachary

Harrington, the man who saved my baby from a maniac."

Theo shook hands with Zach, and Zach could've sworn he'd seen that man somewhere before. "Nice to meet you, son," Theo said. "I do hope you two will join us in a nightcap."

"Of course they will," Elsie said as he pushed them toward that sofa. "Besides, I want to tell you the amazing news."

"What news?" Chante asked.

Theo and Elsie joined hands. "We're married."

Chante hugged her grandmother and Mr. Theo. "This is wonderful! And what took you so long?"

Elsie pointed her finger at Chante. "I wish your mother had been so happy. But she's being such a drama queen right now, I can't deal with her. I just hope she has the good sense to act like she's happy at our garden party on Saturday."

"And then leave for our cruise in Greece," Theo said excitedly.

"There's one more thing," Elsie said. "And I know your mama isn't going to like this either, but I'm having this house declared a historic landmark."

"Why wouldn't she like that? It adds more history to our family."

Theo and Elsie exchanged glances. "I'm not going to be living here anymore. This house represents my past. A marriage that wasn't the greatest . . . But a lot of good things happened in this house that the city and all of her visitors should know about. Plans for the Stono Rebellion started right here on this property. And this was the first house owned by a black person in this county. It's been in our family for centuries, and your mother is going to blow a gasket. But she'll get over it."

Chante smiled with pride. "I think it's a great idea, but where are you guys going to live now?"

"Well, when we're in town, we'll stay at my place," Theo said. "But my Elsie wants to travel the world. And since there has been this renewed interest in my music, we're going to be getting paid to travel."

"I knew you looked familiar," Zach said. "Theodore Tanner, the man with the golden voice."

"Guilty as charged."

"I'm happy for you, Grammy," Chante said. "Let's toast with some of that Magnolia wine from Irvin Vineyards."

"Stay out of my wine cellar, girl!" Elsie joked. "Theo, will you be a dear and bring the wine up?"

A few moments later, the four of them were toasting with the sweet wine. And Zach was sure that when Miss Elsie started yawning, it was because she was tired, not trying to drop a hint to him and Chante.

"Why don't we get together for breakfast in the morning?" Chante asked as she and Zach rose from their seats.

"As long as you mean lunch, I'm all for it," Elsie said.

"Grammy, you're a mess." Chante and her grandmother hugged.

"I'm so glad you're okay. You don't know how scared I was." Then Elsie turned to Zach. "You keep taking care of my grand-baby, and I won't hold being a Yankee against you."

"I'm going to take care of her for a long time," Zach said as he looked at Chante.

"All right, you two, get out of here."

CHAPTER 27

It was close to midnight when Chante and Zach checked into the bed and breakfast. She was glad she'd slept on the way into Charleston because she was wide awake now. "This view is amazing," she said as she stepped out onto the balcony.

"I think I have a better view," Zach said as he leaned on the doorjamb and watched Chante walk the length of the wide balcony.

She turned around and faced him with a saucy grin on her face. "Is that so? Because you haven't seen anything yet." Chante pulled her dress off and stood there in her strapless bra and lace thong.

"Damn!"

She sauntered over to him. Taking her into his arms, Zach brought his lips down on top of hers, kissing her passionately. With one hand, he unsnapped her barely there bra and tossed it aside. Her skin felt like silk underneath his fingertips as he stroked her back. He couldn't believe that just a few hours ago he'd almost lost Chante. He brought his hands up to her breasts, softly kneading them until her nipples were as hard as diamonds. She moaned softly, like the warm wind that blew over them. Zach pulled her thong off and spun her around.

"You're a sexy work of art," he moaned as he led her to the wicker sofa in the corner of the balcony.

"I love you so much," he said before kissing her again. Slowly their tongues danced as Chante reached down and tugged at his belt buckle, but he grabbed her wrist.

"Slow down, baby. I want to taste you first." He flipped Chante on her back and held her wrists. With a deliberate pace, he explored the curves of her body, using his tongue as his guide.

Starting with her breasts, he kissed and sucked until her nipples hardened. Chante moaned as he inched down her stomach, tasting her as if she was made from the nectar of the gods. Clutching his shoulders, she nearly exploded as his lips made their way to the folds of skin between her thighs. Her legs shook as his tongue found her throbbing bud and sent ripples of pleasure through her. She tossed her head back and called out Zach's name over and over again like a mantra. Reversing his direction, Zach found his way to Chante's lips, and she could taste her essence on his tongue as he kissed her deeply, making her heady with passion.

"Zach, I need you," Chante moaned as he covered her body with his. He slipped his hands between her thighs and felt the heat radiating from her core. When he felt how wet and ready she was for him, Zach got even harder. Wrapping her legs around his waist, he fell into her hot wetness and felt as if he'd died and gone to heaven.

No other woman had moved him the way Chante did. It was more than sex; they had a connection that he reveled in. She was a part of his soul, and as they ebbed back and forth on the edge of ecstasy, Zach knew he'd never love another woman as much as he loved Chante.

Wrapped up in each other's arms, the duo fell asleep on the sofa, glad to be high up in the air so nobody could snap a picture of their ecstasy.

The chirping of birds woke Chante, but the warmth of Zach's arms made it hard to move.

"Mmm, good morning," he said, his voice thick with sleep.

"It's a good and beautiful morning," she said. Chante sat up and pointed at the horizon. The sunrise had painted the sky with blue, gold, and a hint of pink. "Grammy used to call this the love sky. I finally get it now."

"The love sky? It's almost as beautiful as you are."

"Zach, we're back where it all started, only there won't be any drinks thrown this time."

"Nope, but we will be eating oysters tonight." He winked at her. "I love you Chante, and I don't ever want to lose you."

"You won't."

"I know I won't," he said. "Marry me."

"I-I don't know what to say."

"Yes would be the appropriate answer. Last time we were here, our engagement was fake, but I heard a rumor that we've fallen in love."

"How are we going to make that work? You live in New York, and my practice is in Charlotte."

"We get a house in Virginia and commute."

Chante laughed. "You've thought about this, haven't you?"

"Yep. And your mama is just going to have to get over having a damned Yankee for a son-in-law because I'm in this forever."

Chante smiled and decided that she and Zach would wait until Saturday before they told anyone about their engagement — including Liza and Jackson.

"Liza would post it on Twitter. She can't help herself."

"She's going to get you when she finds out you didn't tell her first thing," Zach quipped.

"Let's wash up and go have breakfast," she said.

Zach flipped Chante on her back. "Actually, I'd rather have you for my breakfast." He parted her legs . . .

After spending the morning making love, Chante and Zach finally pulled themselves from the bed in time to head back to Elsie's for a late lunch. When they arrived and saw her mother's car parked in the driveway, Chante groaned.

"We were having such a great day," she said as they got out of the car.

"That doesn't have to change. I'm sure your mother will be happy to see you after everything that's happened."

Chante rolled her eyes and held back a caustic comment. "We'll see." They went up onto the porch and were greeted with the smell of grilled chicken and barbeque. "Hello," Chante said as they walked in.

"We're in the kitchen," Elsie called out. Zach followed Chante down the long hall leading to the kitchen. The place felt like a museum. There were pictures that looked to be at least one hundred years old in silver frames.

"Must be nice to know your family history like this," he said. "I'd love to see the baby pictures of you in your little ruffled panties."

"Oh, don't say that around them," Chante whispered as they walked into the kitchen.

"Say what?" Elsie asked.

Chante smiled. "Nothing," she said, then crossed over to her grandmother and gave her a tight hug.

"Baby pictures," Zach said as Allison walked into the kitchen.

"Chante! Oh, Chante, I'm so glad to see you." Genuine tears sprang into her mother's eyes as she rushed over to Chante and enveloped her in a tight hug. "I was so scared, and your father was . . ."

"About to drive to Charlotte and shoot somebody myself," Eli said when he walked into the kitchen carrying a platter of meat. Allison wiped her eyes and then turned to Zach.

"Mr. Harrington."

"Zach, please call me Zach."

Allison crossed over to him and gave him a hug as well. "I'm going to call you a hero. You saved my daughter's life, and there's nothing I can ever say to tell you how grateful I am."

"You don't have to thank me for saving the woman I love."

Allison brought her hand to her mouth. "Love? Is this for real this time?"

Chante smiled. "Yes, Mom, it's very real."

Elsie shot her daughter a cautioning look. "Well," Allison said, "I learned something over this whole ordeal. Life is about more than who gets married and who doesn't. You two just do your thing, and I'm going to mind my business. Though I'd love to be Nana one day — soon."

"That was real subtle, Mom," Chante said as she walked over to her father and gave him a kiss. He wiped the barbecue sauce from his hands and hugged her tightly.

"Chante Britt, I'm glad you're okay, because what you did with Amanda Chavis shows what kind of brilliant mind you have."

"I got it from my brilliant parents," she said as she stole a chicken wing from the tray.

"Well, I'm glad you're taking that brilliant mind of yours and making money for yourself," Elsie said. "A woman like you should never work for men stuck in the dark ages."

"Elsie," Theo said as he entered the kitchen with a tray filled with grilled corn on the cob. "Are you about to start ranting about sexism, again? This is just a nice family lunch."

"All right, honey, you get a reprieve for now," she said with a wink.

Chante took a wing over to Zach and whispered, "You still have a chance to run."

"No way," he said. "You just wait till you meet my sister. As a matter of fact, I might not introduce her to you until we're married."

"She can't be that bad."

"No, she's worse."

For the first time in years, Chante actually enjoyed having lunch with her family. There was no arguing, no judgment, and no pretense. She checked the wine to see what they were drinking and decided she'd take a case of it back to Charlotte if this was how it made people act.

"Well," Elsie said, "I have an announcement."

"Mother, I don't know how many more surprises I can take from you this week," Allison said as she fanned herself. "You go on a cruise and come back married. Who does that?"

"I do, now hush up. Theo and I are having a party here to celebrate the renovations on the house and announce his tour."

"That sounds like a good time," Eli said. "We are invited, aren't we?"

"Eli, you jokester, of course. All of my family will be here, and I couldn't be more excited."

"Chante," Allison asked, "you will be here, right? I know you must be busy with your new business. And just like your father, I'm really proud of you."

Chante wanted to cry. How many years had she waited to hear her mother say those words to her?

Zach stroked her leg underneath the table as if he could feel her emotions. "We wouldn't miss it," Chante said, then winked at her grandmother.

Over the next three days, Zach and Chante played tourist. There were no cameras or bloggers chasing them this time. But when she woke up Saturday morning and he wasn't in bed with her, she felt instantly nervous. What had happened? Where was he? And just when she was about to give in to panic, the door to the suite opened and Zach walked in.

"Where have you been?" she asked as she

tossed a pillow at him.

"Whoa, whoa! I had to meet Miss Elsie this morning."

"What?"

"I may be a Yankee, but I know you don't announce you're marrying a southern belle without a ring."

"Let me see it," she said with a smile.

"After you hit me with a pillow, I don't think so. You can wait until tonight."

Chante hopped out of the bed and wrapped her arms around his waist. "Zach, I'll make it worth your while," she said like a little sex kitten.

"I think it will benefit me more later tonight. You're going to be thinking about it all day too."

"You're so wrong."

"Yep."

"I called Liza and told her about the party at my grammy's, but she and Jackson can't make it. They have a prior commitment in Fayetteville."

"Jackson has to be the first politician I've ever met that I feel I can trust."

Chante nodded and forced herself not to think about Robert. Zach noted her silence. "Did I say something wrong?" he asked.

"No, it's just crazy how Robert's insanity

brought the right man into my life and Liza's."

Zach stroked her arms. "New rule: we never say his name again. He's the past, and tonight is all about the future."

"Right," she said. "The future Mr. and Mrs. Zachary Harrington."

Zach kissed her slow and tender. When they broke the kiss, Chante smiled at him. "Now can I see the ring?"

He tweaked her nose. "No."

Chante pouted and walked away. "Then I'm not going to show you my new bikini until we get to the beach!"

"You're so cute when you pout," he said.

After a day of frolicking on the beach, the couple returned to their suite to get ready for the party.

Chante decided to show off her sun-kissed skin in an emerald-green strapless mermaid dress. She pulled her curly hair up in a messy bun and clipped on a pair of gold earrings.

Zach walked into the bathroom, where Chante was brushing a bit of foundation on her face. "You're so damned sexy," he said as he wrapped his arms around her waist. "Are you sure you're not a model?"

"You're really piling it high and deep."

"Talk your junk now, but when you see this ring, I want to hear all apologies."

"This ring better be everything you're hyping it up to be."

"That little bit of reverse psychology isn't going to work on me."

Chante turned around and faced her handsome fiancé. He looked like a chocolate-dipped James Bond in his tuxedo. Forget Idris, Zach could be the next Bond.

"I know what's working on me," she said.

"And that is?"

"You in this suit. Hot."

"I can't wait until our really nice clothes are lying in a pile in the middle of the floor because what's underneath that dress is what I can't wait to see."

Chante smoothed her hands down his lapels. "We'd better go or we're not going to make it out the door." She reached into his jacket pocket and grabbed his car keys. "And since you won't show me the ring, I'm driving. With the top down."

Zach and Chante arrived at Elsie's house windblown and late. Chante, who hadn't driven the Mustang all week, decided to take the scenic route, much to Zach's dismay.

"You drive too damn fast," he said as they pulled up to the house. And he reached up and smoothed back a couple of curls that had fallen from her bun.

"I only drive like this in a Mustang."

"In that case we are never buying one. Good plan."

She blew him a kiss. "Stop being such a . . ."

"Chante, Zachary!" Allison called out from the top of the steps. "Where have you been? Mother is about to make her presentation." Chante smiled at her mother, who looked fabulous in a goldenrod gown and diamond accessories. "I thought you two had been in some horrible accident in that race car."

"I told Chante, we're never going to own one of these things," Zach said.

"I'm liking you more and more every day, Zach," Allison said. "Now let's get a move on."

Walking into the house was like stepping into the pages of *Who's Who in Charleston, South Carolina*. A few people stopped Chante and asked her if she was all right, but there were no probing questions about what had happened in Charlotte.

Shortly after Zach and Chante finished mingling, Elsie called for everyone's attention.

"This has been a wonderful night, and it

gives me great pleasure to open my home to so many friends, old and new. To my wonderful husband, my daughter, my son-in-law, and my granddaughter, I'm so glad we're here together tonight," Elsie said. "There is so much history right here on this land and in this house. I think it would be pretty selfish if I didn't share this with everybody. That's one of the reasons I had this house restored."

The guests clapped. "And," Elsie continued, "this house will always be persevered as it has been declared a historic landmark."

Allison's face showed her surprise. Elsie grabbed her daughter's hand. "Our family has always been a feisty lot. And that continues through our bloodline. It's our past that inspires our future. I'm hoping all of the great things that happened here will inspire generations to come. Thank you for celebrating this event with me."

Thunderous applause broke out, and Chante saw her mother and grandmother hug for the first time in years. Her heart melted when she heard Allison tell her Grammy thank you.

"This is so beautiful," Chante whispered to Zach. He nodded.

"You know what else is beautiful?" he said, then dropped to one knee. Reaching into his jacket pocket, he pulled out an old velvet box. "I'll never love another woman as much as I love you. I'll never have the honor of meeting a stronger or braver woman than you." Zach opened the box, revealing a white-gold, emerald-cut diamond ring. Chante's eyes stretched to the size of quarters. That was the mythical Cooper stone.

"Oh my God."

"Your grandmother told me that this ring has been in your family for generations, and since you always were a student of history, you know that every Cooper who wore this ring never had a day of sadness when she married the man she truly loved."

Allison and Chante were both about to cry. "Do you love me?" Zach asked.

"With all my heart," Chante found the voice to say.

"So will you do me the honor of being my wife and my lover for the rest of our lives?"

"Yes, yes," Chante said as Zach slipped the ring on her finger. As the room cheered for their love, Chante couldn't wait to begin her future with the man she'd love forever.

The employees of Thorndike Press hope you have enjoyed this Large Print book. All our Thorndike, Wheeler, and Kennebec Large Print titles are designed for easy reading, and all our books are made to last. Other Thorndike Press Large Print books are available at your library, through selected bookstores, or directly from us.

For information about titles, please call:
    (800) 223-1244

or visit our Web site at:
    http://gale.cengage.com/thorndike

To share your comments, please write:
    Publisher
    Thorndike Press
    10 Water St., Suite 310
    Waterville, ME 04901